UNHOLY PLEASURES

DEBRA DUNBAR

*K*ai twisted the boarding pass in her hands, nearly tearing it into two pieces. "So...I met someone."

Why was she so nervous? I was a half succubus. I needed the energy generated by sexual arousal and climax in order to live, and that meant I'd learned to get my mind around the fact that relationships weren't only meaningful if they were monogamous. I loved Irix, but we both needed random sexual encounters to survive. I'd also found there was an odd middle ground where I cared deeply for someone and that caring also involved making love. Kai was one of those friends-and-more. She'd become both my friend and my lover when Irix and I were vacationing in Maui, and we'd continued to keep in touch for the rest of my senior year. When she'd heard I was doing a summer internship on the west coast, she took a week off from her surfing instructor job and flew out to meet me.

We'd had a wonderful week together. And her having "met someone" didn't change that, nor did it change *our* relationship. At least at my end...

"So…tell me about him or her." I reached out and captured her hand in mine, stilling the twisting motion.

"Him. Lee. He's the marketing director at the resort down the street from mine."

And that was it? Was it up to me to pry the details out of her? "When did you meet him? And when did you start dating?"

She shook her head, her eyes looking everywhere but at mine. "We met a month ago when I was subbing there for one of their instructors on maternity leave. We started dating right away."

Oh. Was this trip to see me our last hurrah before she gave me the Dear John speech? I didn't want to, but I could move back to friends-without-benefits territory. Maybe she couldn't?

Maybe Lee couldn't deal with the idea that she could love more than one person.

Kai took a deep breath and continued. "It's not…does this make me a slut? Coming here to see you when I've been dating Lee? I should have told you before I came out. I should have not come out at all." Her eyes finally met mine. I entwined my fingers with hers, her dark, golden-tan against my creamy pale skin.

"No, it doesn't make you a slut. Your dating Lee doesn't make one bit of difference to me. I wanted you to come out to see me and I'm glad you did. I don't regret one moment of our time together—this week or even since we've met."

She shook her head. "You're my friend, Amber. And I love that our friendship extends into the bedroom. Sex with you is amazing. It's so easy with you. It's just part of our friendship."

I got the feeling there was an unspoken "but" at the end of her speech. "Does Lee want you to be exclusive? Are you worried that what we had this week was somehow cheating on him? Talk to me, Kai. I don't know what's going on unless you tell me."

She sighed. "I told him about you. At first he thought it was totally hot that I had a female friend that I had sex with. Then I think he started to get jealous because we're still involved with each other, even if it's long-distance. But when I explained about you and Irix and that the both of you are a committed couple but aren't exclusive, he was intrigued."

Where was she going with this? "Are we still friends, Kai? Friends with or without sex?"

It hurt to think that I might never see Kai again, that what I was would end our friendship. I hated being different. I hated being not human. Up until a year ago I'd thought I was just Amber Lowry, a college girl with a greater than usual sex drive and commitment issues, a human with the uncanny ability to speed-grow and heal plants. But instead I was a half-elf/half-succubus freak that would be killed by the elves as a blemish on their precious genetic purity, collected as an exotic toy by the demons, and reviled as a slut and ho by any humans who found out that I spent most of my free time trolling bars and grocery stores for hit-it-and-quit-it sexual partners.

And who knew grocery stores could be such an amazing place to pick up men? And women?

"We're still friends, but…" Kai shook her head.

I cringed, waiting for the rest of her statement.

"I don't know, Amber. It's hard to be around you and not touch you, not want you. And Lee doesn't want me to have sex with anyone else unless he's a participant."

"But this week…was this okay?" I hated the thought that the lovemaking we'd enjoyed might have jeopardized Kai and Lee's relationship.

"Yes! I told him I was coming out to see you and that after what we'd had I couldn't just throw this at you, not when we'd been planning this get-together since before Lee and I met." Her fingers gripped mine tight, crushing the boarding pass between our hands. "He said this time only. And then it either had to stop, or you and I could only have sex if he was involved."

I wasn't sure how I felt about being her one "hall pass" with Lee, but at least she wasn't ending our friendship.

"Do you want that? Between me, you, and Lee? Because, you know, that isn't a problem for me."

Her brows knitted together. "It *is* a problem for me. I don't like the idea of sharing you with Lee or sharing him with you. Is that weird? I know you have sex with lots of other people, that you and Irix have a loving bond, and none of that bothers me. But I somehow can't mix my relationship with Lee and my relationship with you together. It would feel as if I were cheapening both, turning them into a weird swinger orgy thing instead of the expressions of caring and love that they truly are."

I understood. There was the sex that I had with random people I picked up at the grocery store, and there was what I had with those I loved. If Kai cared about Lee, then I was positive I would, too. I was completely open to the idea that there might be a plus-one to the love Kai and I had together, but obviously that would only happen if the other two in the equation were like-minded.

"It's okay, Kai. You can be exclusive with Lee. If things work out and you wind up married, I'll be thrilled for you. And if they don't and you want to pick up where we left off, I'm here. I'll always be here."

"I want to see you again, Amber, but I think next time I visit I should bring Lee with me." She smiled, a brief twist of her lips before they dropped once more. "That way I won't be tempted to fall into your arms."

My chest felt like it was being squeezed between two

rocks. "We can still e-mail and text, and Skype. And when I get settled this fall in New Orleans, maybe you both can come out to visit Irix and me. Maybe come out for Christmas?"

She nodded, her lips trembling as she forced them into a smile. "Or maybe you both can come out to Maui again. I think it would help if we did a couples thing. I mean, a couples thing platonically."

Of course. I could hardly breathe, my lungs felt so constricted. "I love you, Kai. And if that means just platonic, then I'm fine with that. I don't want to lose your friendship."

She stood and threw her arms around me. Then she kissed me. It was bittersweet, this last kiss. It reminded me of everything that was changing between us, and how very fragile our friendship was. We sat, and this time we didn't hold hands. I wasn't sure we'd ever hold hands again.

"So, speaking of marriage, when are you and Irix going to tie the knot?"

Kai was much more cheerful now that she'd unburdened herself. I, on the other hand, wanted to go curl up in a corner and cry. This time it was me forcing a smile.

"I don't think demons are the marrying kind," I told her. "We have a commitment, and that is unusual enough among demons. I doubt a ring and white dress are in my future."

"Oh." Kai shot me a worried look. "Then kids…"

"I don't know." The thought of having Irix's child, or children, filled me with a sense of longing, but that was probably less likely than the white dress and ring.

"It's alright," I reassured her. "I'll just spoil Darci's kids, or Nyalla's. Well, if Nyalla ever finds the right guy, that is."

She nodded. "You and Irix love each other. You're adorable together. And I can tell you're excited about your career and this internship. That's plenty."

It *was* plenty, but was it enough? I thought about Irix and me at his house in New Orleans, me and Jordan studying the bayou ecosystem and restoring endangered plant life. Yes, it was enough. It would have to be enough. But I still couldn't help but imagine Irix and me pledging ourselves to each other in a church, all of our friends and family in attendance. And babies, little children…. They would be three-quarters demon. How would that work? Could I even *have* children with Irix?

"I need to get through security before they start boarding," Kai announced, reluctantly getting to her feet. We hugged again, and I waited until she cleared security, waving as she headed down the hall. Was this the way it would always be? Irix and I were constants, but I'd hoped that Kai would continue to be a major part of my love life. Would I always be waving goodbye to those I loved because they found someone who wanted a more traditional love affair, or because they needed to move on to a more socially acceptable relationship? It hurt. As happy as I was for Kai, it still hurt that she couldn't find room for me as more than a friend.

But at least I had Irix. We were in love, and there was nothing that could break us apart. Other loves might come and go, but we'd always be forever.

CHAPTER 2

My internship at DiMarche Cellars included a tiny, single-wide trailer just off one of the vineyards. The wooden steps were bleached gray and squawked at each tread. The metal door was so flimsy that I feared it would come off the hinges every time I opened it. The kitchenette had a pink stove and a yellow refrigerator with cigarette burns on the Formica countertop. The wallpaper was peeling over the baby-shit brown, tweed couch, and the bedroom was so small that I had to crawl on the mattress from the foot of the bed each time I went to sleep.

Sleep was about the only time I was in this trailer. I'd come back from my trip to Hel and flown straight out to California, practically going from the airport right into the vineyard. We were removing suckers and excess leaves, trimming vines, tying up supports and moving wires, checking and recording the water content and pH of the immature grapes. The last part of my internship would be in August when we were harvesting some of the early grapes.

That's when the real work began—August to October. Harvest was when the winery employed the majority of their field workers. Grapes were still picked by hand in huge plastic tubs, carried to the line of bins towed behind a tractor, then driven to the winery for processing. Those seasonal employees would leave after harvest, while the key field staff continued on to prune and maintain the vines through the winter and spring.

I went out at dawn, ate in the field with the other employees, and came back at sunset to shower and fall onto the lumpy mattress only to do it all over again the next day. And I loved every minute of it. For the last two days they'd had me analyzing and compiling reports on downy mildew and a troubling cutworm infestation, plus cataloging areas where the irrigation system seemed to be supporting a fungus. They were typical problems that a vineyard of this scale might encounter, but all these issues were intriguing to me.

And the wine. The first day in I'd gotten the grand tour of the winery and had been amazed. I loved the giant casks, the bottling areas, the tasting room with three tours per day, the gift shop. Most of all I was fascinated with the vintners and how they blended the varietals and decided if there would be any special products that year. Nearly all the wine produced at DiMarche was from grapes harvested in their own vineyards, but some specialized grape varieties were purchased and brought in either in pulp or in extract form for the blends. When I had first arrived, I'd been introduced to each of the DiMarche signature products, tasting several years of a wine to get a sense of the differences that a season's temperature, rainfall, and soil quality could make in the final product. I hoped they'd soon transfer me to the tasting room where I could watch the sommelier. Maybe someday, with my half-elven palate, I'd be able to taste, categorize, and even judge wine with that level of skill.

Of course, my obsession over my internship cut into my

time with Kai this past week, but she'd enjoyed following me around in the field, and had loved the tasting room both at DiMarche as well as the neighboring four wineries. It had been great having her here to talk to, having her to curl up with at night, spooning in bed. It was going to be a lonely few weeks until Irix arrived. I hadn't seen him since before I'd left for my trip to Hel, and as much as I missed him, I was feeling guilty. I knew I'd have to confess that I'd gone to Hel all by myself—something he'd forbade me doing. I knew it would cause a huge fight between us, no matter my reasoning for doing so. I hated fighting with Irix. I missed him terribly and wanted nothing more than to have him by my side, but he had been away taking care of a few things in New Orleans, then back in Hel. And as much as I missed him, I was dreading the argument I knew we were going to have.

It seemed like I wouldn't have to wait two weeks after all. As I went to climb the steps to the trailer, I felt him. And even if I hadn't felt him, the BMW M5 parked out front would have clued me in. Stolen, no doubt. Irix never had a problem in taking whatever vehicle suited his fancy, regardless of whose name was actually on the title. It was something I'd learned to live with.

All fears of our inevitable fight vanished with the excitement of having him here. It had been five weeks since I'd seen him last, and that was five weeks too long in my opinion. I flew up the last few stairs and ran through the door, squealing to see him standing in the kitchen, pulling a bottle of ginger ale out of the ridiculous yellow fridge.

His smile tugged at my heart. "My elf-girl, my princess. I finished up early and wanted to surprise you."

I rushed him and fell into his arms, losing myself in his scent, in the warmth of him enveloping me. God, I'd missed Irix. I was so glad we wouldn't need to spend months apart anymore, that I wouldn't need to fear the angels might catch and kill him. I'd gone to Hel and helped the humans there in exchange for immunity for Irix, so that never again would he need to flee back across the gates for three to six months.

"I'm so glad you're here," I told him. "This is the best surprise ever."

"Did I miss Kai? I hope she enjoyed her visit." His deep voice rumbled in his chest under my cheek.

"She flew back to Maui this morning. We'll hopefully see her Christmas. I asked her to come to visit us in New Orleans for the holidays." I didn't tell him about Lee or the change in Kai's and my relationship. We could discuss that later, once the hurt had soothed a bit. I knew he'd understand my feelings, but Irix saw these things differently. As an incubus who was several thousand years older than me, he had experienced lovers come and go, had watched lovers age and die. This was a painful but routine occurrence for him, but for me it was a reminder of how weird I was, how I'd always be a freak in a human world.

"I hope she can make it for Christmas." He bent to kiss the top of my head. "I like her. I like that she loves you."

I winced, but I knew that she *did* still love me, even if that love was going to be different going forward.

And Irix meant what he said. There was no jealousy with him. Of course as a sex demon, he could hardly be jealous of the hook-ups that fed me energy, but my relationship with Kai had been different. He never been annoyed about the time I spent with her, or fretted over whether I cared about her more than I did about him. I didn't. I loved them both, but in a different way. And the feelings I had for Irix were indescribable. He was part of my soul. When the world died at the end of time, I'd still love him.

I wished that Kai could somehow have that with Lee and

not have to push me away. But wishing wouldn't change things.

"You're weak," Irix said, pulling away to look me over from head to toe.

It was an accusation, and not the first time he'd made it. I pulled him close again and hid my grimace in his shirt. Two weeks of hook-ups and a week of gladly given affections from Kai couldn't replace what I'd spent turning a demon into a tree nearly three weeks ago in Hel.

"I had to expend a lot of energy recently. I'll recharge." I was going to tell him. Just not right now, not when I wanted him to do less talking and more getting naked.

"Oh, really."

I froze at his tone, not because of the drawled words, but because beneath them was a thread of anger. Crap. Oh shit, I was so busted. The fight I'd been dreading was coming, and there was no delaying this confrontation any longer.

"Maybe you can tell me what exactly you've been doing the last five weeks, and what this is about?" Irix stepped back from me and pulled something from his pocket. It was a scroll, thick cream parchment that had been tied with a red ribbon and closed with a wax seal. It was slightly squashed, no doubt from being in the demon's back pocket.

I took the outstretched scroll and broke the seal. Inside were line after line of sigils and symbols, none of which I could read. I looked up at Irix, not sure if I wanted to know what it said.

"It's a breeding contract," he told me.

"A what?" Breeding contract for *what*? I didn't own a purebred dog or any livestock. What in the world could this person, whoever they were, want to breed? The cool, impersonal look on Irix's face was scaring me. I'd expected a huge blow-out fight about my trip to Hel, not this cold, detached demeanor. Or this scroll. What was *that* about?

"It seems a high level warmonger, an *ancient*, named Harkel is quite impressed with a succubus named Amber and feels that the pair of them would create notable offspring. He sent the offer through the Iblis as he was told that you were part of her household. She asked me to give it to you and convey her congratulations on what she says must have been the 'fuck of the century'."

Offspring? Babies? I give a demon a blow job and he wants me to have his baby? What the fuck was that about? I'd met Harkel once while I was in Hel. He'd transported a wagon full of plant samples for me and in return I gave him a quick hummer. Actually it wasn't really for services rendered. I liked him. We didn't speak one word of each other's language, and I'd just met him, but I liked him. I felt an attraction to him strong enough that I'd thrown caution to the winds and let him think I was a full succubus who was granting him a sexual favor.

"I…uh, I was in Hel a few weeks ago and met this Harkel. It wasn't 'the fuck of the century'. I mean, it was really nice, and I liked him a lot, but it was just a blow job. Kind of a thank-you for pulling my wagon full of plant samples from Patchine to Libertytown. I don't know where this baby proposal came from."

I was babbling, sweating. Oh God, don't let this be the thing that tore Irix and me apart. I knew he'd be furious about the Hel trip, but why was he upset about Harkel? He wanted me to feed my succubus side. And the demon had given me plenty of energy, even willingly tying himself to me.

"You did *what?*" Irix stepped closer, a spark of anger breaking his cold, impassive expression. It gave me hope that this would end well. Irix yelling at me was familiar. That other Irix wasn't. "You went to Hel, by yourself, I'm supposing, and while there you met a demon and made enough of an impression that he's proposing a breeding incident with you."

"Yes," I whispered.

"You went to Hel where you don't speak any of the languages and know nothing of the customs. You risked coming in contact with elves who would kill you and demons who would chain you to a wall, hidden away as a plaything for a few centuries, until they tired of you and let you go or until I somehow managed to bribe and threaten enough demons to find you."

"Yes." I swallowed hard, trying to remember the reasonable explanation I'd planned to give him, the one I'd been rehearsing for weeks. "I had a demon interpreter, one who helped me navigate the cultural issues, one who would defend me if I got into trouble."

Irix's golden brown eyes bore into mine. "A Low. Sam gave you one of her Lows that speaks English. There are customs a Low wouldn't be familiar with, and that level of demon wouldn't be able to protect you from a mosquito."

"But he did," I protested. "He jumped on a giant cave lizard, got me out of a tight spot with the warmongers, and even helped me lie my way past the elves in the archives."

Shit. That wasn't what I was supposed to say.

A muscle twitched in Irix's jaw. "You go to Hel against my orders, then don't even attempt to hide your presence. Instead you're playing with cave lizards, partying with elves, hauling carts across the desert, and giving warmongers blow jobs."

"It was just the one warmonger." This wasn't going well. Not that I'd expected it would, but I hadn't planned on this discussion derailing quite so fast. "I wasn't running around Hel giving blow jobs to every demon I saw, just the one. The lizard belonged to the dwarves. He was their watch lizard or something and they called him off. And the elves...well I needed to get a Wythyn map of the water sources under Libertytown so they could put together an irrigation system, so I needed to go to the archives."

"And you couldn't let the humans do that? Have them bribe a demon to steal it?"

"No. An elf needed to open the case. It couldn't be broken by a demon."

"Well, then a demon could have stolen the whole case and let the magic users figure it out. Amber, what the fuck were you thinking? Where is your common sense? What is so damned motherfucking important that you'd disobey my orders and risk your life like that?"

Now here was the Irix I knew. He never cursed unless he was furious at me. I chose to overlook the whole "obeying my orders" thing, deciding not to throw gasoline on an already raging fire, and concentrate on the rest of his questions.

"Sam promised you'd receive immunity if I helped the humans in Libertytown. Her archangel agreed. And they need help, Irix. They'll starve if they can't find edible crops that can grow in a Dis-like landscape. The elven environmental modifications are falling apart, and they'll soon be living in a desert. I had to help them."

I felt some of the anger drain from him. The demon took a few breaths and rubbed his face. "And they couldn't just leave Hel and come here?"

"They probably will have to in a few years, but they're scared. Hel is all most of them know. I remember when Nyalla came here. She didn't speak any human languages, didn't have any skills that would translate into a living-wage job. She didn't even know how to work the toaster or the phone, or drive a car. They need time, Irix. I gave them time."

He looked at me again, something unreadable in his gaze. "You risked your life to give a bunch of scared humans time."

"Yes, but this was mostly about you. You have immunity now. No more running for the gates every few months. No more me panicking as I try to explain to some angel that there was no demon where you'd just been standing five minutes before. No more being apart from me. No more me scared to death that you're dead and no one even knows to tell me."

"That's not worth your life," he argued.

I reached out to touch his arm. "Yes, it is. To me it is. That was my primary reason, but once I got there, I realized I needed to help these humans. They had spent most of their lives as slaves. They're scared. They needed me. And, honestly, it was a rush to know that I had the skills and abilities to make a positive impact. I was a hero to them, Irix. I like being a hero."

"I'm assuming my ordering you to never return to Hel isn't going to have any impact on your future actions."

I bit my lip. "I need to go back in six months to check on them and make further modifications. And maybe bring them some canned goods. But beyond that, I'll try to do as you say. If you want me to stay within the confines of Libertytown, or only have contact with humans, or something else I'll make every effort to do so."

This time when his eyes met mine, they were determined rather than angry. "Next time you will take me. That is non-negotiable. You will not go to Hel again without me. Understood?"

This wasn't the moment to protest his ordering me around. "Understood."

He sighed and took the scroll from my hand, shaking his head as he read through it. "Then I guess it's time we discussed this and exactly how the attentions of a high-level warmonger are going to affect your life going forward."

I blinked in surprise. "Um, I can't just say 'thanks, but no thanks'?"

Irix shook his head and led me to the couch. "Sit. I'll explain in a minute, but first I'm going to fix us a drink. Or two. Or possibly three."

Yikes. And my "life going forward"? I didn't like the sound of that. "Better just bring the bottle. It sounds like three drinks might not be enough."

CHAPTER 3

*I*rix plopped the bottle of rum on the table along with two glasses full of ice and several cans of ginger ale. "Go ahead. Tell me everything about this blow job."

I bit back a smirk. "Well he changed into a human form because there was no way I was going to go down on a lion-bear. Then I put his cock into my mouth."

"I think I'm familiar with the step-by-step of the sex act. I mean how did you meet him, how did he end up pulling your cart, and what led to the blow job. Actually, do tell me about the blow job, because there might be something there that sheds light on why this notable ancient demon is so smitten with you."

I poured rum into my glass full of ice, then topped it off with ginger ale, taking a sip while I tried to organize the story in a way that wouldn't end with Irix storming out of the trailer and my life.

"Andor, he's a dwarf and a friend of Kirby's, had led us to his city in the mountain caves where the dwarves gave me a cart full of plant samples to modify and use in Libertytown for crops. So I had this cart, but they didn't give me a lizard to pull it. Andor let me have a transportation thingie that got me and Rutter, he's the Low, to somewhere between Patchine and Libertytown, but that left me in the desert at nightfall with a cart and no animal to pull it. Rutter and I tried, but we're not strong enough and the sand was too soft to really get the cart to roll."

Irix sighed and leaned back in his chair. "Why do I have the Three Stooges theme song running through my head right now? Why?"

I gave him a stern look. "What was I supposed to do? Conjure a horse from the red sands?"

"Leave the cart and hike back to Libertytown so you could send some humans and either an animal to pull it or a magical device to transport it?"

Easy for him to say. He wasn't there. "Rutter said it would be picked clean by the time we reached Libertytown and managed to send someone back for it. Demons roam that area during the night, and they'd trash the cart if they found it unattended. Or a sand wyrm could have eaten it. Or quicksand could have spontaneously formed under the cart and sucked it into the earth. I went to a lot of trouble to get those plant samples. I wasn't about to lose them."

"Quicksand? Sand wyrms?" Irix shook his head. "Never mind. So you and a Low were trying to drag a cart across the sand…"

"And we saw a group of demons—warmongers— approaching from the distance. It was too late to make a run for it. At first I was going to pretend to be a full elf, and Rutter was going to pose as a servant, but when they reached us, things got kind of tense and I inadvertently let some pheromones slip, and they all thought I was a full succubus who'd managed to Own an elven soul and had a really convincing elf form."

Irix did the equivalent of a head-desk, only in his palms instead of on a desk. "There is so much wrong with that... I'm on the edge of a panic attack just thinking about that scenario. You could have been killed, Amber. A group of warmongers would never have allowed an elven woman with only a Low in attendance to pass unmolested. And a full succubus...how did you pull that one off? You don't speak demon."

"Rutter told them I'd been summoned by a sorcerer that had cursed me and the only language I could speak and understand was English. They were actually very nice. They wanted me to come party with them."

"I'm sure they did," Irix commented wryly. "It's most demons' dream to party with a sex demon. Unfortunately, demons can be quite rough, and sex demons are more fragile than others, and you, in particular, are even more fragile than a full succubus would be. If they'd burned you, or twisted you and broken your limbs because they wanted you in a weird position while they had sex with you, they would have realized you weren't a full succubus, then the bidding war would have begun over who would get the pleasure of dragging you home as a fun, half-breed toy."

I shivered, knowing he was right. And I'd known at the time it was happening that my safety, as well as my life, hinged on the warmongers not finding out my deception.

"I'm not stupid. I didn't go party with them, but they were very strong, and this lion-bear guy was appealing, so I had Rutter ask him very nicely if he would pull the cart to Libertytown for us."

Irix shuddered. "You asked a high-level, ancient demon to pull a cart like he was an ox or a draft horse? What did you offer him in exchange? I'm assuming there was more incentive than just a blow job."

My face heated. "I didn't offer him anything. I smiled very

nicely, and I'll admit I did have the pheromones cranking, but I didn't offer him even a blow job in exchange. He just agreed, picked up the end of the wagon, and went."

That received a moment of silence while Irix scowled and rubbed his chin. "Nothing? Demons don't do favors for nothing, and high-level demons don't stoop to pulling carts like a farm animal without significant incentive. Sometimes not even then. Think, Amber. You must have offered him something."

I shook my head. "Rutter was translating for me. I know he's a Low and all that, but I'm sure he didn't commit me to something without my knowledge. The warmonger just agreed and pulled the cart. I walked beside him…and I petted him. His fur was soft, and I wanted to touch him, so I petted him as we walked to Libertytown."

Again Irix put his face in his hands. "You had an ancient pulling a cart, and you were *petting* him like he was some sort of big fluffy dog. I'm assuming he didn't try to bite your hand off, or tell you through Rutter that he was going to disembowel you if you didn't treat him with proper respect."

Yikes. This was making me realize how very, very lucky I'd been. "I think he kind of liked it. After the cart was within the gates, I walked out with him and we ended up sitting just outside the city wall, looking at the moons while I petted him. I told him that I wished we could understand each other, that I wished he had a human form because I wanted him, but I didn't want to have sex with an animal. I know he couldn't understand me, but he must have gotten the impression that he had a chance of getting lucky because he stood and changed into a human form."

"And he indicated via gestures that he wanted or was receptive to a blow job?"

"No, I just did it. I liked him, and I wanted to do it, not just because he pulled the cart for me, but because I wanted to. And the energy he gave me…it was huge. I felt electrified afterward. It was enough energy that I was able to make some significant plant modifications for the humans as well as defend myself and Rutter from a jerk of a demon in the elven archives."

"Energy. Amber, I've had sex with lots of demons, and although it can be a fun experience, the energy I gain is not significant. What we gain from sex with humans if far more sustaining. I know this warmonger is a high level and an ancient, but you shouldn't have received that much energy."

He was scolding me, as if it were my fault. "I don't know! I didn't ask for the energy, I just wanted to give the guy a blow job. Then he pushed enough energy my way to practically light me up like a Christmas tree. He even offered a light tie."

Irix's head popped up from his hands and he fixed me with a hard stare. "Tie. He offered you a tie and voluntarily shared a large amount of energy with you. You had to have understood that those gifts come with strings attached? It's bad enough that you had him pulling a cart, but to take his energy…please at least tell me you didn't accept the tie."

I squirmed. "It seemed rude not to."

"There might have been a way around the cart-pulling favor and the gift of energy, but a tie? Amber, you accepted a tie with an ancient warmonger. There are consequences to that. And this," he waved the scroll at me, "is one of the consequences."

"It was just a blow job," I shouted, starting to panic. What consequences? Why did no one tell me these things? What did Irix mean about "consequences"? "Of course I accepted his tie. He was nice. He'd pulled the cart, and I was attracted to him, and there was this heat-of-the-moment thing with the blow job and the energy lighting up every one of my nerve endings. The tie was freely given and it wasn't an all-consuming tie, it was light. I didn't know he was an ancient. I just liked him, and I wanted him."

"Amber, you can't just go giving blow jobs, accepting energy and ties with demons because you like them."

"Why not?" I insisted. "You're a sex demon and I like you. We have sex and you give me energy, and I can tell there is a tie between us. Why *not* have sex and accept energy from those I like? What's wrong if I wanted to do the same with other demons, like Sam or Rutter—"

"Please tell me you did not have sex with a Low," Irix interrupted.

"Why? What's wrong with having sex with a Low?" I was outraged. Rutter was a nice guy. The idea that just because he was a Low he wasn't worthy of my attentions was wrong. It was just fucking wrong.

"Okay, okay. But I hope you didn't."

"I didn't have sex with Rutter, although I might eventually because I like him. But what's the big deal? What if I did? What if I'd had sex with a dozen Lows? If I'm not allowed to have sex with demons, because then they somehow think they have a right to make babies with me, then you need to tell me these things."

"I would have told you if I'd ever thought you would be in a position to be giving blow jobs to a warmonger. You weren't supposed to be in Hel. You weren't *ever* supposed to be in Hel." Irix ran his hand through his hair. "Amber, you cannot take every tie that's offered, nor go accepting energy from or offering sexual acts to demons without careful consideration. I don't know if you understand that tying with a demon is different than tying with a human. With human beings, they serve you. Tying with the demon is a two-way arrangement, except the more powerful demon in the bond has an expectation of…things. With a Low, you'd be expected to protect and defend him or her. With someone like this warmonger, they expect you to be available to them, and to give their requests for favors, or breeding, a priority. It's similar to joining a household. Normally you could delay responding to this breeding contract, or politely decline, but because you accepted energy from Harkel as well as a tie, he would be within his rights to expect you to join his household if asked, or to enthusiastically agree to at least one breeding incident. These things don't come without strings, Amber. Even blow jobs have consequences, and you did more than just suck this guy off, you accepted his gift of energy and an offered tie. You've linked yourself to him, and by the circumstances that you've told me, he will consider himself to be most-favored in your eyes."

Warmonger aside, this revelation made me wonder about what Irix and I had together. "Then what about us? You've shared energy with me, had a tie with me since last year. Did that come with strings attached? Maybe we need to discuss that."

Irix suddenly shot me a wary glance, then looked down at his drink. "That's different."

"How? Because I don't see it as different. Did I agree to things with you out of ignorance just as I've done with Harkel? Are you going to start telling me I'm part of your household or that you want us to have children, or little demons, or whatever?"

My words were harsh, but in my heart that's what I wanted. I desperately longed for him to tell me that we were bound together forever in a demon sort of marriage, our tie and sharing of energy the equivalent of a marriage vow. And I wanted him to tell me he wanted me to have his children.

"No," he said into his drink, his voice wooden. "I gave all that to you without any strings. You're free to join whatever household you want, to have children with whoever you want. There are no obligations in what I've shared with you."

That was the wrong answer. The chest-crushed-between-rocks feeling I'd had when Kai had given me the "talk" was nothing compared to this pain. I knew he loved me. I knew he thought that I was too young to commit to him as a life-partner, if demons even did such a crazy thing. I knew he feared that in a few centuries I'd tire of him and find someone else, happy to put our relationship into the category of "fond youthful indiscretion". I'd tried to convince him otherwise, but I couldn't force him to give me what I wanted.

Still, the whole thing made me angry. "Then what's wrong with me considering Harkel's proposal? I really like him. I'm very attracted to him. He obviously is unusually attracted to me if he was pulling wagons and letting me pet him and offering me energy and a tie. Maybe I should ask to join his household and consider his breeding proposal. Seems as if an allegiance with a powerful demon like that could only do me good."

I could practically hear Irix grind his teeth. "First, you're not a full succubus and will not be able to produce offspring as a full being of spirit would. Harkel is expecting that, and when you tell him that you can only have his child the elven way by him deliberately impregnating you during a sexual act and that you need a lengthy gestation period, he'll realize that you're not a full demon."

I thought for a second about bearing Harkel's child the elven way, and knew I was making a hollow threat. As much as I liked the warmonger, there was no way I was going to have a baby and give it over to a demon to stuff into a dwarven-run foster home. When I envisioned children, it was with Irix. It was him pushing a little boy on a swing, or helping a little girl doctor her teddy bear.

"What do you think is going to happen once Harkel realizes you're a half-elf?" Irix continued. "Suddenly any contract between you, any agreement you've had, is null and void. You won't have the same rights as a demon. You won't have the same protection of household and affiliations. He'll be able to just haul you away as a thing, and do whatever he wants with you."

I felt a chill run down my spine at the thought. "But I have affiliations. Leethu would kick his ass. And both Wyatt and Nyalla would make sure that Sam would join in on the ass kicking."

He fixed me with a hard look. "Leethu would pout and offer all sorts of incentives in exchange for you, but she wouldn't 'kick his ass'. And Harkel might or might not find her offers tempting enough to give up an exotic plaything. And as for Sam…she's an imp and although she might have the sword of the Iblis, no one in Hel really cares. I doubt Harkel is going to tremble in his boots to have an imp show up at his door with a dozen Lows insisting he give you back."

I bit my lip to stop it from trembling. What had I done? What had I gotten myself into now? Did I even have a choice in this? Would I need to cancel my return trip to Liberty-town in fear that Harkel would seek me out and demand I agree to this breeding proposal?

And if I cancelled my trip, would Sam cancel Irix's immu-nity? Would the people of Libertytown starve?

I felt Irix take the glass from my hand and pull me close, his hands rubbing my shoulders and down my back as he rested his cheek against the top of my head. "I'd come for you, Amber. I'd do anything within my power to get you away from him, but I don't know if I could or even if I'd be able to free you before he accidently killed you. Our best hope is to delay this as long as possible until you build up enough allies that if Harkel ever found out what you were, he'd think twice about snatching you."

I knew Irix would come for me. I knew he loved me

enough to do anything to save me. But having him say it, having him label this as "our" problem when it was so clearly a problem I'd created by flouting his heavy-handed orders and not at least including him in my trip to Hel, made me feel better.

And as much as it would have helped having Irix along early this summer when I'd gone to Libertytown, I was glad I'd gone alone. Yes, I'd obviously made a mess of things with this warmonger, but being there on my own had done things for my confidence, allowed me to grow, in ways I never would have been able to do with leaning on Irix for help and guidance the whole way. I'd made mistakes, but they were my mistakes, and I hoped what I'd learned and gained from the trip would far outweigh the repercussion of one heat-of-the-moment blow job.

"What do I do?" I snuggled closer to him, reassured just having him with me.

"Delay. Patience is a virtue, so demons tend to be incredibly impatient, but they measure time on a scale of millennia as opposed to days. Harkel may be eager to solidify this affiliation with you, but he wouldn't expect an immediate response to his offer. Demons are often in the middle of one project or another, or dealing with a sorcerer summoning, or out of touch, and it's not unheard of for a proposal like this to go a few years without response. Even a few decades wouldn't be considered rude. It's not like you're formally a part of his household. It's not like you *have* to accept his breeding contract or even send an immediate response. I'd suggest we wait for a year, then put forth a counter proposal. That would be a quick enough response that it won't insult him, and the back and forth can take a decade or more. By that time, we'll be able to figure out a way to say 'no' without angering a powerful demon."

"Or I'll have enough protection that when I tell him that I

can't accept because I'm not a full succubus, he doesn't feel he has the right to grab me and drag me off to his castle in Dis."

"Hopefully. But in the meantime, he has expectations that there will be some contact between you going forward. If you're in Hel and he encounters you, or even seeks you out, you'll need to acknowledge him, and greet him as you would Kai or another close friend that you've been intimate with. He'll expect that you will cooperate and collaborate on future items of interest together. That's why I need to be with you if you go back to Hel. He's an ancient. He's unlikely to come here, but once you cross the gates, things can go downhill fast."

I'd need to work really fast when I returned to Liberty-town and try to limit the amount of time I spent in Hel, as well as the frequency of my visits. This whole thing hinged on my not 'accidently' running into Harkel, and buying myself time.

"I think I can live with that. I mean I can say no to projects if he sends a request to me through Sam, right? And what about if I run into him in Hel? I like him. I don't mind seeing him again. In fact, I wouldn't mind having sex with him. If you're there to make sure I don't inadvertently agree to something like having his babies, sex should be okay? Would you mind if I had sex with him, or gave him another blow job? That might satisfy him that I'm keeping our end of the relationship, but not give myself away as a half-elf."

Irix frowned. "He's given you a tie. There's no expectation for you to provide additional sexual favors to him, but he may ask for them. We'll try to avoid him when you're in Hel next, just pop in and out as quickly as we can. And if he does happen to find you, we'll have to be flexible and wing it."

I nodded, thinking that this might not be as much of a problem as I'd originally thought. I'd been this side of the gates my whole life with only two short trips to Hel. The chances that I'd run into Harkel were probably slim to none. I picked up the breeding contract, looking at the strange symbols and what must have been Harkel's bold sigil at the bottom. It made me shiver, and not with dread or fear. I liked the warmonger. I'd liked giving him a blow job, petting him out under the moonlight next to the city gates. I imagined the feel of him above me, the smell of his skin, the thrust of his cock inside me as I wrapped my legs around his powerful hips. But if a blow job had consequences, intercourse would no doubt have even more consequences—consequences I wasn't prepared to face.

"Are you still angry with me?" I asked, putting the breeding contract aside and scooting onto Irix's lap. I'd missed him terribly, and now that all my secrets were out in the open, I was desperate to be with him, to give a physical expression to the love I felt for this demon.

"Yes." He slid his hand up my thigh to the top of my jeans and snapped the button open. "I'm very angry with you."

Oh, I hoped this was going where I thought it was going. "Would it help if you punished me?"

He eased down my zipper and ran his finger along the waistband of my underwear. "No, I don't feel punishment is in order, but it would help if you atoned for your sins."

I snorted. "What, so you're an angel now?"

He took my hand and placed it between his legs. "Do I feel like an angel to you?"

"I don't know; I've never groped an angel before." I palmed the bulge in his pants and wiggled enough to slide my shorts over my hips. "So, tell me what I can do to appease your anger, my mighty incubus lover."

He slid a finger into my underwear and I leaned back, angling my pelvis and spreading my thighs as much as the shorts would allow to give him access.

"I'd like to experience this legendary blow job that causes ancient warmonger demons to present a breeding proposal to young, unknown sex demons."

I caught my breath as his fingers brushed through my wet folds, one finger dipping inside me. "I better warn you. If I do this, you might find yourself presenting me with a breeding petition of your own."

What was I saying? He'd made it clear that there would be no marriage, no children between us. I needed to leave this topic alone before it turned into the sticking point that drove a wedge in the middle of our relationship.

"I think you should concentrate on performing so well that I'm no longer angry with you."

It was my turn to edge my hand upward and unsnap his pants. "Oh trust me, one blow job and you'll be completely besotted."

He pulled his fingers from between my thighs and leaned back, putting his hands behind his head. "I'm already besotted. But I'll keep an open mind."

I scooted off his lap, moving the drinks and the coffee table aside to give myself more room. Then I stripped down to my lacy underwear, taking my time while Irix watched me, his golden brown eyes hooded. Then I knelt before him, brushing my breasts against his lower leg as I removed his shoes and socks.

"Very thorough. And keep the underwear on. I like it," he told me, his voice low and rough.

Getting to my feet, I crawled up his lap, straddling him as I pulled his shirt over his head, rocking against the erection in his pants. A muscle twitched in his jaw, his pupils dilating, but he held back from matching my rhythm.

Sliding back down, I kissed a trail from his torso to his waistband, and finished unzipping his pants. He helpfully lifted his hips and I eased his pants downward, slowly removing them one leg at a time, then turning around and bending at the waist as I placed them across the coffee table, flashing him a view of my ass and my very wet lacy panties.

I heard him catch his breath and smiled, well aware that he would have loved nothing more than to get to his feet, shove my head downward, and take me from behind. But this was his game, and he wanted that blow job first.

Turning around, I knelt once more, kissing and nipping as I worked along the inside of his thighs to nudge the underside of his balls with my nose, licking and sucking at the tendon that joined them to his body. They tightened, his cock hardening even more.

"I'm starting to see why Harkel is so enamored of you," he murmured, edging down a bit on the sofa and angling his pelvis so I could slide my fingers between his buttocks, encircling then pushing gently at the puckered entrance of his ass, all the while I continued to lavish attention on his balls, taking them in my mouth before leaving them to run my tongue up the underside of his cock.

A bead formed at the end and I tasted it, licking along his slit to search for more. Then with my finger still at the edge of his asshole, I took him in my mouth, sucking as I slid the entirety of him in with one long pull that ended with my nose on the skin of his pelvis and the head of his cock at the back of my throat. Slowly I worked my way back, pulling my mouth free with a pop.

With one hand still playing with his ass, I brought the other upward, grasping his shaft at the base and slowly stroked him, all the while keeping my tongue busy flicking and sucking the head of his cock. With a slow steady motion of my hand, I moved my mouth downward, exploring the length of his shaft with my tongue. The whole time he kept his hands behind his head, his ragged breathing and the tension in his legs telling me how much he was enjoying this.

Then I got to work, taking him in my mouth and driving down deep, setting up a steady rhythm with my mouth and hand in time with my finger in his ass. His hips rose to meet me with each stroke, with each suck, and I increased the speed, faster, harder. He thickened, hardened, his balls drawing up tight, then with a sharp breath he pushed me from him, standing and spinning me around in one fluid motion.

I gasped at the unexpected action, then laughed and he pushed me face-down across the coffee table, ass in the air, knocking drinks all over the floor. I felt my panties yanked downward, a knee kick my legs apart, a hand pushing the top of my head onto the table, then the press of his cock at my wet entrance.

With anyone else I would have felt a bolt of fear. I was in a vulnerable position, breathless and disoriented from how quickly he'd flipped our positions. But this was Irix and I knew he'd never hurt me, that I could completely trust him. I'd been vulnerable, both physically and emotionally, since I'd met him, and he'd never betrayed my trust. I knew he never would.

He drove into me, and I gasped, feeling his pelvis smack against mine. Then with a grunt he built a punishing rhythm, pounding into me as his balls slapped against my thighs with each stroke. I closed my eyes, losing myself in the feeling of him inside me, of his fingers curling into my hair, one of his hands at my hip, steadying me and ensuring I didn't bruise myself on the edge of the coffee table. I heard myself make that whimper noise that Irix always loved, felt the pleasure spiral through me, building up from my core until my climax exploded, rippling through me. He groaned and followed, holding my hips tight to hold himself deep inside me as he pulsed. Then he let out a deep breath, his grip loosening in my hair, his hand massaging where he'd dug his fingers into my skin.

I waited for him to thrust one final time then pull free before I pushed myself upright from the downward-dog stance on the coffee table. Irix chuckled, helping me up and brushing his fingers across my cheek.

"We made a mess," he said, indicating the cans of ginger ale and spilled glasses on the carpet. I was pretty sure the floor covering had seen worse over the years.

"You made the mess," I teased. "Neanderthal. Give a girl some warning next time you want to flip her around and take her from behind."

He kissed me, a soft, gentle peck on the lips. "No. It's not as much fun if I warn you."

He was right. I put my arms around his neck and leaned into him, feeling his cock stir against me. It was sticky. I was sticky. My floor was sticky. And damn, I was so glad to see him again.

"Still mad at me?"

He grinned, his hands moving downward to grip my ass. "After that? No, I am most definitely no longer mad at you."

My fingers brushed the hair at the nape of his neck. "Good. Let's take this show into the bedroom then, and see what kind of mess we can make in there."

He picked me up and I wrapped my legs around his waist, tucking in my knees as he carried me through the narrow doorway that led to the tiny bedroom. From the edge of the bed he tossed me onto the mattress. I knew I wouldn't be getting much sleep tonight, but that didn't matter. Nothing mattered except having Irix next to me once more and spending the night in his arms.

CHAPTER 4

I awoke before dawn, carefully crawling my way down to the end of the bed and sliding off to make my way to the tiny bathroom. The joy of working in the fields meant I didn't have to dress up, put on heels or make-up, or do more than stuff my hair up into a pony tail. In ten minutes I was ready to go, giving one last look at the sleeping demon in my bed before I headed to work.

Irix had kicked the sheets off and was sprawled naked, taking up the entire width of the bed with his outstretched arms and legs. I had a clear view of his muscular legs and arms, his angular face, so innocent and peaceful in sleep with a sable lock of hair curled on his forehead and the shadow of stubble on his face. His chest rose and fell with each breath, pecs and abs clearly defined, a dusting of dark hair leading downward between the sharp edges of his hip bones to his cock draped lazily across one thigh. How I wanted to crawl my way back up that bed and make it stand at attention, to see his eyes open, lust in their sleepy, golden-brown depths.

But work. Yeah. That thing I'd spent four years studying for. I'd beat out thousands of applicants for the opportunity to get up at dawn, sweat in the sun and dig in the dirt, vines scratching my skin until the sun went down. With a reluctant smile and one last longing glance, I left Irix to sleep the morning away, and quietly shut the door behind me.

I walked the half mile through the fields, eyeing the rows of young vines tied to their posts and strings. DiMarche had its share of issues, as did any agricultural concern, but in the last few days I'd begun to wonder at the sudden outbreak of a surprising variety of pests and diseases. Downy mildew. Leafrollers that laid clusters of eggs on the leaves, then fed on stem, foliage, and fruit, leaving exposed areas that allowed bacteria to infect the plant. Spittlebugs. Chlorotic spots and tissues that withered and died. Infected canes. Stunted growth. And that was just the plants themselves. The soil required constant monitoring for adequate and consistent moisture as well as any sign of fungus, root boring insects and larvae, molds and mildews. None of these would take out an entire crop, but any plant or fruit losses reduced yield and thus ate into the vineyard's profit margin. When a winery such as DiMarche operated on volume and sold on a mid-range affordable price point, Eutypa dieback could mean the difference between happy shareholders or a painful drop in stock price.

I met up with Jorge, the field supervisor for my assignment of the day. He handed me a set of clippers and pointed me toward field eight with mature vines. "Thinning and tying today, Amber. Be careful, we've got a few issues with black measles in those rows. Note any plants that show signs of infection, and seal any open pruning wounds." He looked up from the clipboard and raised an eyebrow. "You know what to look for?"

Of course. "White grape varieties will show yellow patches on the leaves, while red varieties show reddish ones.

Look for dieback at the cane tip and dropped leaves as well as dark spots on the berries with a purple ring."

Black measles tended to crop up when temperatures in the summer were high, especially in certain areas of California and Arizona. The infection was thought to come through large pruning wounds and related to a type of wood-rotting fungi. What Jorge didn't know was that I could sense the outbreak in the plant even without the outward signs, and with enough time, I could eradicate it and heal the vines. Sadly, I didn't have the luxury of that time in this internship. In spite of the thesis that got me this job, I'd been assigned low-level, laborer work after a brief tour of the winery. It was frustrating. I could heal the diseased vines, but that meant I wouldn't get the trimming and tying done, and would wind up reprimanded or even fired. How ironic that they weren't using me to my potential, that what I could do to heal these vines wasn't part of my job description. But that's what happened when I had to keep my supernatural abilities hidden from the human world. Now that elves were being slowly introduced into the human world—or not so slowly in places like Iceland—I might someday be able to come out of the supernatural closet. Maybe. As a half-breed I still had to worry that one of the elves finding a job among the humans would discover my succubus half and stick a knife in my back.

"Nice." Jorge nodded approvingly. "Make sure you note any diseased plants and symptoms so we can send a team out to spray."

I made a face, hating the thought of spraying pesticides on plants that I could heal on my own. Maybe if I got a bit ahead of schedule, I'd at least be able to fix one or two plants and spare them the toxic spray.

Shouldering my clippers and sticking the smaller tools along with the twine into my belt, I headed to field eight, nodding to other workers as I passed. We were spread pretty far apart, so socializing during the day was pretty much impossible. Beyond that, only a handful of the field workers spoke English, and in spite of my demon heritage, I hadn't inherited a demon's ability to quickly and easily learn languages. English was it. I'd failed high school Spanish, and Nyalla's attempts to teach me Elvish had been hilariously unsuccessful.

By noon I'd managed to cure two small incidences of downy mildew, repair some leafroller damage, and trim and tie two long rows of vines. I was soaked in sweat, my hair sticking to the back of my neck. I'd skipped lunch to try to get ahead, and my stomach was growling loud enough that I was sure Carmen two rows over could hear it. At the end of the third row I saw something that nearly brought tears to my eyes. The vine there was the worst, with small, circular, light green circles with dark bulls-eye centers on the leaves. Black veins had stretched out and cracked, leaving seeping wounds on the cane stems. Young grapes were beginning to rot and shrivel. I went to the adjacent rows and found signs that the infection had spread. Phomopsis cane and leaf spot. The odd thing was this type of infection happened during very wet summers, and we'd had very little rainfall the past month. Black measles I could see based on the temperature we'd had this year, but Phomopsis? This shouldn't be happening.

I noted the affected plants on my clipboard and headed in. Jorge took one look at my notes and wrinkled his nose. "Are you serious? Tell me you're not serious."

"I'm serious." When I'd first been assigned to field work, Jorge had questioned every infection I'd logged, assuming that a freshly graduated student with a BS in botany wouldn't know a mealybug from a cutworm. Within two days, he realized that I was spot-on with every diagnosis, pun intended.

"We haven't had enough rain for this." Jorge made a frustrated growl. "I swear this year it's one thing after another. It's gotten so bad that Richard is hiring an expert."

I was an expert. But I was also not quite twenty-two years old, and didn't have the sort of credentials that would land me that kind of job, no matter how good I'd proven myself to be at identifying fungus and bacteria and insects. It was frustrating, but I needed to pay my dues, show that I could be of value to the organization and slowly move upward in my career.

Although, as much as I loved this internship, I didn't see myself working for vineyards long-term. The money was in commercial enterprises like DiMarche, but my heart was in environmental work, like what Jordan did. I was most enthusiastic about the prospect of joining her in New Orleans, making my home with Irix there and working with Jordan to rebuild the wetland areas in the Gulf States. But even in the low-paying world of non-profit, grant-funded studies, I needed to have credibility. And jobs like this built that credibility, even if I spent most of my day thinning leaves and tying vines to the strings and posts.

"When does the expert get here?" I asked Jorge as he finished calling the pesticide crew and telling them what to spray where.

"Tomorrow morning. We're having a meeting of all the field hands first thing to do introductions. Everyone will be expected to cooperate." He gave me an odd look, as if he didn't expect me to cooperate. What was that about? I'd proven myself to be a team player, getting along with everyone from the field hands to the snooty production manager.

"Looking forward to it," I told him. "Anything to help us bring in the best harvest we can."

Okay, that was a bit of a suck-up, but I really wanted good references when I put this job on my resume.

"It's only an hour until your day ends. There's no sense in your going back out into the field." Jorge reached into the back of the Gator he drove and pulled out a spade and a small rake. "Head over to the retail store and tasting room and spruce up the beds out front."

He had to be joking. No he wasn't joking. I was a half-elf who'd spent a week genetically modifying crops in Hel to be drought resistant and to thrive in both high heat and an acidic soil, and I was being sent to pull sorrel and broadleaf out of the geranium beds. I took a deep breath, bit back what I truly wanted to say and smiled. "Sure. No problem."

Without even the slightest bit of grumbling under my breath, I headed to the retail store. The brick facing had been beautifully and artificially aged. The huge oak double doors sported brass handles and hinges, with stained-glass inserts. Little sprinkler heads protruded from the black mulch in between carefully spaced annuals. I eyed them, hoping that if they were on a timer, they weren't set to go off until after my shift completed.

It was boring and uninteresting work, and I was surprised when, after an hour, two other farm hands approached, each carrying hedge clippers. Scotty and Manny. The pair waved at me and got to work trimming the sharp lines of the boxwoods that lined the front of the tasting room and the pathway that led to the parking area. Either they'd finished their rows early, or they'd also found an alarming infestation that prompted them to report it imme-diately to Jorge. It was a disturbing thought that things were going so very wrong in the fields this year. One virulent strain of black measles or fungus was upsetting, but it was to be expected. These things happened, even in large, well-maintained operations. But in the past week, we'd all observed at least six distinct diseases, and over a dozen insect infestations. No wonder Richard was bringing in an expert. Such a mixture of problems, all persistent and recurring in spite of herbicides and pesticides...it made me wonder. I hated to suspect the influence of paranormal beings of magic around every corner, but after what had happened in New Orleans and in Maui, I didn't feel comfortable ruling it out.

But why would someone target a well-known, stable vineyard this way? I could see a hostile stock takeover, but this kind of sabotage was weird. Although given what I'd seen in the past year, weird wasn't so weird. In New Orleans, magic groups had used spells to alter the flow of the river and control the ley lines. In Maui, a farmer had invoked an ancient goddess to assist him in his failing agriculture business with disastrous results. Was this what was happening here? Had the executives and board of directors of DiMarche gotten so greedy that the healthy profits they made weren't enough? Had they tried to increase production only to have a spell backfire on them?

Or was I just imagining it all?

My wandering thoughts took a hard right turn as a familiar energy signature grated along the edge of my awareness. I felt him before I saw the shoes at the corner of my vision, dress loafers sinking into the loamy dark earth. Stabbing my spade into the soil I looked up and saw Harkel. The demon was haloed by the sun behind his head, inky black hair in a neat man-bun, face the familiar warm, dark gold I'd remembered. He was dressed in black slacks with a white button-down shirt, a jacket slung casually over one shoulder making him look like Attila-the-Hun on his way to a stockholders' meeting.

My heart stuttered, and I battled the very conflicting

urges to jump up and flee like a crazy person with the desire to jump him and screw him right on the well-manicured lawn of the tasting room.

"What...what are you doing here?" Fear was giving way to curiosity. And desire. There was nothing threatening or menacing in his expression or stance. Actually for a warmonger, he seemed rather bashful looking down at me as I crouched in the black mulch.

"Amber Shania Lowry." He bowed, his voice deep and gravely with a heavy accent. "I trust you received my proposal? I know it is uncivil to expect a response this soon, but thought it would be better received if I made my offer in person."

He'd learned English. Was that effort for me? I felt the energy from our tie, felt something stir within me at the memory of our night together. Normally sex for a succubus was a one-time thing, but I'd learned there were exceptions to that rule—individuals who meant something to me. Like with Kai, I still wanted this demon, and in spite of all Irix had said about the dangers and how I needed to be cautious, I was delighted to see him.

That worried me. Irix had said to keep my distance, to avoid both giving a response and any chance of encountering this demon again, but Harkel had risked everything to come across the gates to see me. It was flattering, and I *was* excited to see him again, even if in my head I knew the danger I was facing. He thought I was a succubus, but here I was at a winery, digging in the dirt. What if he suspected my half-breed status? What if he guessed the truth?

"Harkel, I...I...I" My words completely failed me. All I could do was crouch there like a rabbit in the briars and eye him nervously.

His brows came together, but an expression that should have been fearful and menacing seemed instead as if he were merely perplexed. "I have crossed a line of protocol, and upset you. That is not what I wanted at all. I haven't offered a breeding proposal in tens of thousands of years, and I apologize if my etiquette is a bit rusty. I did not mean to rush or pressure you in any way. Please take all the time you need to consider my offer—centuries if that is what you wish. I only wanted to see you again, to assure myself that you weren't a figment of an old warmonger's imagination." His dark eyes grew intense, and I felt the pull of attraction between us. "I relive that night together. I close my eyes and feel your hand stroking me as I assisted you with that wagon. I remember the way your fingers tugged at my fur as we sat under the moonlight. I remember your sweet mouth on me, giving me the joy of release and a feeling of connection that I have not experienced since my banishment from Aaru so long ago."

I stared up at him, also relieving those moments with his words. I'd been on my knees before him, his hands on his hips, letting me take the lead and bring him to orgasm. It was so hot, such a turn-on. And Harkel was one impressive demon, whether in human or in lion-bear form. Quiet. Strong. Stoic. A deep river of power under a calm exterior. Damn, I was hot for this guy.

"Amber, in my eagerness I fear I have committed an indiscretion more expected of youthful demons than one of my age. Please tell me that my sudden appearance here has not ruined any chance I have at a recurrence of our encounter. Please tell me that you are as delighted to see me as I am to see you."

I was. And the expression on his face was so adorable, so endearing on a demon of this level and power that I couldn't help but be flattered. "I'm surprised, Harkel. Shocked. But I'm not...dismayed."

He smiled, and it looked oddly natural on a warmonger's face. "Then perhaps I can have an enthusiastic greeting?"

He spread his arms wide and I couldn't resist smiling back. I jumped up, not even wiping the dirt from my hands before throwing my arms around him and planting my lips on his. He hesitated a second in surprise, then wrapped me in his arms, pulling me close and returning the kiss with an intensity that sent heat pooling down between my legs. I liked this demon. I really, really liked this demon. Irix wasn't going to be happy, but I couldn't deny that I *was* delighted to see Harkel once more.

His lips left mine to quirk up in a questioning smile. "Does this welcome mean my proposal is under consideration?"

Uh, no. It meant I was thrilled to see him, wanted to fuck him. It didn't mean I wanted to have babies with him. Besides, from what Irix said, he'd be sadly disappointed that baby-making with me wouldn't be the same as baby making with a full demon, although from the erection I felt pushing against me through his pants, maybe not.

But as displeased as Irix had been to see Harkel's breeding contract, he'd counseled me to delay. Giving a negative response right now would be insulting, and it wouldn't be wise of me to insult a war demon as highly placed as Harkel. I'd take Irix's advice, partially because I liked Harkel far too much to give him the cold shoulder or send him packing back to Hel.

"It's a very flattering offer, but there is much I need to think about. I'm young, and I've never had offspring before."

"Of course. It's only natural for you to want to take time to reflect upon what legacy you would like to leave as a demon and what traits you value, as well pondering the connections you will choose to make." He stroked my back, his hands wandering downward to grip my ass. "I'm flattered that a talented young succubus such as yourself had unreservedly accepted a tie, an intimate and significant link with me. I know I can be intimidating, and I find your open and giving nature to be refreshing."

Uh oh. I needed to tread carefully and never forget that under this attractive exterior lay an ancient and powerful warmonger, who thought that my affiliation with him held far more significance than I'd planned when I agreed to it.

"I'm flattered at your attention and interest, Harkel, but I have to let you know that I also have a previous significant link with another demon. I have a long-standing tie with an incubus named Irix, and his breeding proposal is also under consideration."

It wasn't. Irix had never expressed an interest in having children with me. Admittedly, children with me would require more commitment than between two full demons, but it still stung. Once again, old thoughts of marriage and kids sprang to life, only this time it was Irix as my husband, as the father of my children. It hurt to think that would never happen.

"Irix?" Something sparked in Harkel's eyes at the mention of the sex demon. "The pair of you would create an impressive sex demon. I can understand why his proposal would be at the top of your many offers. Perhaps mine will be next? I do not demand exclusivity."

I'd been told that demons seldom did. And although there was no breeding proposal from Irix, that excuse did buy me some time.

Harkel leaned down to kiss me again, slow and deep. "Perhaps, since I am here across the gateways from Hel...?" he murmured against my lips.

I understood. I'd tied this demon to me and he wanted me just as much, if not more, than I wanted him. My heartrate jumped at the thought of repeating the encounter we'd had in Hel, or maybe this time something different.

"Perhaps a brief encounter. I'd hate for you to return to

Hel unsatisfied, but I do have some business I'm completing at this vineyard during the next few months."

Again there was that spark of interest in his dark eyes. "I don't see what could possibly interest a succubus such as yourself in the dirt outside this winery. And wine? Such an elven beverage. Although since you appear to have Owned the soul of an elf, perhaps you've learned to enjoy such things as plants and fermented grapes."

"I'll admit I do enjoy them." I thought for a second. "And I need to let you know that Irix arrived last night for a lengthy stay with me. The nature of our relationship is such that it would be rude of me to engage in physical intercourse with another demon at this time without at least notifying him first."

He blinked, tilting his head as he regarded me. "You have a tie with me. Any demon would understand that leads to a certain familiarity. There should be no need for Irix to grant permission, or to even know about anything that happens between us."

I felt the sweat pool between my breasts. I couldn't keep Harkel's presence from Irix, nor could I have sex with the warmonger without Irix's knowledge. But how was I going to explain this in terms that wouldn't reveal I was less than a full succubus? "The next few months I've dedicated to Irix. I also have a tie with him, and your arrival here is unexpected. I'm not sure what sort of encounter you have in mind, but I will definitely make time for you. I vowed to Irix that I would tell him about any planned sexual act with another demon during the time he's with me. It's simply a formality."

That sounded horrible, like I was trying to squeeze Harkel in on the side. Like he was an illicit affair that I needed to schedule around my other lovers. Irix would be so angry, but I didn't see any other way out of this. I'd let him know about Harkel's arrival, let him know that I needed to have sex with the warmonger, then hopefully afterward, Harkel would return to Hel for another few decades at least.

Irix would just have to be angry, because as much as I wanted to keep this from him, he had to know. I needed to tell him that Harkel had sought me out across the gates, and that I'd consented to a sexual encounter with him, not just because I owed him that due to our tie, but because I wanted this warmonger as much as he wanted me.

Harkel smiled, leaning back so he could cup my face in his hands. "Then I will indulge your silly request to alert Irix of my presence as well as your intention to have sex with me. I want you, little succubus. With you I feel like an angel again. Read my fantasies, Amber. Read them, and then you'll know what I want from you."

There was a thread of command in his words, a knowledge that I would never be able to deny him what he wanted. And as his desires spooled into me, I realized he was right. Wow. My legs were weak just thinking about it.

"I will be happy to oblige, Harkel. As soon as I'm finished here at work and consult with Irix, I will fulfill all of those fantasies and more."

Work. Oh crap, I was standing in the middle of the walkway holding and kissing someone. Scotty and Manny were just ten feet from me. What must they be thinking? They'd seen me in passionate embraces with Kai, and now Harkel, and no doubt they'd see me with Irix within the next few days. I pulled slightly away from the warmonger and turned, expecting to see the two men scowling at me in shock, or at the very least disapproval over my less-than-professional behavior.

They weren't paying one bit of attention to me because they were fighting. As in, exchanging blows, fighting.

I turned back to Harkel. "Seriously?"

He gave me a sheepish grin and shrugged. "I am a warmonger. It is what I do."

I swatted him playfully on the shoulder, pulling out of his arms. "Well, don't do it at my place of employment. Go cause strife somewhere else."

"You are killing my joy. Spoiling my sport," he teased, but with a wave of his hand Manny and Scotty stopped fighting. I hoped this didn't ruin their working relationship.

It didn't bother me that he'd made two of my co-workers fight. He was right, it was who he was. And the fact that he was a warmonger, that he'd no doubt been responsible for vast numbers of human deaths throughout the centuries didn't dull the attraction I felt for him.

"Can I see you tonight? Perhaps in one or two hours?" His fingers traced along the edge of my jaw. "After you finish this strange work thing you are doing in service to the humans?"

Definitely, but where? And when? I couldn't risk getting fired for doing someone in the tasting room. Irix was probably out taking care of his own needs and wouldn't return until sunset. We could use my trailer. I'd tell Harkel to come by late tonight, after I'd had a chance to break the news to Irix and plan on how I could make this happen, how I could satisfy Harkel without exposing myself further.

"Nine o'clock tonight," I told him. "There are a few things I need to finish first, and I want to prepare if we're going to do...what you want to do."

This felt weird, like I was planning on cheating, even though Irix had never been jealous of my succubus needs, or even my relationship with Kai. I knew it wasn't that Irix was jealous of Harkel. He was only worried that with repeated contact, Harkel would eventually discover what I was. I'd tell Irix. I'd enjoy a wild romp with this warmonger. Then he'd return to Hel satisfied and Irix and I could go back to business as usual.

But Irix would want to stay while I was fucking this warmonger. I knew he wouldn't want me to be alone with Harkel, just in case he needed to intervene. I'll admit there was a part of me that hoped he would watch the pair of us, his eyes dark with passion. Hmmm. I'd known that Kai would never have been interested in having a threesome with Irix and I, but Harkel…

"My place." I told the warmonger the address, again emphasizing that he should be there at nine tonight.

He smiled, brushing his thumb across my lower lip before turning to go. "I count the hours, Amber."

CHAPTER 5

I didn't feel like a femme fatale succubus as I made my way back to my trailer that evening. I stank with sweat. My hair was a damp mess. I was covered in dirt and mulch, and I was tired as well as hungry, having missed lunch. My growling stomach probably had as much to do with my exhaustion as the work I'd done today.

Irix had left a note for me that he'd gone out to recharge and would be back at dusk. I eyed the sun low on the horizon and realized that I'd have time for a quick shower before he got back. Unfortunately, his arrival time was dangerously close to when I was supposed to be having a passionate encounter with Harkel. Hopefully the incubus would be early, otherwise I'd need to stall the warmonger until Irix returned. Just in case either arrived while I was in the shower, I wrote a quick note and stuck it on the front door.

I was starting to regret my agreement to have sex with Harkel. Yes, I still wanted him, but with the warmonger's absence, the reality of my situation hit me hard. I was just making things worse by prolonging this relationship with Harkel, but I couldn't figure a way out of this situation I was in. He was an ancient, and my actions in Hel led him to believe our relationship was more than it was. I needed to be respectful. I needed to fulfill my obligations, no matter how unintended they'd been. And I needed to walk a tightrope of familiarity and distance to ensure I got out of this alive and didn't wind up as an ancient demon's dungeon toy.

I showered, then puttered around the trailer in my underwear, getting a bite to eat and opening a bottle of wine. At a quarter to nine I heard a knock at the door and cringed, wondering if I could climb out the back window and escape. Irix wasn't back yet. The sun was just setting, and he should be here any minute. I just needed to stall.

I couldn't run away from this. If Harkel had tracked me down this time, he certainly could do so again. The warmonger seemed earnest in his affections. I didn't want to piss off a high level demon, but I didn't want to hurt him either. And I wanted him. I returned his affections. I might not feel about him the same way I felt about Irix, but I still cared for him in a way that led me to believe we might have a future together. I'd just lost a future with Kai, possibly even our friendship. Perhaps this sort of love would be easier with a demon who didn't feel the need to comply with human ideas of monogamy. If only I didn't have to worry about him discovering I was a half-elf. If only I was a full demon and could enter into these sorts of relationships without having to hide half of who I was.

I answered the door, realizing too late that I was still in my underwear, my damp hair hanging down my back, a glass of wine in my hand. Harkel was looking like a Wall Street executive in his silk suit, one hand in his pocket and the other holding…a flower?

"In keeping with your elven appearance, I brought you a rose."

Oh my God, the demon brought me a flower. How could

I not like this guy? Irix's warnings faded away as I opened the door wide to let Harkel inside my trailer.

He extended the rose toward me and I took it, smelling the rich fragrance. The tea roses that were typically found in floral shops and in Valentine's Day arrangements were beautiful but without much of a scent. This was an old fashioned rose, not the newer hybrids, so it looked more like the ones that grew on the briars along the roadside, and had a sweet complex smell. It was a thoughtful gift.

I smiled and motioned for him to sit. "Would you like a glass of wine?"

He raised an eyebrow.

Okay. "Or perhaps some rum?"

How horrible was it that I was offering Irix's rum to the warmonger? The whole thing made me uncomfortable. If only the incubus would hurry up and get home so we could all three sit down together and hash this out.

"Is an alcoholic beverage prior to intercourse a common ritualistic practice?" he asked.

Here's where I recited what I'd learned during the nineteen years I'd thought I was a human. "Actually, yes. The ritual is that you arrive and present me with a small gift, which you've done quite admirably. Then we have an alcoholic beverage, sit on the very ugly couch over there and make small talk about the weather in Dis or the prospects of the local sports team. You give me extravagant compliments concerning my appearance and repeatedly mention your undeniable attraction to me. I return those compliments. Then we enjoy some food, and perhaps an additional alcoholic beverage. After a few hours of this, we let passion take the ball and run with it."

And hopefully within those few hours, Irix would return.

He blinked in surprise. "Can we just fuck?"

"No, we cannot. The build-up makes sex more enjoyable

because the whole time we're talking about the weather, we're eyeing each other's bodies and thinking of all the incredible sensory experiences we're about to have. It's foreplay. Think of it as revving the engine at the starting line."

"Then I will have some rum to start my engines."

I poured him a shot and handed it to him. We sat side-by-side on the couch.

"Dis is hot," he announced, throwing down the liquor.

"We too have had a hot summer here in Napa—"

The rest of my sentence was lost as Harkel knocked me backward onto the cushions, his hands in my hair, his lips crushing mine. Heat raced through me. It reminded me of making out with boys back in high school, when they were frantic to get it on, without any ability to restrain themselves whatsoever.

But in the middle of the kiss, something changed. Harkel's gentle bites on my lips became painful. I tasted my own blood, felt the sting of something sharp rip through my shirt and graze the sensitive skin of my side. I gasped into his mouth and struggled to get out from under him, the curl of fear in my belly quickly replacing the lust.

He pulled his mouth from mine, trailing blood down my neck with his kisses, tearing my shirt at the neckline with sharp claws.

"Harkel, no!" I gasped. "Gentle. Don't, please don't."

"Beg, little elf. Beg. This is better than I'd imagined."

It wasn't. It was a whole world of difference from the fantasies he'd sent my way in front of the tasting room. I reined in the pheromones and clamped my lips tight, hoping that if I didn't cry out or encourage him, he'd at least dial it back.

He didn't. And when he buried his fangs into my breast, I screamed.

The door crashed open. Harkel was lifted from me and

thrown across the room where he hit the refrigerator hard enough to knock it sideways into the stove.

I looked up and saw Irix, his golden eyes ablaze, his hands curled into fists. He didn't look at me. His entire attention was on the ancient warmonger who was picking himself up from the kitchen floor and repairing an arm that had been twisted at an unnatural angle behind his back.

Harkel snarled and the air crackled with tension. His hands sparked, talons lengthening. I knew that in a fight between him and Irix, Irix would lose. I'd need to get in the middle of this, to somehow diffuse the situation before the demon I loved wound up dead.

Irix snarled back, but the glow in his eyes changed and suddenly the room was thick with pheromones. They were so overwhelming that I nearly came lying bleeding and in pain on the sofa. The two demons crashed together. Harkel's claws raked Irix's back, his fangs biting down on the incubus's shoulder so deep that they had to have hit bone. Irix never flinched, his face elongating into the beak of his demon form, his hands forming sharp talons. The sex demon pulled back and slapped Harkel across the face, raking furrows in neat red lines on the warmonger's cheek.

The whole time, Irix kept pumping out the pheromones. I was scared. I was in pain. And I couldn't help reaching between my legs through the tears in my underwear to stroke myself. The demons pulled apart, Harkel's form shifting, broadening to the point that his nice suit split and tore. Out of his pants shot an erection of such length and girth that I winced. Had that been intended for me? Because there was no way I could have survived that sort of impalement.

Irix wrapped his hand around it, digging the tips of his talons into the demon's cock and scratching along its length as he gave it two quick pumps. Harkel roared, and I waited for him to rip Irix's head off, but instead he thrust his hips forward, jabbing claws into the incubus's chest and tearing loose bits of skin and muscle. Irix continued to stroke the demon, ripping skin along the warmonger's shaft until his cock was red and torn. Still, Harkel thrust his hips, his member hardening to the point where it seemed as if Irix was jacking off a bloody pike of steel. Claws flashed, fangs bit, and it was hard to tell which blood was the incubus's and which was the warmonger's. The entire time Irix kept the pheromones at maximum, and as scared as I was, I kept stroking myself, working my clit until I was writhing on the sofa, unable to take my eyes off the two demons.

Harkel gripped Irix's hip, impaling his claws into the flesh. With his other paw he palmed the bulge in the sex demon's pants and squeezed to the point that I was sure Irix would cry out, if not pass out. Instead he took a step forward, working the warmonger's cock and bringing it between his thighs. His beak opened wide and bit down on Harkel's shoulder. The warmonger shouted, slamming his pelvis into Irix's and throwing his head backward. The pheromones stuttered. Cum shot all over my floor and carpet, on top of the pools of blood. I felt my approaching orgasm slip away from me, replaced once more with pain and fear.

Claws, fangs, and talons retreated. Irix's beak shifted back to his normal, human face.

"You had no right to interfere," Harkel growled. "We have a tie. The succubus Amber and I were only continuing to solidify our relationship. You had no right to interfere."

"I had every right." Irix's voice was low and husky, sending a shiver of need through me. He reached up to grab the back of Harkel's head and pull him forward. There was a shared breath, then Irix's lips met the warmongers in one of the sexiest, most passion-filled kisses that I'd ever seen.

"We will discuss this," Harkel murmured, his hand stroking Irix's bloody cheek. "I will return in two nights, in the evening, after Amber has finished her ridiculous duties with the humans at the winery, and we will discuss this."

Irix ran his thumb across the warmonger's lower lip, his eyes watching the motion. "In two nights. I look forward to it."

There was such innuendo to his statement that I had no doubt what Irix meant. Harkel's huge cock stiffened again and he smiled, opening his mouth to suck on the tip of Irix's thumb. "I look forward to it, too."

Then the warmonger left, his clothing ragged, his body bloody, an erection that was beyond the scope of the human body poking from his torn pants.

I let out a breath and turned wide eyes to Irix. He grinned, his teeth red with blood. Then he staggered backward and slid down the side of the leaning refrigerator to collapse on the floor.

CHAPTER 6

*J*jumped up from the sofa and ran to Irix, ignoring my own injuries to attend to his far more significant ones. Grabbing a towel off the sink, I pressed it to his shoulder, checking the gouge marks along his waist and hips.

Wait. He was a demon. And now that he had immunity, he could repair himself without fearing that the angels would catch him.

I threw the towel aside and swatted him on the shoulder. "Fix your injuries before you get any more blood on my floor."

He winced. "That's the thanks I get? I'd hoped to lay here in a pool of my own blood while you fussed and cried over me a little. Can't a guy enjoy a little attention before he repairs his wounds?"

No, he couldn't. "I want to hug you and cry on your shoulder and tell you how scared I was and that you arrived just in time like my own personal sex-demon knight, but I can't do that when you look like I should be measuring you for a casket."

He sighed, and with a flash his flesh was once more smooth and olive-tanned. His clothes were still tattered. His skin was still red with blood, but he was no longer injured.

So I threw myself at him, wrapping my arms around his neck, and sobbed. He held me tight, rocking me back and forth while I let all of my fear release. I had a bite mark on my breast, a bite on my lip, and a shallow but bloody scratch on my waist. I'd heal quicker than a human, but not nearly as quickly as if I'd been a full demon. If Harkel had been overcome with passion, if he'd done to me what he'd done to Irix, I might have died.

And wouldn't the warmonger have been shocked to find himself holding a corpse in his arms when he was doing nothing that a demon wouldn't have found completely normal in a sexual encounter? I really liked Harkel and I wanted to have sex with him, to have a relationship with him. But I wasn't what he thought I was. I couldn't do these things, and I didn't know if he'd be interested in something with me that was more human and less demon.

When I was done sobbing, Irix lifted my head from his shoulder and brushed away my tears, leaning forward to kiss my nose. "I did what I had to do, Amber. I would never let him hurt you. I only wish I'd come back a few minutes earlier."

He'd taken my place. He'd turned Harkel's lust from me to him and in his expert incubus fashion, had given the demon exactly what he wanted.

"I'm so sorry. I feel horrible that you took that…endured that for me. I'm so sorry."

He smiled, smoothing the hair from my face. "Don't be. I actually enjoyed it. Harkel was gentle by demon standards. I get the impression he's quite a bit more moderate and sane than most of the ancients. If you wanted to be entangled with a demon, I think he'd be the right choice."

Why did Irix's words make me feel so much better? But he'd enjoyed that? What he'd just done with Harkel wasn't anything he could have done with me, even if I'd had the correct body parts. Maybe both of us could find something of value in a relationship with this warmonger. Well, if I could somehow convince Harkel that I needed to be handled with the demon equivalent of kid gloves.

"And when he comes back in two nights?"

Irix smiled and I caught my breath, suddenly wanting him even though my lip and breast were still throbbing in pain. "In two nights we will meet, talk, then come to an agreement. Trust me, Amber. I've survived as an incubus unaffiliated with any household my entire life. I've never needed another demon's protection because I'm good at what I do. I'm very good at what I do. By the time he leaves, either Harkel will be the most gentle, loving sexual partner you've ever had or he'll be ripping up the breeding contract he sent and vowing to never see you again."

I had a bad feeling in the pit of my stomach. "And why would he do that?"

That golden spark was back in Irix's eyes, his smile turning lascivious. "Because after tomorrow night, all he will be able to think about is me."

And when his voice grew deep and husky, when he smiled like that, his golden-brown eyes lit with an unnatural glow, I believed him, because all I could think about was Irix, as well.

"So how did this happen?" he asked. "I come home from hunting and find Harkel on top of you, biting you while you screamed. Did he break in and attack you? Because if that's the case we're going to have a very different conversation in two nights than I'd imagined."

"No, he was actually very nice until he started the biting stuff," I explained. I told him all about Harkel showing up at my work, and how bashful and sweet he'd been. "I think he was just overcome with passion, and since he assumed I was a full succubus, he didn't think anything was wrong about clawing me and biting me hard enough to draw blood."

Irix stroked my shoulder. "No, he probably didn't. That's gentle as far as demons are concerned. And your squirming, your fear, and your screams would have only encouraged him. We're predators, Amber. And even when two predators meet, they enjoy the fear and the pain. Never forget that you're only half of us. Never forget that we're capable of killing you and not even realizing we're doing harm."

We. He'd included himself in that statement, but I knew Irix was different. Whatever he felt, he was able to hold it all in check for me. I wasn't sure Harkel would be able to do the same.

"You're hungry," he told me, leaning forward to place a gentle kiss on my bruised and cut lip. I felt a tingle and knew the skin was knitting together.

"Did you just heal me?" I accused him. Demon's didn't heal, they fixed and fixing wasn't a perfect science when it came to repairing injuries that weren't their own. Irix might do a great job, but I'd wind up having to repair and deal with whatever long-term damage his "fixing" had caused.

"No. You're an elf. Elves heal. I'm just jump-starting that process in you since you're only a half-elf."

I was starting to feel better already. "Sex? That will definitely help me heal."

He stood, pulling me upright with him. "Yes, it will. Come to bed Amber so I can share my energy with you. Tomorrow you can go out to hunt, but let *me* be the one to feed you tonight."

I had no desire to go out and hunt for sexual partners tonight, not after what had happened with Harkel—what had almost happened with Harkel. I wanted to be cherished. I wanted to be loved. I wanted to have someone fuss over me and take care of my every need.

"Can you see my fantasies," I whispered to Irix.

He smiled. "Always, Amber. Always."

CHAPTER 7

The next day I felt like I'd been worked over with a tire iron. The remaining bruises and sore muscles from Harkel's affections combined with a very late night that included lots of affection from Irix left me both aching and sleep deprived.

Even after Irix had dozed off, I'd tossed and turned as I worried about how this thing with Harkel was going to work out. Then I kept reliving the image of Irix, torn and bloody after sex with the warmonger.

It wasn't just my safety I was concerned about. It wasn't just worry that Harkel might find out I was a half-elf and drag me off to his lair. It was something else, and I couldn't quite put my finger on it.

Jealousy? Was I some crazy woman who was jealous that the warmonger's affections had so easily turned to Irix? Compared to Irix I was young and inexperienced, so of course he could command even an ancient's attention.

Or was I jealous that Harkel could fulfill what the demon in Irix wanted, that he could give him the rough sex that was out of the question even if I could physically make it happen?

Irix had never been jealous of my sexual partners, even Kai. But I was of his. Maybe the fact that Harkel was a demon bothered me. Maybe the fact that Harkel was a higher-level, older, powerful demon bothered me.

Yes, I was smitten with the warmonger, and it seemed he returned that affection, but Irix held a place in my heart that no one else would. As often as I told him that, he never seemed to believe me. His response was always that I was young, that as I gained experience I'd change. And here I was worrying that he'd change *his* mind, that I'd become boring to him, that he'd want what someone like Harkel could give him—sex that crossed the line into violence as well as offspring between two beings of spirit. I'd love Irix forever, but was I just an exotic fling? Would he miss the things I couldn't give him? Would he want to leave his genetic mark with someone that didn't insist he change diapers and deal with spit-up burps?

I guess I'd find out tomorrow night when Irix, Harkel, and I had our sit-down. Until then I had a vineyard full of disease and pests to deal with. When I arrived where Jorge always gave out our daily assignments, there was a group of the field workers standing around the Gator just outside the equipment sheds. For a second I wondered what the commotion was, then I remembered that today was the day that the "expert" would arrive.

"Is he here yet?" I asked Manny, taking the Styrofoam cup of coffee he handed to me. Wow, this expert rated coffee? He must be important for Jorge to have pulled out the huge coffee urn and drag it into the field with a box of cups and little bags of sugars and powdered creamer.

"Not yet." Manny rolled his eyes, one of which was shadowed right above his cheekbone, no doubt from his warmonger-inspired altercation with Scotty last night.

"I'm guessing he's some French dude with knife-pleated, black silk pants and a cravat," I told him.

He laughed. "And a jaunty beret tilted rakishly to one side."

"And he'll lecture us that the reason our crops are having these blights is because our grape varieties are inferior and the soil a poor substitute for what they have in Bordeaux or Champagne," Scotty added, reaching over Manny to grab a sugar packet.

"French grapes, pfft," Rosa chimed in. "*They* are a poor substitute for what we have in Chile."

"Nobody grows chardonnay like northern California. Nobody," Henry added. "And as far as vintnering goes, our red blends are putting us on the map."

"Ah non," Manny said in a fake French accident, waving his hands in the air. "The red blends, they are a sacrilege to fine wine. The uneducated peasants may buy them by the caseload, but those who have even a modicum of palate will turn away their noses in disdain."

I laughed. "He's not a sommelier, he's a pesticide or insecticide expert. I'm thinking some old dude who spent the last forty years of his life working for DuPont."

"Or a twenty-year-old hippy from the co-op who is Richard's cousin's wife's stepbrother's nephew or something," Scotty conjectured.

A shiny black F350 pulled up and we all fell silent, trying to catch a glimpse of our expert through the dark-tinted windows of the truck. Jorge hopped out of the driver's side. The passenger door opened, and we craned our necks.

First, expert dude wasn't a dude. He was a she. And she was a diminutive woman wearing clothes that looked like they just came off a hanger at Nordstrom's. Her make-up was subtle and tastefully applied, her long blond hair clipped back at the nape of her neck with a gold barrette. She wore an oversized pair of designer sunglasses, expensive, yet comfortable Italian leather flats, and a pair of thin leather gloves that looked more suitable for driving a sports car in the French Riviera than handling thick vines and wires. In her hand she carried a clipboard that was a duplicate to the one in Jorge's hands.

And she had pointy ears.

"Whoa. An elf." Scotty elbowed Manny in the ribs. "I thought they were all in Iceland."

Manny elbowed him back. "Nah, there's an island of them somewhere in the South Pacific where they learn about money and how to drive cars and operate cell phones."

"And shop at Nordstrom's, evidently," Rosa added.

"Yeah, that, too." Manny nodded. "But when they're ready, they are supposed to join society and get jobs or something. Weird, huh? Elves running around. A dragon in the British Museum. And angels. Although I've never seen one of the angels. I'm not sure where they all hang out."

"Probably on the island with the elves," Henry commented. "Right, Amber?"

I didn't reply because I was frozen like a deer in headlights, watching the elf woman's head swivel as she eyed our group of field hands clustered around the Gator, drinking coffee. Maybe if I hid behind Henry she wouldn't see me. I wasn't in Hel, so my ears weren't pointy and my mirror told me I looked like a human, but Irix had always said even without the distinctive tips on my ears, I looked just like an elf.

At this moment I didn't want to look just like an elf. Why was this happening to me? My mother had sent me to live here in a changeling swap so I'd be safely away from both elves and demons, and here I was with a warmonger literally bringing me flowers and wanting me to have his baby, and an elf who would be walking the fields beside me. Two races who couldn't know what I was, right here right now. Was there nowhere safe for me anymore?

"We've got a busy day ahead of us," Jorge announced. "But before we head out, I want to introduce the expert that Richard hired to help us combat the insects and blights we've been having with our vines and fruit this year. Hallwyn will be working with all of you in the fields over the next few months, and I expect you to give her your full cooperation."

Manny's hand shot up. I cringed, trying to distance myself from him. "Hallwyn is an elf? Is this legal? I mean, I had to practically get fingerprinted here to prove I could legally work in the U.S. She got her social security card, H1B, and all that other stuff?"

Jorge fixed him with a stern look. "Here at DiMarche we comply with all federal, state, and local labor and employment laws."

Rosa's hand shot up. "Yeah, but she's an elf."

"And you're from South America, Rosa. She's an expert. She knows more about powdery mildew, cutworm, and black measles than anyone in this field."

Well, anyone except me. Suddenly my fear vanished and I eyed Hallwyn, feeling incredibly bitter that I, who most likely knew even more than she did about the plants, bacteria, fungus, and insects indigenous to this area would be sweating in the field with a set of clippers, while this elf got to prance around in her Italian leather flats and be the hero who saved the harvest. And she probably got paid five times as much as I did, too.

"I'm thrilled to be helping you," Hallwyn announced, her accent lilting with rolling lls and long vowels. "I will begin with the mildew and the measles, then look at the others."

Rosa sniggered. "Her English is worse than Manny's."

"Hey," Manny glared at her. He didn't have time to do

much more than glare because Jorge had started handing out the day's assignments.

"Amber, field eight. Show Hallwyn where you found that Phomopsis."

I caught my breath, hesitating a moment before walking forward to grab my tools and clipboard. Then I walked to the elf, giving her a stiff smile. She was staring down at her clipboard, but the moment she looked up from it, she did a double take.

"You're Am-burr?" Her eyes narrowed, her gaze swinging from my face to my ears. I had my hair in a high ponytail today, my rounded, very human, ears clearly on display.

"Yes. I'm Amber Lowry. I'm here this month on an internship. I graduated in May from Penn State with a degree in botany. You're an elf?" I looked at her ears, as if I'd never seen such things before.

A shadow passed across her face. "Yes. Formerly of Wythyn. My family managed the royal gardens."

I nodded. "Well, let's go look at some Phomopsis."

She followed me through the fields, removing her gloves and brushing her hand along the canes. A few times she had me stop while she examined the underside of some leaves or a bunch of immature fruit. Each time I watched carefully, trying to see why she'd needed a closer look at those particular plants. None of them were diseased or damaged. Perhaps she was trying to get a baseline on what a healthy vine looked like so she could detect subtle differences in the infected ones that had left them open to disease. Or perhaps she had no idea what she was doing, and was faking expertise. I wasn't sure what foliage the Wythyn elves had in their royal gardens, but from my short visit to Hel, I knew similar plant life didn't mean they were exactly the same.

"How long were you on the island?" I asked, looking back

at her. It was hard to read her expression now that she'd put her sunglasses back on.

"A few weeks."

That didn't sound right. "You learned all about human culture, human language, and our flora and fauna in a few weeks? You somehow became an expert in pests and diseases of grapevines in a few weeks?"

"Elves are very intelligent. We learn exceptionally fast and your plant life here is remarkably basic. Becoming an expert took only a few days, but I was not allowed to leave until I had secured an assignment and a means to both support myself and provide a service to human society."

Well, la-de-da.

"How do you elves get assignments? Is there a placement service? Do human employers post job openings somewhere? I had to apply for this internship, submit a copy of my senior year study, and interview, competing against thousands of other applicants."

I don't know why I told her all that. It wasn't like she'd care, and it made me sound as if I were desperate for validation of my intelligence and worth from her. I shouldn't be bothered about what she thought of me, but it rankled that she was the expert while I was the field hand. And it irritated me that she'd been handed this assignment on a silver platter while I'd needed to work my butt off to get this internship.

"We each have areas of expertise. There is someone who coordinates connecting us with positions where humans can benefit best from our superior knowledge and abilities."

I was beginning to hate this woman. And I knew that wasn't exactly fair. They'd spent their whole lives thinking of humans as slaves—some with talents in magic, but most just grunt labor. They'd come here thinking they were going to rule only to have their ruling-class elves mostly killed off and the rest of them shuffled onto an island to learn to be of service to the humans they'd originally planned to lord it over. They were arrogant, smug jerks as far as I could tell, but it's not like they'd had a chance to form a different opinion in their lives, and now they were being thrust into a strange world, made to bend their customs and culture to suit a foreign one, and told by the angels that they must be of service, or else be sent back to Hel.

I was pretty sure most of them wished they'd never left Hel at all.

Hallwyn said something in elvish, in a loud clear voice that I was clearly meant to hear. None of it involved the few curse words I'd managed to memorize, so I had no idea what she was saying. I ignored her and kept walking.

"You look very much like an elf woman," she told me, lengthening her stride to catch up and walk beside me. "A very low-class elf. And the resemblance when I am closer is only minor. Still, if you had more symmetrical features and elegant ears, I would have thought you to be a child of a basket-weaver, or perhaps a semi-skilled fletcher."

Screw her. My mother was of the Wythyn royal family. And the only reason my features weren't the perfect elven symmetry and my ears weren't topped with tall points was that my succubus half allowed me to blend in with the humans—something *she'd* never be able to do.

"I was raised in Frederick County, Maryland, by my mother. I'm not aware that either of my parents had elven ancestry, but perhaps if some basket-weaver or semi-skilled fletcher had an illegitimate child with a human, that would account for my somewhat elven appearance."

I was thrilled at the horrified expression on her face. "That would *never* have happened. Even the lowest of the elven classes has a sacred responsibility to preserve the purity of our race. Elves would never stoop to having inti-mate relations with humans or any other being. And to have children with a partner outside of the elven race is to commit a crime where the punishment is execution. No elf has ever done so. None ever."

Well, there was that one elf, namely my mother. And she had been killed for it, even though they'd never found me and there had been no substantial proof of her crime.

Remembering what they'd done to my mother, what this woman's kingdom had done to the mother I'd never even had a chance to meet, the elven woman who'd sacrificed so much, including her life so that I'd be safe, just made me hate this woman even more.

But I swallowed it all down, knowing that to her, I needed to remain a useless human field hand who just happened to look a little bit like a low-class elf.

"Guess that just makes me a pretty human, then." I smiled at her, and wished I could punch her in the face instead. "Here's row eight. We've had black measles in a few of the younger vines, which isn't surprising with the hot summer we've had so far. The Phomopsis was a surprise. It tends to flare up when there has been an abnormally large amount of rainfall."

"I know that." She sniffed and walked over to a plant, rubbing a leaf between her thumb and forefinger.

Bullshit. "These first two plants have shown signs of lead-cable-borer damage," I lied. "The Phomopsis is further down, toward the end of the row."

Any reasonably knowledgeable botanist, human or elven, would have immediately checked the lower trunk of the vine for the round holes the borer larvae left behind as they emerged. If this vine were infested with leadcable-borers, it would have long meandering tunnels on the vine stem even if the trunk hadn't shown signs of housing the larvae. A few of those tunnels might even have the cream-colored, c-shaped larvae with their dark heads nestled into the stems as they fed. They weren't common pests, and as with many of the fungal and insect infestations, a leadcable-borer infestation resulted from carelessly leaving dead trimmings around on the ground near the vine trunks.

Hallwyn didn't look down at the trunk, or along the vine stems. Instead she glanced at the ground beside the vine then back at the leaf. "Interesting."

Seriously? Did she have the skill to sense the black beetles from just the leaf? Did she know I was lying but didn't want to confront me about it? After her rude remarks about my parentage in particular, and humans in general, I couldn't believe she'd think twice about calling me out on my falsehood.

"Yes. It is quite interesting." I led her down to the last few plants where I'd seen the Phomopsis and halted, waiting for her to check the leaves and fruit. Detecting this would be no judge of skill. A blind man could see the damage the plant had suffered.

She didn't disappoint, touching the bulls-eye spots on the leaves, running a finger along the puckered veins. Then she pushed the leaves aside, checking the black streaks and cracks along the stems with what seemed like a knowledge-able eye. Turning to the last vine in the row, she immediately looked at the grapes, frowning.

"I told Jorge about the infection yesterday afternoon and he sent out a crew to spray," I told her. "Today I need to trim back the diseased wood and remove the clippings, but I'm concerned I won't be able to prune the vine hard enough to fully rid it of the disease. Too much, and there won't be enough of the vine to survive. Can you tell if the spray is working? And if so, how little can I get away with in pruning the plant?"

She was an elf. She should be able to feel how the vine was responding to treatment and let me know the areas that were too far gone and needed to be removed as opposed to the portions that could be left behind and re-treated. And if she were truly skilled, she should be able to fix the entire vine, rid it of the disease and repair the damaged areas to full health. I watched her carefully, waiting, and wondering what course of action, what level of skill and power a full-elf would have as compared to my abilities.

She nodded. "The treatment is having an effect. Remove these stems and all the fruit, leaving the main trunk and these canes. This section will be fine, but these other two need to go."

Guess she wasn't going to heal the plant. Not that *I'd* healed the plant yesterday, but I had my reasons. There was only so much energy I had to spare, and this vineyard had a lot of problems. Plus, I didn't want the owners to realize that their minimum-wage intern had supernatural powers to heal their plants. From there it would be one quick step to rumors of my abilities, and discovery of my half-elf heritage. Normally that wouldn't be a big deal, but with ninety percent of the elves migrating from Hel, I had to be careful. Hallwyn wasn't the only one who viewed an elven hybrid as an abomination, and if discovered, every elf would be eager to have me meet the same fate as my mother.

"Got it." I pulled a set of pruning shears from my tool belt. "Manny is one row over, and I know he had some spider mites."

Without a word she left, moving swiftly and silently as all elves did. I watched until she'd vanished into the next row, then slid my shears back into the belt, and reached out to touch the plant.

It had gotten worse. Somehow the spray had delivered no lasting effect, and the blight was spreading. I bit my lip and looked at the plant, knowing I'd need to trim back far more than Hallwyn had told me to. This plant wasn't going to make it, and the thought of losing an entire vine to this disease had me feeling just as sick as the leaves I was touching. I pulled my pruning shears back out and got to work, removing exactly what the elf had told me, then gathering the clippings up into a bundle to take to the end of the row where they'd be collected tonight and stuffed into an incinerator. Then I looked around to ensure no one was watching and touched the plant once more.

I closed my eyes and fell into the leaves and stems, seeking out the blackness of disease and pulling it from the plant and into myself. My stomach rolled, my head pounded. I felt a bead of sweat slide down my nose and heat rush through my body as I burned and destroyed the blight inside myself. Then I turned my attention back to the vines, soothing every gnarled vein, repairing cells and healing fissures. Done, I let go of the plant and opened my eyes, fighting the urge to throw up. I was tired and shaky, but this plant would live.

The plant would live, but the worst part is that Hallwyn would take all the credit. I continued to work down two more rows, healing what I could until it was the end of my shift. Walking through the fields, I saw Hallwyn putting her gloves on, muttering to herself in Elvish. What did the elf do when she went home for the day? Did she sit in a trailer staring at her dinner? Did she fraternize with humans? How isolated was she? Did DiMarche give her a tiny rusted trailer like mine, or did they put her up in a swank hotel more fitting for an elf?

I checked my phone and decided I had time for a quick trip. Then I ran after Hallwyn at elf-speed, catching up to her just as she pulled out of the driveway in a new Prius. Figures. I was driving an ancient Toyota pickup that I'd had since I was sixteen, and she had a new car not two weeks after leaving Elf Island.

Hoping old Bessie started, I jumped in, dug my keys out of my pocket. The engine reluctantly turned over, and with a cloud of stone dust, I tore out of the driveway and gunned it in an attempt to catch up.

Hallwyn was the worst driver I've ever seen in my life. I'd seen Nyalla behind the wheel, and this elf was worse. Clearly the angels in charge of Elf Island needed a better driver's ed class. Instead of pulling into the road with the line of trailers, or turning onto the freeway that would take her into town and the imagined apartment, Hallwyn kept going. Ten miles later she was making a left into a neighboring winery, Boone Valley.

What the heck? Was she spying on us for the competition? Something sour curdled in my stomach as I began to wonder about all the varieties of diseases and pests the DiMarche vineyards were suffering this year. I'd suspected a supernatural cause, maybe I was following the person, or elf, responsible. Maybe Hallwyn wasn't inept, she was very skilled—skilled at causing disease and damage, then looking like she was making every attempt to fix it. What was Boone paying her?

I held back and watched while she parked up near the tasting room, then I swung around to the side lot and pulled my Toyota in behind a box truck. Then as stealthily as my elven feet could move, I edged my way up to the tasting room and peered in the window. I expected to see Hallwyn receiving an envelope full of cash from a man twirling a black villain mustache, but instead she was sitting at the tasting room bar next to another blonde, impeccably dressed woman with pointy ears.

Boone had their own elf. I just hadn't expected them to know each other. So these two were…friends? Were there elves at some of the commercial orchards and vegetable farms that they knew? Were they all in league together to run competing businesses into the ground for a payoff, or were they just lonely?

I guess if I were the only elf at my place of employment, any elf within a hundred-mile radius would wind up being my friend. It's not like Hallwyn could socialize with humans without getting cooties or something.

Was this just an innocent social visit? Or was there something to my theory that Hallwyn was causing the troubles at DiMarche?

I wanted to look into this further, but it would have to wait until tomorrow, because I was tired and hungry, and if I was going to single-handedly fix the problems at DiMarche, I needed to have a whole lot of sex.

CHAPTER 8

*T*rix was in the trailer when I'd returned, an excited expression on his face and a heavenly smelling meal in the oven. There might have been paper plates on the table, but there were also candles, wine, and fresh flowers. He'd put Harkel's rose right in the middle of his bouquet, and that more than the dinner and expensive wine told me how he was feeling.

"It's going to be okay?" I asked.

He smiled. "Yes. I've got an idea that will make Harkel happy, and give you the satisfaction of an alliance with him that won't get you killed. It's all going to be okay."

I choked back a sob and ran into his arms, letting all the fears I'd locked away this morning out into the open. I'd been so scared that one foolish blow job was going to ruin everything.

He rubbed his cheek against my hair. "I'm sorry. I should have instructed you on how to act in Hel and around other demons. I've been slacking in my tutoring duties, and I intend to make up for it. You can go to Hel and help the humans. You can have sex with Harkel. You can even have sex with a Low if you want. I will coach and guide you. I'll be there to keep you safe. I'll let you know if I think your course of action is ill-advised, but I won't forbid you from anything. You are so young, but in the human world you're an adult and I promise to respect that."

"But the tie with Harkel…how are we going to work that out? I know that bothers you."

He sighed. "I'm worried about what that meant in terms of Harkel's expectations. He's an ancient, a powerful warmonger, and you're not a full demon. There may be things he wants that are beyond your ability to provide."

"Like the breeding contract."

"Yes, or other things. He's strong enough to break the tie with you if he chooses, so either we work this out, or we manage to convince him to break it. My hope is that if he persists in wanting an affiliation, he'll become so attached to you that even if he finds out you're not a full demon, he won't harm you."

I thought about that a moment. "He needs to see me as more than a plaything, see a value in me beyond sex. Maybe then it won't matter that I'm only half-demon."

Irix nodded. "Yes, but that will be difficult. Demons gain respect by being…demonic. I love you, Amber, but beyond your succubus ability, you're all elf. Actually you're very human, but that's not surprising given how you were raised."

How to get an ancient warmonger to respect a young half-elf who has succubus skills and acts like a human. This wasn't going to be easy. Was it worth the effort? Maybe I should just hide somewhere for a few centuries.

But then I thought of Harkel with his sweet smile, bringing me a rose, learning English and risking a trip through the gateways just to see me. I had to try.

"How are you feeling about this?" I pulled back to look up at Irix, searching his face. "With Kai we were all friends, and she and I would have our private time together, but with Harkel, you're going to be very involved in this relationship."

The idea turned me on. Even the other night, with that violent hand job, I still felt a thrill when I imagined the three of us together.

"I don't know." Irix pulled away from me and grabbed a pair of mitts, pulling the roast from the oven. "I won't deny that I'm attracted to the warmonger, but honestly I'm not thrilled with the idea of sharing you with another demon. I've been urging you to feed your succubus self through sexual activity, yet at the same time I was expecting a sort of human monogamy when it came to our bond and your having sex with other demons. So I guess I'm jealous. Irrationally jealous to expect I'd be your only demon lover, the only demon you'd bond with."

He wasn't the only one. "I've been jealous of you, too. It's been so difficult not to care about your one-night stands with humans but the thought that you might have a tie with another demon makes me stabby. And here I am doing the very thing that would crush me if you were to do it."

"Then maybe the key to this is that we're all three in this together, as opposed to the type of arrangement you share with Kai. At least until I trust that he won't hurt you, then I'll just have to reconcile myself to the fact that there are times that you may want to have a few weeks, or months, or years, one-on-one with Harkel."

"No. Irix, he's not going to replace you. Kai didn't replace you, and Harkel won't either, if we somehow manage to make this work at all, that is."

He started slicing the beef and putting it on a platter. This calm resignation of his bothered me more than anything. "You say that now, Amber, but you're young and might change your mind. I need to look to the benefits that will come with your affiliation with Harkel. If you join his household, if you continue to secure his affections, then perhaps he'll protect you as a half-breed from the other demons. He'd be in a much better position to protect you than I ever would."

There was a world of pain in that last statement of his. "I love you, Irix. I've never felt the same way toward anyone else, and even though I like Harkel, even though I'm sexually attracted to him, it will never be the same as what I feel for you. Please stop doubting that. Please stop thinking that my love for you will fade in a few centuries, and trust that you're the one constant in my life. You're the one who I always want with me. And if I need protection, I want you to be the one protecting me, even if you enlist another demon's help."

He took the platter of food over to the table. "Tonight I want to be only about us. I need that. I need us to share a meal together, to make love, to sleep together in each other's arms, because tomorrow when we meet with Harkel everything will change. I'll either convince him to accept a three-way tie where I can intervene and protect you as I did last night, or I'll make sure he transfers his affections to me and drops the tie with you. But if we wind up together, then this will be different than how things are between just you and me. This will involve three demons, well two demons and a half-demon. That makes this tricky and we'll need to work at it to ensure there are no jealousies, or power plays or sabotage of each other's relationships. I worry, because Harkel is a warmonger, and warmongers don't have an easy time making peace with someone they see as a rival."

I grabbed the tray of roasted vegetables and followed him to the table. "Then he needs to not see you as a rival. He needs to see you as his, too. He needs to feel like he's getting the attentions of two sex demons for the price of one."

I remembered the admiration in Harkel's voice when I'd told him that Irix had petitioned me for a breeding incident.

I remembered the way he'd looked at the incubus even as they were gearing up to beat the snot out of each other. I remembered the way they'd both enjoyed ripping each other to shreds last night as Irix jacked the warmonger off. Harkel was as attracted to Irix as he was to me. And I got the impression that although it wasn't quite as strong on his part, Irix had the same feelings toward the warmonger that I did.

Would this work? Could we possibly have a threesome relationship where no one felt left out, where each had a separate role and identity but where we could come together in mutual affection? And the sex…holy cow, the very idea of it was turning me on.

"I don't know if this will work. I've been in threesomes and while they work fine for the occasional kinky sex, they don't always work well in relationships, especially with demons. Three sex demons, maybe, but a warmonger is going to want to win, and that usually means being the sole focus."

"What if he *was* the sole focus?" I asked. "He can't be here forever. He's got to go back to Hel. Let's say he comes across the gates once every decade or so, spends a week with us, and during that week, it's all about him?"

Irix frowned. "I won't pretend, Amber. I won't fake devotion for someone, even an ancient. I'm willing to meet with him, to entertain the idea, but if I don't feel about him in a way that would create a stable threesome relationship, then the answer is no. And if the answer is no, I'll use every bit of my incubus power to pull him from you so he willingly transfers the tie to me."

At least he was willing to try. And as much as it made me ill to think that Irix would take on my debt to the warmonger for me, I got the feeling it wouldn't be such a burden. Yes, Irix had always worked solo, but by his own admission, a link to a powerful, ancient warmonger wouldn't exactly be a bad thing. I was glad he'd decided to keep an open mind as well as make a romantic dinner that smelled amazing.

Speaking of which… "I'm dirty and sweaty. I'm guessing I don't have time for a shower before we eat?"

He lit the candles and that slow sexy smile of his spread across his face. "No, you don't. Eat. Then we'll both take that shower together."

He didn't have to ask me twice. I washed my hands and face, then plopped down at the table while Irix poured me a glass of wine. Whatever demons had formed Irix, they must have added in culinary skills because the guy could cook. The beef was tender with a crisp pastry crust. There were twice-baked potatoes with cheese, and roasted honey-glazed carrots. He'd made roasted brussel sprouts with a balsamic drizzle and a side of grilled fruit with a yogurt dressing. For dessert he pulled an apple crumble out of the oven and scooped vanilla ice cream on the top from a local creamery. I was stuffed, but I made him sit on the couch with his wine while I cleaned the dishes and put on a pot of coffee. This was perfection. This was the life I wanted. Rewarding work. Amazing food and drink. An easy sharing of chores. A smoking-hot incubus boyfriend whose presence I enjoyed in and out of the bedroom.

Rewarding work without having to deal with a snobby jerk of an elf, that is.

"As if worrying about Harkel figuring out I'm a half-elf/half-succubus isn't bad enough, I now need to work side-by-side with an elf," I told Irix as I put the last pan away and got out a pair of coffee cups. "Actually I need to 'cooperate with her in every way' because apparently she's a botany expert who is at DiMarche to save our crops while I just point out diseased plants and prune shit."

The wine glass stopped halfway to Irix's mouth. "An elf?

You're working with an elf? I'm guessing since you're sitting here alive and in one piece that she is blind or so stupid she didn't immediately realize what you were?"

"I'm beginning to think the latter. She told me that my appearance was similar to an ear-mangled, ugly peasant-class elf. I think I was supposed to be flattered."

He snorted. "Right. You look exactly like an elf except for the ears right now. And you clearly look like you're descended from a high elf. She's blind *and* stupid. And I'm grateful she's such an idiot."

"Me too, especially after she told me that there was no way I could have elf ancestry since no elf would stoop so low to have sex with a human, let alone procreate with one."

"Elves," Irix muttered, draining the contents of the wine glass and setting it on the coffee table.

"Yes, elves. And she's an expert," I grabbed the dish towel and began drying. "How fucked up is that? I study my butt off, spend a week helping the humans in Hel, and DiMarche brings in an elven expert."

I heard Irix snort. "*You're* the expert. There's no one they could bring in that would possibly know more about this stuff than you."

I flushed at the pride in his voice. "I know, but I'm a recent college graduate, a twenty-one-year-old human girl as far as they know. They might think I'm super smart, that I have a great future ahead of me, but they'll never take my advice and assistance over that of an expert."

"Especially when they think you're human."

I knew what he meant, but there was no way around that. Jordan, Darci, and the covens in New Orleans knew the truth. Kai and a few others in Maui knew the truth. But no one else could. Elves might be welcome in this world, but I wasn't sure I would be, at least not right now. The humans were probably at a point that they'd accept me, but the elves that would soon be working side-by-side with them wouldn't. I'd find a knife in my back one night, or poison in my thermos of iced tea.

Irix frowned. "How often do you have to work with her? I'm concerned that if she spends enough time with you, she might suddenly realize you're more elf than she thinks. Or if she sees you heal a plant or grow something at super-speed."

"I was careful that she wasn't around, and that any healing I did was subtle. Manny has her occupied with black mildew right now, so I probably won't see her again for a few days." I thought about the Phomopsis and felt angry all over again. "It was weird, Irix. I got the impression that she didn't know a cutworm from a borer. She didn't seem to know the symptoms of disease or infestation. And she gave me instructions on what to do with a vine that would have resulted in the whole thing dying and the disease spreading on down the row."

He shot me a concerned look. "Are you sure she wasn't just testing you, that she suspects what you are? Was that the plant you healed? If she goes back and finds that you didn't follow her advice, and the plant is disease-free, she'll know you at least have some magical ability, if not skills that are suspiciously like those of the elves."

"I trimmed it exactly as she said and healed the rest, so if she's double checking, she won't know who healed it, or if the human chemicals finally did their job. Honestly, I don't think she'll double check. I don't know if she lacks the skills to detect these things, if she lacks knowledge about the diseases and pests affecting plant life here, or if she just doesn't care. She said her family were in charge of the royal gardens in Wythyn, so maybe she just doesn't give a shit if this crop succeeds or fails."

"She should. The angels are probably watching this first group of elves carefully. They'll want to make sure they're assimilating and becoming productive members of human society. If she fails at her first job off the island, they'll ship her right back for re-training. And if they suspect she's done it on purpose, she'll go right back to Hel."

I shrugged, handing him a mug of coffee. "Then she's probably in over her head. Maybe she lied about her knowledge and experience just to get this job and get off Elf Island as quickly as possible."

I didn't know much about the hidden island where the angels sequestered migrating elves until they were deemed ready to enter the human world, but it couldn't be pleasant going from a place of privilege and status to a world where humans were in charge, and you needed to serve them in order to have basic food and shelter.

"That could be the case."

I sat beside Irix and we sipped our coffee in silence while I thought about the cutworms, the leafrollers, and the Phomopsis. And those were only three of the issues plaguing the DiMarche crops this year, all of them seemingly occurring out of the blue and all at the same time.

"I need to pick your brain on something," I told him.

He smiled. "Pick away."

I explained all of the myriad issues affecting leaves, stems, trunks, fruit, and soil and how darned near statistically impossible it was for all these things to happen at once in plants right next to each other.

Irix tilted his head, a quizzical expression on his face. "It might be a coincidence, but I ran into someone today down at the Santor Winery. Harkel and I seem to be not the only demons in Napa Valley right now. I was in the tasting room, making plans with a few of the employees to slip into the back room with me, when in walks Txipa."

I blinked. "Do I know him? No, I don't think I've ever met

this Txipa. And I can assure you that I've never given him a blow job either."

Irix smirked. "She. And Txipa is a plague demon."

Holy crap. "Do we need to call the CDC? Are we all about to come down with norovirus or something?"

"Maybe. I've got no idea what her game is, but where plague demons roam, disease follows in their wake. Txipa focuses on human disease, but her sister leans toward the famine side of pestilence. She likes to infect plants."

Double holy crap. "Seriously? Plague demons come in pairs, like evil disease-spreading twins?"

"Exactly, although they don't always travel together. Demons are created singly, and those with the correct traits can create an individual plague or pestilence demon. Sometimes a powerful demon will decide to combine skills that affect the animal kingdom with skills that affect the plant kingdom into one being."

"So this Txipa is a blight *and* pestilence demon?"

"No. I've only known one demon that has the combined traits. Usually as they're created, the powers are too great for one being, and the spirit-self divides into two."

"So they *are* twins. One gets the plague toward humans and animals and one gets the pestilence toward plants?"

"Exactly, although there is some overlapping in the skills. If a demon infects a crop, it can transfer to humans, although that's a very limited set of bacteria in my experience. Txipa is one of the unusual ones who was supposed to have both traits, but split at creation. She has a twin, who imaginatively was named Apixt."

Demons. Not exactly the most inventive when it came to naming conventions for their young.

"Do you think Apixt is nearby? And that she, or he, is having a merry old time killing off my vineyard?"

Irix shrugged. "Could be. They both like to travel

together. I managed to shoo Txipa off before she infected my chosen sexual partners with something annoying like genital warts or herpes, but I think she just moved on to another winery."

Ugh. Hopefully not my winery.

"If we manage to track her down, do you think we can convince her and her sister to go elsewhere? Like Antarctica or something?"

"Yuck. You seriously want to go find a pair of pestilence demons? I was hoping we could head for that shower. Then head for bed. Then maybe around four in the morning or so, actually go to sleep."

I hesitated. This wasn't my responsibility. I was an under-paid intern who just noted damaged and diseased plants on a chart and trimmed vines exactly as instructed. Yes, Jorge did seem to appreciate my knowledge, but I was only here for a month. They had an expert. Let Hallwyn deal with it. She could run around the fields healing plants, then run around Napa Valley to chase away a plague demon and her plant-killing sister. Let her handle it. I'd do what I was paid to do, and spend this evening having so much sex with Irix that I had trouble walking tomorrow morning.

But could I do that? This was my vineyard. I had no faith that Hallwyn could identify the cause of any damage, let alone heal it. And even if she could, I couldn't imagine her recognizing the work of a pestilence demon or knowing where to find the culprit. The Phomopsis seemed like a normally occurring disease to me. Nothing screamed demon about it. Unless she somehow managed to find out, she'd spend her whole time here curing one plant only to have it fall sick again the very next day.

"How do they operate, these pestilence demons? Our vineyard is pretty bad off, but between the elf expert, the pesticides, and me, I think we can turn it around. Assuming they don't keep coming back in the middle of the night and hitting us with more disease."

He chuckled. "That's not likely unless one or both of them has a grudge against this vineyard in particular. Plague demons hit something, then move on. They'll drop a bunch of *E.*coli at a senior center, or aphids into a lettuce farm, then go do something else. They're probably just passing through."

Good. That meant that things would start to look up for the vineyards at DiMarche Winery. "Awesome. In that case: shower, sex, and sleep. But if you see either Txipa or Apixt around again, can you let me know?" *Not my problem. Not my problem*, I chanted in my head, trying to get my mind off the diseased vines and back on a night of sin with my incubus lover.

Irix took the coffee cup from my hand and helped me to my feet. "You're hungry."

I knew he wasn't talking about food because I was stuffed to the point of explosion. "Yes. I healed that vine and it was pretty rough. It took a lot out of me." I looked up at him, realizing that I just expected him to share his energy with me. How screwed up was that? When I was in Maui with him, I made it a point of pride to learn to go out and gather my own energy sources, even if he needed to supplement them. When Irix wasn't around, I took care of myself. But as soon as he was back living with me, I got careless about finding my own supply of energy and began to rely on him. Sharing was a wonderful thing, but I needed to be more self-sufficient.

I reached out to touch his hand. "Are you sure you want to stay in? How about we shower up, then we both go out together and pick up some snacks?"

"I don't mind feeding you, Amber. In fact, I enjoy taking care of you."

"Sometimes. And sometimes you badger and scold me to

be an adult and go take care of myself. You helped me last night when I was shaken and upset and just wanted to stay home in your arms. Tonight I feel better. Let's get dirty in the shower, then go hunt. I'll let you pick my prey if I can pick yours."

He smiled. "Now that sounds like a fun evening."

By the time we headed out the door I was clean and satiated, my body humming from the energy that Irix always shared through our bond. I still put on a skirt and heels, and my tightest tank top and push-up bra in anticipation of scoring some supplemental energy. Tomorrow I'd need to be in a condition to do some damage control and healing at the vineyard. Especially since Hallwyn seemed to be unable to do so.

CHAPTER 9

This morning we'd been treated to coffee again, and had traded stories about the elf. She was universally despised as haughty, rude, and an idiot, although Manny did grudgingly admit that she'd done some "glowy-hands magic" on the vines with black measles, and that they looked better.

Looked better. She should have been able to cure them. She was a full elf, and with her family heritage, this vineyard should be the picture of health with double the crop yield. Although maybe I was being too hard on her. The woman hadn't been out of Hel for long, and I knew first-hand how different the plant life was here as opposed to in Hel. She said her family had been gardeners, so they hadn't probably done more than forced blooms and ensured that already-perfect plants were pristine. She'd probably never experienced all of the things that were thrown at her yesterday.

Jorge drove up in the truck, and just like the previous morning, Hallwyn climbed out of the passenger side. This time she had on jeans so dark that I feared the dye might discolor her legs and a leaf-green button down with a Peter

Pan collar and cap sleeves. Instead of the low, neat pony tail, her hair was wrapped around her head in a series of blonde braids. I noticed with some satisfaction that the tips of her ears were slightly pink. Perhaps someone should offer the elf a tube of sunscreen.

This time Hallwyn went off with Rosa, and I almost felt sorry for the elf. I'd worked with the Chilean woman when I'd first arrived for my internship, and she didn't take shit from anybody. One wrong word and Hallwyn was going to wind up with her ears yanked off.

I got my assignment for the day and headed out, making a quick detour through the row Manny had been working yesterday. The vines with the black measles did look better. Some of the spots had faded from the leaves and the grapes seemed to be sound. Looking around to see if there was anyone near, I put my hands on the plant and sent my energy into it.

There was still black measles. And while the leaves seemed to have improved on the outside, the reduction in disease was strictly cosmetic. Inside, the vine was struggling just as much as it had been before. If anything, this was worse. The humans tending these vines would think all was well—or at least well enough to not raise the alarm. With Hallwyn doing her "glowy-hands", Jorge might not even send the crew out to spray again, putting his faith in the elf. The woman was a downright menace. And I couldn't leave this plant like this, not in *my* vineyard.

Once more I pulled the disease from the vines, absorbing and neutralizing it then repairing the plant. That was what Hallwyn should have done. Idiot. Or maybe just lazy. Either way, I couldn't keep doing this. Well, if I went out every night and managed to pull together enough energy, I could. If Harkel and Irix shared enough with me, I could. And with Hallwyn here, I wouldn't worry about the humans thinking it odd that seriously ill plants had suddenly and miraculously recovered. All my work would be attributed to the elf.

And that irritated me the most. Lazy, stupid, arrogant elf. And she'd be getting all the credit for my hard work. Ugh. But what was more important—that this annoying elf woman fail or that the DiMarche vineyards have healthy plants and a bumper crop of quality grapes?

Yeah. I left the vine and headed further into the field to check on the case of Phomopsis I'd healed yesterday. Rounding the end of the row, I came to an abrupt stop and stared with horror at the mess before me.

The vines that were the picture of health when I'd seen them last were now black and rotted, the leaves slimy and decayed. If that wasn't bad enough, the canes had been ripped from the ground and crushed as if someone had driven back and forth over them with a cement roller.

What had happened? I glanced around to see if anyone was watching then bent down to touch the stems, nearly vomiting from the foul sensation. Had this been one of the plague demons, pissed off at DiMarche for some reason and determined to see them fail. Or...I looked around once more...was it an elf? Had Hallwyn come to check on the plant, sensed that someone had used magical means to fix it, and reversed the process with a vengeance? She needed job security to stay here and off Elf Island. A rival healer might take her job.

The plant wasn't just sick. The healing hadn't just been reversed. Whoever had done this had been pissed. And if they demonstrated this much rage on a grapevine, then what would they do if they discovered I'd been the one who had healed it?

I scurried over to where I'd been assigned to prune and tie for the day. If Hallwyn really was that much of a bitch that she couldn't deal with a mystery person anonymously healing the vines, then fuck her. And if Richard or one of the executives at DiMarche had screwed over a pair of plague demons, then fuck them. I hated the thought that these plants were going to suffer, though. Maybe if I just went behind Hallwyn and healed what she'd attempted to, I could fly under the radar.

Or maybe I should mind my own business, learn all I could at DiMarche, then head for New Orleans at the end of the summer.

This internship wasn't exactly as I'd expected. I didn't seriously think I'd be coming to a well-known, high-volume operation and jump into their management team, or have a significant role, but I did have visions that I'd be doing more than manual labor for the month. It sounded horribly snobby, but I had a botany degree and although I liked my co-workers, none of them had college degrees. Most of them had backgrounds in landscaping, and a few had worked commercial farms. I'd learned everything I needed to about pruning and tying and record keeping in the field. Maybe I'd soon be moved to the winery to shadow those doing production, or work with the distributors, or learn the role of their chemist, then I could forget all about these poor vines.

Determined not to be the crazy overachiever, I actually took my lunch break today. All the field employees took lunch at the same time, giving us an opportunity to get out of the worst of the midday heat. Tromping back through the fields to get my cooler and join the others, I gave Rosa a wave and jogged to catch up with her.

"Trade ya lunch?" I teased her.

She shot me a narrowed glance. "Right. Like I'm going to trade my cazuela for a bologna sandwich on white bread."

"I've got lemon cookies."

For some reason Rosa couldn't resist cookies. The more mass-produced, the better. She wouldn't be caught dead buying a box of them at the grocery store, so I acted as her supplier.

"An empanada for two lemon cookies," she proposed.

"Chicken? Or cheese?"

"Pork."

Yum. I'd never had her pork empanadas before. I wondered what kind of spices she was using. "Deal."

Rosa smiled smugly. "Not a word, right?"

I'd keep her Keebler cravings a secret. "I'll slide them to you when no one's looking. Maybe even wrap them in brown paper." Like sex toys or a porno mag.

She nodded. "So what do you think of this elf woman? You know more about plants and their diseases than anyone I've met. Do you think this magic stuff of hers is really going to work, or did Richard just blow a ton of money on a pointy-eared figurehead?"

I decided to walk a political middle line on this one. "Even if the magic doesn't work, the elf-employee is going to be a status symbol. Richard can always slap her on the ads next to Matthieu."

Rosa laughed. "Right now they're exotic and strange, but that won't last if they don't prove their worth or pull their weight. The corporate world runs on profit and loss and shareholder return. A pointy-eared blonde isn't going to be worth squat if all she can do is smile for a couple of ads. And I'm not even sure she can smile."

I wasn't sure she could smile either. We rounded the tool shed and saw the others already sitting in a shady spot, opening their lunch boxes and coolers. Some had little folding chairs that they kept next to the shed for breaks, others just sat in the dirt. Shockingly, off on her own sitting in a golf cart next to the Gator was Hallwyn. I mean, of course she had to eat. I just expected that maybe she'd be up at the winery eating with the management, not down here in the trenches with us peons.

"Manny said the vine with black measles did look better after she magic-handsed it," I told Rosa as we scoped out a spot where we could lean our backs against the shed. "So maybe she'll be of more use than a publicity stunt."

"As long as she's not so good that we're out of a job. I'm all for a healthy vineyard and all that, but if she starts magically tying and trimming, I'm gonna shank her."

Rosa looked around, then slid me a brown paper bag. Inside were empanadas. With my mouth watering, I took one out and handed the bag back. With the same care to secrecy, I slid her a plastic bag with two lemon cookies inside. She crammed one in her mouth, quickly hiding the other as Manny approached.

"Did you notice? We have been graced with the presence of royalty." He jerked his head toward Hallwyn who was sitting primly in the golf cart, frowning at a strawberry.

"She ate inside yesterday with Matthieu," Rosa told him. "Guess he either scored or she was so icy-cold that he gave up."

I winced. Matthieu was notorious for offering a private tour of the cellars to any attractive female employee. And in this case, "tour" was a code word for a quick fuck against the wine racks. There wasn't usually a second invitation, so anyone who took the tour pretty much knew this was a hit-it-and-quit-it encounter. Not that anyone had a problem with that, but the thought of Matthieu trying to get into Ms. Genetic Purity's pants was disturbing.

"Maybe she's just too busy to go all the way back to the winery for lunch," I said. "She's probably swamped running back and forth across a thousand acres, trying to diagnose at least twenty different diseases and heal damage."

Manny snorted. "Henry said she made the powdery

mildew in field twelve worse. He finally made up some mite infestation to get her out of the way so he could spray. I saw you detour down row six, Amber. What do you think about that black measles case?"

Crap. "Looks better."

Rosa shrugged. "I guess she's on the level then. Either the powdery mildew is gone by tomorrow, or her skills are disease specific."

Or she's a fraud. I looked over at the elf. Hallwyn was picking at a piece of bread, and for a second I felt sorry for her. She looked so wooden, so numb sitting there alone with her lunch. But she was an arrogant jerk who was supposed to be an expert. It's not like she'd been friendly or tried to be civil to any of us. She'd insulted me, insulted the others, acted as if she were better than any of us here, better than any human. What did I care if she was eating all by herself?

CHAPTER 10

The heat was so bad that everyone was soaked in sweat at quitting time. Jorge was late getting to the field, so I offered to collect everyone's clipboards and wait for him while they all headed back to their air-conditioned trailers and homes. Once my co-workers were gone, I read through everyone's notes, writing down what problems were in which field and row, and the plants infected.

I know. I couldn't help myself. In spite of chanting "It's not my problem" all day, I still felt very much like it was my problem. I'd just make note of all this to help Jorge. Yeah. Or I'd use the list to check up on Hallwyn and make sure she was doing what she was hired to do.

Or I'd sneak out and heal things on the sly, a tiny bit at a time and hope that whoever was infecting the vineyard didn't notice. And that Hallwyn didn't notice. *Nobody notice the half-elf sneaking around after work doing her weird laying-on-of-hands.*

After I'd compiled everything, I looked at the paper with the tightly written lines both front and back. This was bad. Even if Hallwyn had the skills she was supposed to have I doubt she could have turned this vineyard around in time to save the harvest. No wonder Jorge was looking stressed lately.

"Those for me?"

I looked up and saw Jorge with his hand outstretched. I hadn't even heard him drive up.

"Yeah." I handed him the stack of clipboards. He took a look at the list I'd been compiling.

"What happened to that vine in field eight?" he asked. "The one with the Phomopsis?"

How to explain this one? "It looked like vandals. It was yanked out and squashed."

He sighed. "At least they didn't destroy one of the healthy vines. I'll need to talk to Richard about putting in some additional security cameras." He read down the list and shook his head. "This is bad. If we can't turn this around, we're going to go under. Maybe not this year, but soon. With all these diseased plants, I'm worried the only solution will be to uproot them all, treat the ground and leave it fallow for at least a season, then replant."

"That would mean four to five years before you get a decent yield." I frowned, knowing he was right about his prediction. During that time DiMarche would need to buy grapes and/or extract. They'd be at the mercy of what was available in the market. It's not like they were a boutique winery, but they were at the high end of the middle, mass-produced market. It would be difficult to maintain their brand without their own vineyard supplying at least some of their grapes, and they wouldn't be able to produce any wines with the estate label.

He looked down at the clipboards again. "Hallwyn seems to be helping, but not enough. There's just too much for her to handle, I think. We called her in too late, and she just can't get ahead of it all. Maybe Richard can get a team of elves in here for a one-time contract job, then Hallwyn can maintain the vines afterward."

Hallwyn couldn't do shit. Although I couldn't get ahead of it all either. The last time I'd been able to heal plants on this scale had been the pineapple farm in Maui, and for that I had a goddess feeding me energy through Irix. Pele wasn't here, and even if she was I didn't think she'd be willing to help in this circumstance. Or maybe she would. She did seem to have a thing for Irix, and might be willing to assist in return for another sexual encounter.

But there was no Pele coming to the rescue of this vineyard. There wasn't even a full elf coming to the rescue of this vineyard. All they had was me, and I could only do so much.

"Who did you get Hallwyn through? Maybe they *can* get some elves here for a one-time job." Although if they were all like Hallwyn that would be a colossal waste of money.

"Magical Interventions. Sounds hokey, I know. A guy came around a few months ago dropping off cards. We were still getting used to the idea that there were such things as elves and angels. It seemed a bit of a stretch to imagine actually hiring one, but when Santor Winery brought one on, then Boone Valley, Richard started considering it. And when these infestations kept getting worse no matter how much we sprayed or dusted, he figured we had nothing to lose at this point. Well, beyond money. The placement fee was exorbitant, and she's paid more than most of the management here."

I frowned. It sounded like a scam to me. Although, elves were supposed to be skilled in these sorts of things. Maybe DiMarche had just gotten the one lousy elf. It made me wonder if Santor and Boone were having any better luck than we were.

Jorge patted me on the shoulder. "Go home. Manny said

your boyfriend is in town. Relax. Enjoy the evening, and we'll continue to fight the good fight tomorrow."

I didn't have the heart to tell him that Manny had seen me with Harkel and not Irix. Great. I was going to have such a reputation as a ho by the time this internship was over.

Watching Jorge leave I made a decision. Taking one more look at the huge list of infected plants, I texted Irix that I'd be late tonight, then headed out to the fields.

Starting with the nearest field, I went down my list row by row and began to heal the plants. Two rows down I decided that I needed to change my plan of attack. It would be easier for me to keep track of the infected plants if I could clear each row and field before moving on to the next, but some infestations were less energy-consuming than others. If I kept on like this, I'd be worn out before I could finish half of this field.

Looking through my list I dug a pen out of my pocket and began to circle the plants that would be easiest to heal. My business classes called it the "low-hanging fruit" method. I'd take care of as much of these easier cases as I could tonight, then continue to work on the tougher ones in succession. Of course that meant I'd need to get more energy. How I was going to balance the day job, this second healing-the-vines job, then find the time to score sexual partners and maybe actually eat and sleep was beyond me. Somehow I'd make it work.

It wasn't going to work. Jorge was right, we needed an army of elves, not one half-elf and a completely useless full elf. After healing two dozen plants, I realized that I just couldn't do any more and be able to walk out of here under my own steam. Plus Irix would be furious if I pushed myself so hard that I could barely manage to hunt. I was done. Time to go back to my trailer, throw down a quick meal, then see who in one of the neighboring towns would be up for a quick fuck.

I came to an abrupt stop just as I was about to round the next row. I wasn't the only one in the fields after hours. Hallwyn was standing in front of one of the vines, muttering under her breath in what sounded like Elvish. She reached out to touch the leaf, a warm glow around her hands. Then she pulled back and spoke something that sounded suspiciously like a curse.

I took a step back to leave, but her super-duper elf hearing must have caught the sound of my foot on the soft ground because she spun around, green eyes huge in her pale face.

"What are you doing here?" she snapped, the look of panic quickly replaced by a haughty expression.

I held up my sheet of paper. "Working. How about you?"

She straightened and lifted her chin. "This vineyard is a mess of disease. I am eradicating the black measles on this plant."

I walked closer. "Um, that vine has bunch rot. Botrytis bunch rot, to be exact."

"Yes. I see that. But it also has black measles." She turned her back on me dismissively.

"No, it doesn't. Bunch rot and a minor cutworm infestation, no doubt spreading from the plants further down the row, but there is no sign of black measles."

"That's because I cured the black measles and healed all of the infected areas. I'm about to work on the other diseases. So if you'll excuse me…"

I was smelling some serious bullshit here. And I really wanted to box this woman into a corner. "Oh, please proceed. I'm eager to see an elf work their magic." I held my sheet of paper in front of me and stood respectfully, staring at the plant.

She turned to glare at me for a few seconds, then also looked at the plant, reaching out to touch a leaf. Again her hand glowed golden, but when she pulled her fingers away, there was no noticeable change to the vine.

"This branch rot often takes several healing sessions, and most likely won't show an improvement until tomorrow morning."

I nodded. "Bunch rot. And what about the cutworms?"

"They too will be gone. There is much to do here, and I only have the strength to do a few plants at a time."

She did look tired. Actually she looked defeated, but still she straightened her shoulders and attempted to push past me.

"You're a fraud."

She froze at my words. I shouldn't care. I should just let her run around pretending to help with her glowy-hands crap, but there was something seriously wrong at this vineyard. All this disease and infestation at one time, some of them only occurring with completely different environmental conditions. It wasn't natural. In fact, I was pretty sure it was supernatural. Maybe it was those pestilence demons causing this veritable plague. Maybe it was a sorcerer, or another elf, or a rogue angel who was working this as a racket to get elves employed and take a cut. Maybe it was a rival vineyard paying a demon or magic user to take out the competition. I had no idea who or what, but something stank here at DiMarche and it was going to drive me crazy until I figured it out.

And this elf prancing around in her fancy shoes wasn't helping at all. Did she not care? If she was in over her head, she needed to fess up and ask for help. Maybe Richard could hire another elf. Or a different elf.

Or maybe I could help her, if I wasn't afraid that she'd kill me.

"I should execute you for such slander." Her voice was low with a tremble that could have been rage or fear. "You should die for your insolence, but things here are not as they were in Hel and I am forbidden to harm a human. Instead I will tell you to keep your false accusations to yourself before I alert the management."

"You're a fraud," I repeated. "You don't know anything about grapevines, or their diseases, or the pests that damage them. The pesticides do a better job than you. You can't even manage to heal plants, let alone eradicate the infestations. Was your family truly gardeners to the Wythyn royalty, or were they just in charge of the floral arrangements in the ballroom?"

I felt the slap across my cheek before I even saw her move. So much for harming a human. Although in all honesty, I wasn't a human.

Hallwyn stomped out of the field, while I stared after her in shock. She hit me. An elf slapped me. I put a hand up to my stinging cheek and wondered what the heck I was going to do about it.

Well, I wasn't about to hit her back. Things would escalate, then she'd wind up knowing I was at the very least half-demon. But there was something very suspicious about Hallwyn. How had she gotten this job when she seemed so terribly unqualified? I knew that happened with humans all the time, but elves weren't padding their resumes and bluffing their way through job interviews. Well, maybe they were, but angels were pretty good at detecting lies and I assumed they were the ones coordinating the job placement through this Magical Interventions company.

Although, come to think of it, that was a weird assumption. With few exceptions, angels weren't familiar with how the human world worked, at least not to the level that they'd know about career websites or head hunters. They must have

completely outsourced this kind of thing. And if their placement folks were anything like those in the human world,
they were getting a percentage of that hefty fee that Jorge
had mentioned.

I watched Hallwyn pull her gloves on and hop in the golf
cart, gunning it as she headed back, I supposed, to leave for
the day. Glancing down at the vine with the bunch rot and
the cutworms, I decided to do one giant "fuck you" toward
Hallwyn and heal it. Of course, she was stupid enough that
she might think the ridiculous glowy-hands shit she'd done
actually worked, but part of me hoped she'd think there was
another elf coming in behind her and fixing her mistakes.
Maybe she'd worry that elf would take her job. Vindictive, I
know, but I hated that elf and I wanted her to be watching
over her shoulder.

So I reached out to touch the plant, closing my eyes as I
pulled the disease into me. My stomach rolled as the blackness poured through my veins. Then taking a deep breath, I
began to destroy the bunch rot that I'd just sucked into me.

When that was done I took a few cleansing breaths,
preparing myself to heal the plant before I dealt with the
cutworms, but just as I exhaled I heard a sound behind me—a
snarl, then a whoosh.

Pain blazed like lightning through my head and I felt
myself fall.

It seemed like seconds later that I was opening my eyes
and staring at the dark, loamy dirt of the vineyard. I lifted a
hand to my head and felt the sticky wetness of congealing
blood. And as I looked around I realized that I was no longer
in front of the vine with the bunch rot. Whoever had hit me
on the head had dragged me off somewhere.

And dragged was the operative word. My clothes were
filthy, and I had scratches on my arms and chest where my
V-neck shirt had exposed my skin. My wrists were bruised

and sore, and my head felt like a split melon. I rolled over and groaned, pulling my phone out of my pocket and squinting as I held it up in front of my face. It wasn't broken. And the time it displayed let me know that I'd been unconscious for longer than I'd thought. I hoped my elven half would heal head trauma with the same accelerated pace as other injuries, because I'm sure I had a concussion.

And I was late. I'd told Irix I'd be back half an hour ago. I'd need to run, and the prospect of racing through the vineyard and to my trailer with this headache wasn't at all appealing.

I carefully stood, testing my ability to remain upright and decided against running. I'd walk. And I'd text Irix to let him know that I was okay, and was heading home as quickly as I could manage.

CHAPTER 11

*A*t my trailer, I walked in on a Mexican standoff. Irix had his arms folded across his chest, leaning against the wall that separated the living area from the bathroom. Harkel was mirroring his stance, only he was in the kitchen area, leaning against the side of the refrigerator. Both stared at each other with hooded eyes, the air crackling with tension.

Tension and pheromones. Crap. Crap. I'd known Harkel was coming over tonight for our "talk", but hadn't expected him for another hour at least. So much for hunting. Actually, so much for sleeping. Whatever happened, I *had* to make time to recharge myself tonight or I wouldn't be able to do anything in the vineyard tomorrow after work.

They both turned toward me, their expressions changing dramatically. I would have laughed had I not felt like I'd been hit in the head with a bulldozer.

"You are injured!" Harkel was on me in two strides, but so was Irix. The incubus examined my head wound while the warmonger looked at the scratches on my arms and chest.

"Were you in a fight?"

"Who did this?"

"Why have you not repaired your injuries?"

It was Harkel's last question that caused me to catch my breath. I didn't repair myself with the same process and speed as a demon. Nor was I as quick at healing as a full elf. This was one of those times where I'd need to tread carefully, and by that I meant ignore his question and hope he didn't repeat it.

"I was healing plants in the vineyard and I was attacked."

Which meant whoever attacked me had seen me healing that vine. They knew. Whether it was one of the plague demons or a sorcerer hired by a rival winery, or Hallwyn come back to make good on her threat to kill me for my insolence, whoever attacked me knew.

"Who would dare attack a demon?" Harkel curled his lip. "Unless it was an angel. But angels do not hit demons on the head with blunt objects."

"The elf." Irix shot me a worried look.

"We argued. I think she came back and hit me." And I was such an idiot for letting my temper and pride get the best of me. It made sense. She'd been furious that I'd slandered her, called her a fraud. She'd come back, no doubt to punish me, and seen me working what was clearly elven magic on a vine. I was lucky to be alive. I was lucky she hadn't finished me off after braining me with some farming tool.

Why hadn't she? I was an abomination, a half-elf, a blot on their precious genetic purity. And I'd called her a fraud. The first alone should have signed my death warrant. Both together should have *definitely* signed my death warrant. Why had she dragged me through the dirt and left me there alive?

"An elf dared to assault you?" Harkel looked as if he were about to go postal on every elf this side of the gateways. If this is how he looked as he went into battle, then I was surprised the opposing army didn't just turn around and flee.

"You need to leave," Irix told me. "I know this internship means a lot to you, but your life is more important. We'll go back to New Orleans, and hope she doesn't trace you there."

"Why would she run and hide from a paltry elf? I realize that sex demons are not as skilled in physical confrontation as other demons, but surely she could decapitate an *elf.*"

"I'm not running away to New Orleans," I told Irix. He was right. It was too dangerous for me to stay here now that Hallwyn knew what I was, but I hated the thought that I was going to spend the rest of my life, or at least the next few centuries, hiding away from elves and demons. I was going to have to face this sometime. And now that it seemed the truth of my genetic makeup was coming out into the open, I wanted to deal with it head on.

"Good for you," Harkel slapped me on the shoulder and nearly knocked me over. "And to show you how sincere my affection is, I will kill this elf that has assaulted you."

"No, don't kill the elf." Crap, this was just getting more and more complicated.

Harkel frowned. "No? You would prefer I keep her alive? Actually, that is a far more satisfactory response. I will incapacitate the elf, bring her here and together we will torture her. She will regret the moment she hit you. We will fill the night air with her screams, coat the floor with her blood and excrement. Slowly we will peel the skin from her body, allow her to heal herself, then do it over and over again."

That sounded horrific. "I think that's a bit excessive. I'll handle it. I'll go over there in the morning before my shift and talk with her and we'll work it out."

Irix glared at me. "No, you won't. You're going back to New Orleans where you'll be safe."

"What happened to not ordering me around? Not forbidding me to do this or that? I'm not leaving my internship. I'll handle it."

I hoped I didn't end up having to kill Hallwyn. I really didn't want to, even if she was a hateful bitch and had hit me over the head. Plus, Jorge and the management at DiMarche would wonder where their elf had gotten to. The police would get involved, and possibly the angels. No, I somehow needed to make this right without strangling Hallwyn.

"Perfect," Harkel announced. "And now we can have sex. Irix, you leave us. Amber, may I offer you a glass of wine and discuss meteorological conditions with you?"

He was so adorable. Well, when he wasn't talking about stripping the skin from my elven co-worker, that is.

"I'm not leaving," Irix crossed his arms in front of his chest and transferred his glare to Harkel.

"My bond is with *her*, not you," Harkel snapped. "Get out. Leave us. You have no business being here."

"You hurt her last time you were here," Irix replied. "She's young. And she's mine. I won't let you hurt her again. We're both willing to discuss options and come to a mutually agreeable solution, but two things—I'm not leaving, and you will not hurt her again."

Something that looked like regret flitted across the warmonger's face. "She's a demon. True, sex demons are not as hardy as others, but regardless of her youth she shouldn't have had any problems with the relatively gentle approach I took."

He hadn't seriously injured or hurt me the way that Irix had been. I'd been told some demons enjoyed getting rough when playing with a succubus or incubus. I'd just never thought Harkel would be that way with me. I hadn't been afraid of the warmonger when we'd been together in Hel. He'd been a bit forceful during my blow job, but I'd actually enjoyed that. If he could dial it back to that level, we could totally have some fun together. If not, well then Irix was right, we would have a problem.

"She doesn't like rough." Irix took a step forward. "She likes gentle, and if you can't be gentle, this isn't going to work."

"Perhaps the succubus should speak to what she likes and doesn't like." Harkel also stepped forward. "She's not in your household. She's not accepted a breeding contract from you yet. You might have a tie. You might have a sexual history with her. But none of that means she is yours to speak for or even demand exclusive access to."

I opened my mouth, but shut it after a quick look from Irix. What was he up to? Whatever it was, I hoped it didn't end up with him being sliced to ribbons.

"She *is* mine. At less than a century she should still be under the care of a dwarf. The only reason she is here is because her sire, the succubus Leethu, gave her to me to train and guide. I am her mentor, her tutor, and her lover. I decide what is best for her until she is of an age to do so herself."

Okay, that annoyed the crap out of me. By demon standards, I *was* a minor, but I'd been brought up as a human, and at twenty-two I was legally an adult. I got what Irix was trying to do, but it bothered me that he had resorted to calling me an infant.

"She seems like an adult to me. And when I met her in Hel, she was unaccompanied and fully willing to accept all I offered. She's not yours. And if she so chooses, she'll be mine."

They were nose to nose and all I could do was stand by the door and hold my breath. This wasn't going to end well.

It didn't. Irix punched Harkel in the stomach, following it up with a quick uppercut to the chin. The warmonger rocked backward, but shook off the blow. With a snarl he grabbed Irix's head and slammed him downward onto an upraised knee.

Blood poured from Irix's nose. He wrapped his arms around the warmonger's hips and drove him backwards into the stove, denting the front with the impact.

"Stop! Both of you, cut it out right now." I threw my pheromones into the mix and cranked them up to eleven. And just for good measure, I stomped over to the demons as if I planned to get in between the two.

They ignored me, continuing to whale on each other and smash into my cabinets. I wasn't stupid enough to actually get between two fighting demons, so I did the next best thing —I whacked them over the head with a chair. Since they were grappling, one swing managed to hit both at the same time. Just in case they didn't get the memo, I hit them twice more.

"Stop."

Finally, they pulled apart and looked my way. In addition to the cuts they'd inflicted on each other, both were bleeding profusely from their heads. I threw the broken chair aside and folded my arms across my chest.

"Irix is right," I told Harkel. "I'm not quite twenty-two years old, and I can't take the kind of sex you were trying to dish out last night. You can't claw me or bite me like that. I'm too young to repair those injuries quickly and I'm not the sort of demon that enjoys them. What you did with Irix would have probably killed me. If that's what you want, then I'm not the succubus for you."

The warmonger's jaw dropped. "You're *how* old? When he said less than a century, I thought he was lying. You shouldn't be able to Own at your age. You shouldn't have the sex demon prowess that you have. You shouldn't be out of the nursery."

"I'll be twenty-two in another two months. I swear on all the souls I Own, that is my true age. I have skills that have come to me very early, but there are those I lack. I can't handle the kind of rough sex you want. I don't know if I ever will be able to, but I definitely can't do it now."

He took a step away from me, a look of horror on his face. Was this the demon equivalent of being a pedophile? Maybe demons didn't have sex with those under a century old?

"But in Hel…you were clearly willing. You made the advances, accepted my energy and my tie. And when I came to see you at the winery, you were open to the idea of another encounter with me."

"I still am. Harkel, I'm very attracted to you. I want you. But not if you can't have sex with me as you would a human. And I need to have Irix present. Leethu sent him to tutor me, and I trust his guidance. I was in Hel without his knowledge, and did many things out of youthful ignorance. I don't regret them, but I need to make sure he's present to supervise any sexual encounters with other demons in the future—at least until I'm of an age to make informed decisions on my own."

I'd been pissed at Irix for making me sound like an infant, and I'd just done the same. But it seemed to work. Harkel was no longer backing away with an expression of shock on his face. He seemed to be carefully considering my words.

"She's an amazing succubus," Irix added. "I completely understand how you would want her for your own—whether that's through a bond, a household affiliation, or a breeding contract. And from what she's said about you, I can see she is quite interested in furthering your acquaintance, and possibly exploring a long-term relationship with you. But given her age, I need to guide her."

I had dialed back the pheromones once the two demons had stopped fighting, and noticed that Irix was increasing his. It was subtle, not the smack-in-the-face he'd done two nights ago. This was a hint, an invitation. It was as if he wanted Harkel to reach out and meet him halfway.

Harkel's gaze locked on the incubus's. "I did enjoy the other night."

And now the sexual tension was thick enough to spread on toast.

"Me, too." Irix smiled. It was the sexy little smile he gave me when he wanted to drag me off to bed, only this time it was directed at the warmonger. "And unlike Amber, I like a bit of blood and guts in my sexual encounters."

Harkel caught his breath, then looked my way. "I still want you, Amber, but I worry I won't be able to restrain myself. The other night, when you were afraid and crying out…it pushed me over the edge. I lost control. Now that I know your limitations, I worry that I will damage you and that you will no longer want me afterward."

"Which is why I need to be present," Irix said. "Not just present, but a participant. If you feel the urge to bite or shred skin with your claws, I'll be there to take care of that urge."

"So you will stand by our side and intervene?"

Irix took a step toward the warmonger. "There is no way I could just stand there and watch you and Amber together, not after what I experienced with you the other night. I respect your tie with my young succubus charge, and acknowledge that your presence here is because of her, but I can't deny that I too am attracted to you, Harkel. I want you. And I want you in a very different way than Amber does."

The warmonger's brown eyes flared with orange lights, and the smile that curved his lips made me shiver. "I will be in charge, and you will both do as I tell you to do."

His fantasies spooled into my mind, and I could tell that Irix was also receiving the images.

"But I am the buffer between you and Amber," Irix warned. "If you so much as scratch her, then she leaves and it will just be you and me."

I wasn't sure if that was a threat or an erotic promise, and judging from the expression on Harkel's face, I got the feeling he would be thrilled with either outcome.

"We have a deal." The warmonger leaned against my dented stove and watched us with hooded eyes. "Strip. Slowly. First her, then you."

"Can I shower first?" I asked. "And have Irix help me fix my head wound?"

Harkel's eyes danced, a wicked smile curling up one corner of his lips. "No. Irix may assist you with the wound, but I want you all sweaty and dirty."

Ugh. But I'd been with human men who had similar fetishes. Irix walked up and I felt the tingle of his energy, my scalp knitting just enough that my elf-healing jumped into overdrive. I went to shed my T-shirt, but Irix stopped me, gently easing it up over my head then ducking down to trace a line of feather-light kisses up my stomach to the band of my bra. Meanwhile his hands were busy unzipping my shorts and sliding them down to my ankles. Then he worked his way down my stomach and thighs with his lips, bending to carefully remove my sneakers and socks, and slide my shorts all the way off.

I was relaxing under his gentle kisses and touch, our pheromones dancing and swirling together, creating an intoxicating mixture. I heard Harkel's growl of approval and looked over to see his eyes nearly orange as he looked at me.

"Now Irix."

The incubus stood at Harkel's command. I eased the shirt over Irix's head, then running my hands down the hard planes of his chest, I unsnapped his shorts and slid them down his legs. Irix was commando, and his cock sprang free, tapping me on the cheek as I helped him step from the shorts. Leaning forward, I couldn't resist taking him in my mouth, sucking gently on the head of his cock before pulling away and licking my way back down his shaft.

Irix sighed, his fingers caressing my cheek. As there were no other commands from Harkel, I went with my impulse and reached up to stroke his balls, continuing to kiss, lick, and suck. I felt a hand grip my hair, twisting it around a fist. Harkel forced my head away from the incubus, and to his own cock. He had removed his clothes while I'd been busy with Irix and was now on my other side, one hand tight in my hair and the other working himself with a firm grip. I was sandwiched between the two men, crouched on my haunches with two dicks in my face.

And one of those dicks was alarmingly large. I eyed Harkel's member nervously, hoping he didn't get any bigger or I was going to have difficulty getting my mouth around him.

"My turn," he whispered.

Irix's hand was reassuring on my shoulder, so I tamped down my nervousness and tried to relax. He wouldn't let anything happen to me. Irix wouldn't let any harm come to me. He was here to make sure Harkel didn't cross any lines.

And he was obviously here for another reason, too. As I worked my way to the base of Harkel's cock, I noticed that Irix slid his own member along the warmonger's, both men stroking themselves. With a quick squeeze of my shoulder, Irix's hand left my skin and reached down to touch Harkel, his nails lengthening and sharpening as he scratched a line along the warmonger's cock.

Harkel gasped, thrusting his hips forward. He returned the gesture, but instead of scratching, his embedded his claws into the flesh around the incubus's testicles. I heard Irix grunt in pain, smelled the copper scent of blood. Fear spiked through me and I looked up to Irix for assurance that all was okay.

It was obviously more than okay. There was agony in Irix's eyes, his mouth twisted and clamped tight, but there was also an unholy light of passion. I'd never understand how demons could enjoy this sort of thing. I'd been with humans who appreciated a spanking or light biting, but it was inconceivable that anyone could be so turned on from pain this intense.

Harkel's cock bumped against me and I turned to him once more, tasting his blood as I continued to lick his shaft. My tongue reached the head of his cock and swirled around it, dipping into the slit. And then I did what I'd done with Irix—I took my fingers and slid them back along his bridge to tease the puckered opening of his ass.

Harkel hummed, and I took that as a sign to ease the tip of my finger inside. Some guys didn't like this. Well, actually all guys liked this, but many of them didn't want to like it. Harkel wasn't one of those guys. I felt him harden as I wrapped my lips around him, taking as much of him into my mouth and throat as possible, at the same time pushing my finger inward to curl against that oh-so-sensitive spot. The warmonger growled deep in his throat and rocked forward, slamming himself so deep into my throat that I couldn't breathe.

Again I felt Irix's hand on my shoulder, the gentle scrape of his claws, the wet smear of blood from his nails onto the skin of my back. Steadying myself, I began a rhythm between my finger and my mouth, easing in and out, my other hand resting on Irix's hip.

I tasted Harkel's blood on my tongue, felt Irix's blood drip from his balls onto my shoulder. I pressed myself against the incubus, using him for leverage as I worked Harkel. I felt him swell and pulse in my mouth, his hole tightening around my finger, but before he tipped over the edge into orgasm, the warmonger pulled himself free, hooking a claw around the band of my bra and slicing it in two.

Damn. I really liked that bra, too.

"On your back," the warmonger commanded.

I went to comply only to hesitate when I saw what he was obviously intending to shove into me. Uh, no. Just, no.

"That better be meant for me," Irix said, his voice smooth but with an edge of steel to it. "If it's not, then you need to make it smaller. No more than ten inches long. And reduce that girth by at least half."

Harkel snarled, and Irix edged himself slightly in front of me.

"Or you can leave it as is, and fuck me instead," the incubus continued.

The warmonger hesitated, then looked down at himself. I held my breath.

"There. How's that?"

Irix moved aside and I eyed Harkel's cock. "Smaller."

He sighed, reducing his size a fraction of an inch.

"Smaller."

That was better, but there was something I needed to clarify. "Front door or back door?"

The warmonger tilted his head, eyebrows coming together. "You want me to leave? And there is more than one door to this domicile?"

I smothered a laugh. "It's slang. Are you intending to screw me in the ass at all? Because if that's the case then you need to be a bit smaller—both length and girth."

His shoulders slumped, and I actually felt sorry for him.

"This is humor, no? Because it's humiliating to be forced to take you with a mouse's cock."

"She's not even twenty-two years old," Irix reminded him. "Take me with a warmonger's cock, or take her with a mouse's cock. I vow on all the souls I Own that no details of this will be mentioned with anyone outside of this trailer."

The warmonger looked at me, then down at his erection. Then back at me. Then down at his erection. "This is a very hard decision."

I snickered. "He said hard."

Harkel shot me a mischievous glance, his member doubling in size. "You are a very naughty succubus. For this time, Irix will fuck you, and I'll fuck Irix, that way I can show you the amazing power of an ancient warmonger. Next time I will be gentle and tiny like a mouse, but today I will be a lion."

A lion-bear, to be exact. Before I could speak, Irix had me on the couch, legs in the air. He ripped through my panties with a claw, then looked up at me and winked.

I couldn't help but laugh. He was literally between me and the warmonger. He was going to take that enormous…thing in the ass while I got perfectly sized-and-shaped him instead. God, how I loved this demon.

And I'll admit to some very fond feelings toward Harkel, also. He had a sense of humor that I'd never expected in an ancient. As I looked up into his dark eyes, I saw him wink as well, and suddenly felt that all of this might work out okay.

Irix plunged into me, blood from his balls trickling down my thighs and onto the cushions. I was so not going to get my security deposit back on this place, but I didn't care. All that mattered was the feel of Irix inside me, his normal, human-like hand on my breast, his golden eyes so very warm as they looked into mine. He eased in and out of me with slow deep strokes, then leaned forward to kiss my bottom lip, pulling it gently with his non-fanged teeth. Then I felt him tense, a grunt of pain tearing out of him. Huge claws dug into Irix's shoulders and he pulled his mouth from mine. Each time Harkel buried himself into Irix's ass it drove the incubus forward and deeper into me. I could feel the warmonger's balls smacking against my legs and rear along with Irix's, and felt the way Irix tensed and jerked each time Harkel slammed into him.

"Damn, this feels so fucking good," the incubus growled against my ear.

I caught my breath in surprise, and realized that he wasn't lying in some attempt to keep me from fretting about him, he truly *did* enjoy getting stuffed from behind by some giant cock all while he was burying himself deep inside me.

That was the moment that I truly relaxed. Irix wasn't taking some horrid torture to protect me, he was doing something he enjoyed—something that he knew I wouldn't enjoy. I stopped worrying about him, stopped worrying about me, and put aside all my preconceived notions of pleasure to lose myself in the experience. Reaching up, I stroked Irix's face, running my hands down his neck to his shoulders, wrapping my fingers around the non-sharp portions of Harkel's claws.

The warmonger grinned, increasing the pace, which in turn increased Irix's pace as well. I slid my hand between the pair of us on an outward stroke and touched myself, rubbing my clit in time with the feel of Irix's wet cock plunging in and out of me.

My pheromones surged back to life, building with Irix's until all I knew was the slap of four balls against my skin, the fullness of Irix's cock inside me, the pressure of my fingers against my clit. I heard Irix catch his breath, heard Harkel roar as he dug his claws deeper into the incubus's shoulders. They both came at the same time, and me right afterward, all of us sloppy and adding to the horrible mess on the sofa and the carpet. Harkel collapsed against Irix and I could feel the incubus's body jerk with each pulse of the warmonger's cock. Arms straining, Irix managed to hold himself upright and not squish me into the sofa with the weight of the pair of them. The three of us held still, the only sound our ragged breathing.

CHAPTER 12

*H*arkel pulled out, standing upright and stretching his arms to the ceiling. He said something in demon and Irix responded, hesitating a few moments before sliding out of me and pulling me upright as he stood.

They were quite the pair. Blood, cum, torn skin and stab wounds. But even with all that, they were two impressive demons: muscular, powerful, and sexy as all hell. They stared at each other and for a moment I wondered if I was going to need to break up another fight.

Then Irix grinned and Harkel threw back his head to laugh. The warmonger patted Irix on the shoulder, saying something else in demon. Irix nodded and returned the gesture. They looked like two naked gladiators congratulating each other on a battle well-fought.

Then Harkel leaned in and kissed Irix, his hand drifting down to squeeze the incubus's ass. He whispered some additional words, giving Irix another quick kiss before heading to the door, stopping to look at me as his fingers wrapped around the handle.

"I need to go encourage some activity in Central America

for a few days, but I hope to see you when I return? Both of you?"

I smiled. "I'd like that. Be careful. Don't let the angels catch you."

He snorted. "The angels are busy with the elves and their own conflicts. It is the perfect time for a demon to walk among the humans. But just in case I need to return immediately to Hel, I will send notice so you will not be concerned."

Harkel said another few words to Irix, then left. It wasn't until he was gone that I realized that he hadn't fixed his injuries or put any clothing on. The idea of him walking around naked and bloody was pretty funny.

"What did he say?"

Harkel had said he was going to return, but was the breeding contract still on the table? I continued to feel the warmonger's tie, as well as the energy from our encounters. Would he expect this kind of threesome to continue? I could do this. And I hoped Irix had enjoyed this encounter just as much as I had. In all honesty, Harkel by himself was too much for me. He'd probably always be too much for me in a one-on-one relationship. If this was going to work, it would need to include Irix, and I wanted him to *want* it, not just tolerate the situation because I wanted it.

I hadn't been able to keep Kai because human society encouraged monogamy. Irix would be with me until the end of time. I might never have the ring, white dress, and kids running around the backyard, but I'd always have him, and if he was okay with it, I wanted to include Harkel in our strange set of connections.

"He said that as much as he wanted to continue to see you, he'd been too hasty in offering that breeding contract and that he intended to withdraw it until you were more mature. He asked if I would be open to such a proposal, as he was eager to create offspring with a sex demon, and after tonight, felt I had the mix of seduction and stamina he was looking for. He was impressed with how I withstood and even enjoyed his baser needs, and that this was the very thing he wanted to foster in his offspring—to create sex demons who were inclined toward more violent encounters."

"So he wants you, but not me." It hurt to think that. I'd lost Kai. I'd lost Harkel. And Irix…would I lose him eventually too? Would he someday decide I wasn't demon enough for him?

"No, silly elf-girl. He wants you, he just doesn't feel it's proper to propose a breeding incident with a succubus as young as you are. He'll be back, and I'm pretty sure next time he'll be sporting the mouse cock."

Irix's eyes twinkled, and I smiled in return.

"Good. You can have the lion cock, and I'll stick with the mouse one." Which reminded me… "Did you *really* enjoy that?"

It had been so hot to watch the pair of them, but even though it had seemed that both parties had relished the experience, I still wondered if Irix had done that for me. Had he just endured it, or had he actually wanted Harkel's warlike sex?

Irix shot me a sheepish grin. "Yeah, I did. It was an incredible experience, especially with you there as well."

"Okay." I tried to keep the doubt from my voice, and failed.

"You were raised with humans, but I grew up in Hel," Irix explained. "I've had encounters that have left me scooping my guts off the floor at the end. It's not just the act that's enjoyable, but the status. There's a certain cache in being able to match a high-level demon blow-for-blow, to withstand that sort of 'affection' and survive it. It's a badge of honor to leave yourself unrepaired and walk around Hel for a few days to show off the extent of your injuries."

I'd never understand demons. I might not ever be able to enjoy that sort of thing myself, but I was glad that Irix had. His explanation made me feel much better.

"Good. But please don't think you need to walk around here for days looking like you were run through a chipper shredder," I told him. "You've got immunity now. You can fix yourself without fear that some angel is going to be knocking down our door."

Irix visibly relaxed, a relieved smile on his face. "I'd almost forgotten. And I have you to thank for that, even if I'm still a bit pissed at you for risking yourself to go to Hel alone. I guess of all the things that could have happened to you, meeting Harkel wasn't all that terrible. He does have an affection for you. I wouldn't be surprised if in a few centuries he sends another breeding contract your way. And in the meantime, I get the feeling he's going to be a regular in our lives, both here and in Hel."

I took a deep breath and let it out in a whoosh. "So I'm off the hook as far as baby-making goes? He doesn't think I owe him anything for the energy he gave me or the tie I received during that blow job in Hel?"

Irix shook his head. "He'll expect a level of relationship, more than what you had with Kai, but less than you have with me. And yes, I've taken your place with the breeding contract."

I threw myself into his arms. "Thank you. Isn't he fun? Don't you like him? It's not just the power that's an attraction, but him as a demon. He's sweet and funny—which is a weird thing to be saying about an ancient warmonger. I won't mind being a part of his household, or getting naked and sweaty with him."

He kissed my forehead. "Have sex with him all you want as long as I'm present to jump in if things get too violent."

"So you're going to be a daddy, then?" It boggled my

mind, the thought of Irix and Harkel having offspring together.

He hugged me close. "Probably. I'll have to read what he's proposing, then there will be some back and forth, but I'll most likely accept. I've always remained unaffiliated with another demon's household, and have never accepted a breeding contract, but it's far past time for me to start doing so. Harkel would be a good ally, especially as he's tied to you. We'll probably wind up with the same arrangement that you and he have, except I'll sire a demon with him. I'll support him in Hel if he needs a sex demon for an ally, and speak favorably of him to others."

"Forever? As long as you both shall live? Until death do you part?" Why was I jealous? I was truly one fucked up girl.

"Hardly. We'll probably continue like this for a century or so, then he'll lose interest. It might end sooner if there's a conflict this side of the gates that he's involved in, or something in Hel that catches his attention. It's not a big deal, Amber. These ancients know how to play the game. And as demons go, Harkel is fairly reasonable in his demands. He's not like Ahriman or some of the others. We'll get along just fine."

"Good." No, it wasn't good. I wanted this threesome thing, but the thought of Irix and Harkel—allies, having a demon-child, doing demon things together that I couldn't. It made my stomach churn.

He checked the wound on top of my head. "This is looking better, but it's still healing. Don't hunt tonight. Harkel poured enough energy into me that I can take care of your needs. We'll clean up and go to bed, and make love. This time it will be all about you."

I looked down at the disgusting, wet-and-stained carpet. "Clean up as in us or the trailer?"

He followed my gaze. "Can we just burn this place down and get another?"

"The fire marshal might have a problem with that."

He sighed. "Then you shower. I'll repair my injuries and see if I can get the worst out of this carpet and cushions. I'll join you in bed as soon as I can."

The guy cooked, cleaned, and made love like a boss. Who could ask for anything more?

"Love you," I told him as I headed to the tiny bathroom.

He grinned back at me. "Love you, too."

CHAPTER 13

I got to sleep in the next day. Or rather I got to wake up and have leisurely morning sex with Irix, then doze in bed while he made coffee and threw some mini donuts onto a plate for me.

"So what's on our agenda today?" Irix nuzzled my neck at I munched on a donut.

"We're going to visit Boone Valley and Santor Winery, and then we're going to try to track down a pair of plague demons."

I'd spent some time while the coffee was brewing thinking about the attack on me last night. Hallwyn was still my top suspect, her possible motives both revenge on the slight I'd delivered to her, and my disgusting half-elven parentage. But I couldn't completely discount that others might have motivation to both take me out of the picture and ensure the vineyard, and Hallwyn, failed. Another elf who wanted her job—perhaps the one at Santor or Boone who was looking to change employment, or plague demons who had an axe to grind with DiMarche management. Or maybe a sorcerer, although since I hadn't seen any indication of a magic-wielding human, that one seemed a remote possibility.

"Or instead of touring wineries and hunting down plague demons, we could just stay in bed and have sex." Irix reached out and examined the spot where my head wound had been yesterday. It was healed, but he clucked over it like a mother hen.

Staying in bed all day with my lover was a tempting idea, but I knew something Irix would like better. "Or after we tour the wineries and look for these demons, we could go hunting together."

He grinned. "Oh yeah. Do you want to drive separately so people don't suspect we're in a relationship?"

"No, I don't just want to hunt together, I want us to feed together. Do you think we can make that happen?"

We'd hunted together, but we'd always gone our separate ways once we'd found our partners for the evening. The closest thing to feeding together had been in New Orleans when Irix had arranged an orgy for my own personal pleasure, but I'd needed to leave before anything interesting had happened to take care of a supernatural problem.

He tilted his head, lifting an eyebrow. "Seriously? I will absolutely make that happen if you're game. Do you want to tag team, or threesome, or side-by-side?"

Wow, this was so sexy. "What do *you* want to do?"

He chewed on his bottom lip as he thought. "Tag team. Two and two then switch, although it might wind up just being the four of us together."

"Fun," I breathed, getting turned on just thinking about it. Watching Irix work his magic right beside me, then switching mid-game, or combining it all together would be seriously hot.

"It might take us a while to find the right pair, though," he warned.

"So, like swingers?" I asked. "We each take one of a couple?"

"Yeah, but one step further. We have sex in the same room, and if we can manage it, we switch halfway through or merge the action."

Kinky. "Let me clean up and get dressed, and we'll head out."

I ran into the bathroom while Irix went through my clothing, asking me what I wanted to wear and pulling items out of the closet.

"Think we can actually get brunch, too?" I called out, scrubbing as fast as I could. "I didn't eat much yesterday and mini donuts aren't going to stick with me for long. We have all these diseases and pests in the vineyard and that elf woman is worthless. I was so busy that I didn't get much of a chance to breathe, let alone eat lunch."

"Do you think it's one of the pestilence demons?" I could hear the worry in his voice. "It might be due to any number of causes. A sorcerer? Perhaps a disgruntled employee or a rival vineyard hired a sorcerer to produce a spell."

I wasn't ruling any of that out. Now that the elves had migrated from Hel, the humans had suffered a rude awakening about magic as well as the existence of beings who had powers they'd never imagined. Dragons. Elves. Trolls. Mermaids. And with the elves, several sorcerers from Hel had decided they could expand their operations this side of the gate and find customers willing to pay top dollar for a spell. It used to be that a mage's only career option upon escaping from slavery and running from his elven master across the gates would be as entertainment at children's' parties. But the world was now a different place.

"I don't know. It could be a natural phenomenon. I mean,

with all the pesticides and lack of biodiversity, the humans have set themselves up for a perfect storm of chemically resistant diseases and pests. Maybe their luck has run out, and vineyards are the first to be hit." I hated the thought. I'd almost rather have found out a sorcerer had cursed the vineyard than think there were a dozen fungus and bacteria strains along with an equal number of insects that would be near impossible to kill. Vineyards first, food supply next. If that was the case, the human race would be looking at a serious famine and food shortage in the near future.

It would be more than one young half-elf could handle. It would most likely be more than a hundred thousand elves could handle. Hopefully it was a spell. Spells weren't easy, but at least they could be broken. And when they were, the damage stopped.

"Confronting a plague demon is going to be tricky. I'll expect you to stay as much in the background as possible and let me do the talking, if we can even manage to find her, that is. They're not the brightest bulbs in the pack, but I don't want her to realize what you are."

He was right. I was playing a dangerous game here. Harkel thought I was a full succubus with an Owned elven form. Hallwyn thought I was a human that bore a slight resemblance to a low-level elf. The elves in Hel had thought I was a full elf. I wasn't sure how to play this with the plague demons. And I wasn't sure that Hallwyn's pride-fueled blindness would extend to the elves at Boone Valley and Santor.

"Do you think the other elves are going to know what I am?" I worried. "What am I going to do, Irix? There will soon be a hundred thousand or so elves spread all over the world, working side-by-side with humans. One is going to figure it out sooner rather than later, and I'm scared that I'll end up with a price on my head. My mother hid me here to protect me, but now even hiding among the humans isn't safe."

He sighed. "I'm hoping by the time an elf figures it out, you'll be strong enough to defend yourself, or have valuable allies to shield you. Right now the elves are completely off balance. They came here expecting to rule and establish their own kingdoms with the humans as slaves, and instead the angels have shoved them onto an island and forced them to bend to human culture and society. Right now they feel powerless and confused, and I don't think they'd do more than start a rage-fueled catfight."

"I'd totally win a cat-fight," I told him.

"Yes, you would. Even if Hallwyn or these other two elves find out, what can they do? Most of them can barely speak the language or drive a car. They wouldn't attack when they are strangers in a strange land, and you obviously have grown up here and know your way around this confusing human life. What worries me is that elves are patient. And they're not above pooling their money and hiring a demon to take you out."

So I'd have time if I was discovered, but how much time? I was so sick of hiding and living in fear. I'd grown up thinking I was a human, that the worst thing that could happen to me was dropping my iPhone in the toilet. This knot in my gut every time I saw a demon or an elf was driving me nuts. And it seemed I'd be seeing demons and elves a whole lot more than my mother had ever planned.

"Here." Irix handed me a soft cotton dress in navy blue. He was naked and edging beside me to grab a washcloth. I wiggled past, giving his delectable ass a quick squeeze on the way out of the tiny bathroom. By the time I had the dress on and had slipped my feet into some strappy sandals, Irix was out of the bathroom, devastatingly handsome in a pair of distressed jeans and a snug T-shirt advertising the happiest place on earth.

"Seriously? Do you plan on changing your shirt before we hunt?"

"No. Why?"

Silly incubus. But he was the expert when it came to seduction. "You're going to try to pick up a swinger couple with a Mickey Mouse on your shirt?"

He nodded. "It's quirky. Hot guy. Beloved cartoon character. The perfect combination."

I had a feeling he was right, as usual. Irix was sweet, fun, devoted. He was also smolderingly hot, sexy as anything that ever walked the Earth, and outrageously good at what he did. No sex demon hunted like Irix. I couldn't imagine that even my own succubus sire, Leethu, was as accomplished in seduction and pleasure. He had an uncanny ability to hone in on what people wanted that lay deeper than just their sexual fantasies, and his one night with them satisfied everything— emotional needs as well as physical. He tied his humans to him, but the tethers were so intricately woven that the humans were able to love and continue a healthy life, never forgetting that stranger who in one night made them realize that they were more than just a body.

I admired him. I hoped that one day I could come close to his level of expertise. I'd come so far in the last year. I'd gone from denying who I was, starving my succubus side, to embracing it and trying to refine my technique so that my encounters were as beneficial to the human as they were to me. But I had a long way to go, and I was thrilled to soak up every lesson Irix gave me.

We headed out in Irix's stolen BMW, windows down as the warm morning sunshine bathed us in light. The road out of our little trailer park for the DiMarche field hands went past row after row of vines, all in neat rows, their huge green leaves waving in the breeze. It was beautiful, but even from the car I could feel the diseases. I closed my eyes, sending a net of sensory awareness outward, and saw it all like a color-coordinated map. There were hot spots of infestation, and large areas of healthy plants. The sick vines seemed to be clustered near roadways, the equipment sheds, and the tasting room and winery. I would have expected it to be more random, or to have at least infected the vineyard in the depths of the fields as well as the outskirts, but the portions far from the roadways were the healthiest. Clearly this wasn't due to heat or wetness or another natural cause. The pattern once more made me believe that someone had come along the roadways and either sprayed a biological component to infect the vines, or cursed them via a spell, or rubbed their plague-demon fingers all over the nearby leaves and trunks.

I resisted the urge to have Irix stop the car so I could get out to heal some of the plants and instead tried to plot a course of action for today. The plague demon was one thing. Irix could help with that, and I could either play the human expert or a young succubus. The two elves at Boone Valley and Santor were another thing. Should I pretend to be a concerned and helpful scientist-type human? A demon? If the other elves and Hallwyn were friends, no doubt my co-workers would soon hear about the elf-looking blonde woman who showed up asking questions. I'd pestered Hallwyn too often about the infestations to remain anonymous, and after calling her a fraud, I wouldn't be able to slide under the radar.

I didn't have long to ponder my plan, because the first place Irix pulled into was the neighboring Boone Valley.

"They've got a good brunch tasting," he explained. "And I think you need some solid food and an alcoholic beverage or two before we go tracking down Apixt and her sister."

I took a deep breath to steady my nerves, and smoothed my dress as we walked up to the tasting room. The place was packed, their sign advertising a brunch buffet with a crepe station and a wine pairing all for one low price.

Irix paid at the door, the cashier's eyes wandering up and down his body with open appreciation, snagging on his T-shirt. "Did you go down to Disney?" she asked.

He leaned over the counter on his elbows, biceps bulging as he gave her a slow smile. "The one in Florida. I don't think I'll have time to visit Disneyland this trip, but maybe next time. I've got a fondness for the Magic Kingdom."

She giggled, her face flushed. "I'm more into anime, but I wouldn't kick Mickey to the curb."

"See, I'm a bit old-school." Irix's voice was like dark chocolate on a sweet strawberry. "Disney. Scooby Doo and the Hanna-Barbera crowd. Yogi. Banana Splits. Josie and the Pussycats."

"Teenage Mutant Ninja Turtles?" she asked hopefully. "Johnny Quest?"

"Totally." He reached out and gave her hand a squeeze, his fingers lingering against hers. "Are you working tomorrow?"

She caught her breath. "Yes. Noon to close."

His smile was warm, conveying every intention of fucking her senseless. "I'll swing by around close and maybe we can grab a coffee?"

"Yes," she breathed. "Oh, yes."

I bit back a smile, staying quietly in the background so the woman didn't suddenly see me and think she was breaking the girl-code. Irix had lined up an easy score for tomorrow, and judging from the energy pouring from this woman right now, it would be a very satisfying experience for the both of them.

"I'll be here." He met her eyes as he brought her hand to his mouth and kissed it, nipping the skin at her wrist before releasing her. Then he turned away, but not before giving her one last steamy glance over his shoulder.

"I so want to fuck you," I told him as we walked into the tasting room and found our table. "I worship at your feet, oh incubus master."

He snorted. "At nearly twenty-two you're damned skilled. By my age, you'll be Mata Hari, or Helen of Troy."

"Fuck that. Mata Hari, maybe. Or Cleopatra. I don't want to be some beautiful trophy-wife that gets kidnapped by a pretty-boy and hauled away against my will."

Irix laughed. "I pity the fool that tries to kidnap you. And Cleopatra wasn't as powerful as legend would have it. Women back then were pawns to a patriarchal society. Except for prostitutes. Skilled concubines have always ruled the world. Sex, my dear elven princess. It's what makes the world go round'. It's what brings powerful men to their knees."

I looped my arm in his, waited while he pulled my chair out for me, and let him scoot it in after I sat. We enjoyed savory chicken and mushroom crepes with an amazing flight of white wines and a sweet Riesling to finish. Irix had been sending sultry looks toward the guy who was clearly the manager, but backed off once he realized the man was more interested in me than him.

The manager came over to see how our dining experience was, and I let loose a curl of pheromone. Irix might not need to turn on the demon lures as often as I did, but I was inexperienced compared to him, and this was important.

"I loved the Chardonnay," I gushed, blinking big doe-eyes up at the man. "Are you open for tours? I'm a recent graduate with a botany degree, on an internship at DiMarche for the summer, but I'm trying to get as broad an experience as possible about the best grape varieties for this type of soil and climate, as well as styles and branding of the local wineries.

He glanced over at Irix. "Maybe a short tour."

"You go." Irix leaned back in his chair, swirling the wine in his glass. "This is so not my thing, girl. I'll just have another glass of this…whatever it is, and you go look at the wine stuff."

The manager looked quite a bit more excited at the prospect of a tour without the incubus along. I slid out of my seat and put out my hand. "I'm Amber."

"Sean Bell."

Sean led me through the retail store, and into a small-scale production facility that had been the original site of the company's wine-making enterprise, but was now used for specialty wines and these tours. Unlike the much larger DiMarche winery, Boone Valley specialized in Chardonnay, Riesling, and Pinot with some award winning small-batch dry Rieslings.

"How's your harvest looking this year?" I finally asked. "Quite a few of the larger vineyards and orchards in the state are really struggling with black measles, leafrollers, and other blights."

He shot me a quick, nervous glance. "You've got a botany degree. I'm sure you realize that agriculture is a constant battle against pests and diseases. Boone Valley has been forward thinking and hired an elf to assist us in keeping our vines healthy and producing the highest quality harvest. She's out in the field now, working her magic on our vines."

I shrugged. "I think it's all a bunch of hype. Elves, angels, dragons…pffft. Are they really doing any good, or at the end of the day are you going to discover that the chemicals are doing a better job than the pointy-eared dude with the glowy hands?"

"Well, between you and me, I have my doubts." Sean grinned sheepishly. "Party line is that we've got an elf and everything is going to be pristine. Reality? I don't think she understands our crops and the issues we're facing. She tries. She is helping, and I think she's probably doing a better job than the pesticides would, but the elf is no miracle cure."

"But everyone is going to hire one now, because shareholders will demand it."

He nodded. "Yeah. It will be the new quality control trend. TQM, ISO9000, Six Sigma, elves."

I laughed. "Okay, isn't it kinda weird that this year all the big vineyards are having horrible problems with blight and pests? The very year elves are available to save the day for only one small fee?"

Sean snorted. "What are you calling small? She's costing us a freaking bundle, not including the recruiter fee. It's not like we had a choice, though. Even if she doesn't miraculously cure every spot on our vines, the pressure is already on to have an elf on the payroll. Even the commercial farms have jumped on the elven-bandwagon. Three orchards, two vegetable farms… I've even heard a few of the hospitals have brought elves in to help battle antibiotic resistant bacteria and other infections."

Interesting. This Magical Interventions company must be making a bundle on placement fees. For a second I wondered if they could be behind these outbreaks, but then why continue them after the elf was hired? It would be in their best interest to have the elven employees seen as miracle workers. I mulled it over as we'd made our way back into the retail store. Knowing I should do something to show appreciation for the manager's time and attention, I pulled a couple bottles of wine off the shelf to buy and thanked Sean with a warm smile.

"Anytime. If you'd like to see the larger production site or have a private tasting…?"

"Tuesday night? I finish work around four."

He grinned. "I'll be here. Whites or Reds?"

I waved one of the bottles in my hand. "Today was all about the whites, so let's try some reds."

"Perfect. See you then." Sean took off and I paid for the wine, motioning for Irix to follow me out to the car.

It seemed like Santor Winery was having the same issues as Boone Valley and DiMarche, and the manager there had the same doubts about the effectiveness of their elf. Something or someone was causing these diseases in the crops of large commercial farms, orchards, and vineyards. And that someone's motivation seemed to get the elves jobs.

But these elves weren't going to have jobs for long if they were getting blocked at every turn. I thought again of the vine, rotted and ripped from the ground, crushed in an act that seemed full of anger. I thought of the attack on me, pretty sure that I'd find that particular vine dead when I returned to work tomorrow.

"Any handle on either plague demon?" I asked Irix as he handed me an ice cream cone. We'd stopped in town at a little roadside Mr. Frosty, which served the dual purpose of satisfying my sweet tooth and nosing around for any signs of the demons. According to Irix, they would leave a fairly obvious trail of destruction in their wake.

"Yep. But I'll wait until you're done with your ice cream before I fill you in on the details. No sense in turning your stomach."

I took a lick of my ice cream cone. "Tell me." I'd been dealing with some truly disgusting plant diseases and pests in the last few weeks. Nothing could be grosser than borer larvae or bunch rot.

"Shigella."

I blinked. "In a vineyard?"

"No, silly." Irix shook his head. "In a restaurant."

Yeah, I was totally put off my ice cream. I might not ever eat again. Shigella was a feces-born bacterium. Dysentery.

Projectile pooping. Dehydration. But as horrible as the symptoms were, they didn't come close to the repulsiveness of the way it was transmitted. Somebody didn't wash their hands after wiping their bum and then went and touched food. Since it had been traced to a restaurant, that someone was most likely a kitchen employee.

I eyed my ice cream, shot a quick narrowed glance at the Mr. Frosty, and dumped it in the trash can.

"Disgusting, but this happens with food service occasionally. What makes you think this is one of the plague demons?"

"Because it happened in three different restaurants in the last twenty-four hours and every one had a new employee who matched Apixt's and Txipa's description." Irix grinned, taking a huge bite out of his ice cream. Clearly the thought of explosive diarrhea didn't bother him one bit. "That guy over there? He's an imp and not thrilled with the idea of a plague demon, or in this case plague demons, in his territory."

What the fuck? Were there demons everywhere right now? Was Harkel right when he'd mentioned that the angels' distraction meant the time was right for demons to flood across the gateways?

"So where do we find her? Either one? I'm assuming by the time the dysentery is reported, they're long gone."

Irix grinned. "My bud Lektian over there would truly love some assistance. He doesn't mind sex demons or warmongers, but as an imp running an ice cream shop, he isn't happy about plague demons nearby. We help run Apixt and her sister out of town, and he owes us a favor."

I was suddenly glad my ice cream was in the trash. "An imp running an ice cream shop? An imp?"

Irix shrugged. "The Iblis is a slum lord. Demons gotta work. I'm sure he's got some scheme going on off-hours, or maybe there's something in the ice cream." He eyed his intently. "Possibly drugs. Is pot ice cream a thing?"

After he finished, Irix drove us into town, parking outside of a vegan café. "Don't eat anything," he warned as we walked in.

I had no intention of eating anything, possibly ever again. It was horrifying to think that a plague demon was right now running his feces-laden fingers over all the arugula and bean sprouts.

Irix scanned the room. One of the waiters froze, glaring at the incubus, then turning that frown my way.

"Get out," he snarled.

"We were thinking of ordering a healthy salad, but that's not likely with you here, Txipa." Irix looked down at the plate in the plague demon's hands. "Nice job, by the way. Very skillfully done. I can't even tell you've contaminated it with my eyes alone."

Txipa looked like a human woman—a woman so thin her skin was stretched across her bones giving her a mummified look. Her skin was sallow and chalky, her hair dry and lank, the color of straw. Her eyes were bloodshot, her nose red and dripping. I couldn't believe the management here had hired her. She looked like she should be in a hospital, not waiting tables. A few of the patrons turned to stare at the three of us as if they were noticing Txipa for the first time. One put a twenty on the table and scurried out the door.

"Get. Out. I backed off your hunting ground. You back off mine." Txipa put the plate down at an empty table and poked a finger at me. "And you...you're lucky to be alive. We were here first. I'm willing to share territory with a few sex demons, but not one who is deliberately messing with our work."

"Why?" I asked. "Why DiMarche? Do you have something against the management?"

She snorted, then spat into the plate of greens. "I don't even know their management. Girl, we're plague demons. This is what we do. I'm willing to step aside and not infect prey in specific hunting grounds as professional courtesy, and I expect you to do the same."

This was ridiculous. All I wanted to do was save my vineyard, but I couldn't do that without admitting to my half-elf side. A succubus shouldn't care about grape vines. By demon standards of behavior, Txipa and her sister were being extremely courteous and accommodating.

"Can you just leave the one vineyard alone?" I pleaded, hating that I was most likely dooming the others.

"Uh, no. Why the fuck do you care? Go screw some humans next to the rotting vines. It will be extra romantic. We do our thing. You do your thing. Lektian runs his ice cream stand, and maybe if the three of us come to an agreement, we don't rub our filthy hands all over the cones."

"Push too hard and the angels will come," Irix warned. "And then we're all screwed. You and Apixt have been focusing your efforts in this area for too long. You can't whither and infect every person, animal, and plant within a fifty-mile radius and *not* expect the angels to notice."

"If you haven't figured it out yet, fuck-boy, the angels are busy. They've got a war going on. There's the whole Elf Island thing. And for some reason, most of them are wandering around here among the humans looking as if they were hit with a stun gun. I could probably walk up to one right now and hit him over the head with a cow turd and he wouldn't notice."

She was right. And that put a sick feeling in my stomach. "Please?" I begged. "Just the one vineyard. That's all I ask."

"No. Go fuck in a vineyard on the east coast if that's your kink of the day. We're busy here. And stop messing with our work, or next time we'll do more than split your head open."

Irix shot out a hand and grabbed Txipa's arm. "Threaten her again and I'll be the one splitting *your* skull."

She laughed, giving me a disgusting view of black and rotted teeth. Irix's hand grew white and withered where it touched her skin. "I've heard you're a good fuck, Irix, and I don't like to kill sex demons, but if you don't take your hand off me, you'll be an exception."

There was a tense moment where I wasn't sure whether Irix would comply or fight. A few more customers bolted from the café, leaving us alone with a scared member of the kitchen staff peering around the swinging half-doors.

Irix let go of the plague demon. "I'm asking you kindly to discontinue your work at DiMarche vineyard, but I'm telling you to leave Amber alone. It won't be just me you'll be facing if you harm her again, it will be Harkel. He's taken an interest in her, even presented her with a breeding contract. He's this side of the gates, and would be quite angry if something were to happen to his succubus."

Txipa waved Irix's threats away with a sneer, but I noticed how the plague demon's already pale skin had become chalk white. "Harkel and I respect each other's work. If this little bitch means so much to him, then he needs to rein her in and tell her to keep her hands off what my sister and I have claimed."

Irix shot me a quick warning glance, then reached out with his non-withered hand to grip my arm. "We've given you the courtesy of coming to discuss this in person instead of assaulting you. Amber and I will continue to work as we see fit. Both you and your sister don't have an exclusive claim on DiMarche. If you don't want your work interfered with, then I suggest you spread your diseases elsewhere."

He spun me around and practically dragged me from the café before Txipa could respond, stuffing me into the passenger seat of the BMW and squealing the tires as we left.

"The nerve of her," I fumed. "If they want to throw down some black measles, then fine, but they don't have the right to assault me or prohibit me from trying to fix those vines."

"They do." Irix's hands were tight on the steering wheel. "Amber, you're a sex demon in their eyes. They feel what you're doing is an insult toward them. Let Hallwyn heal the vines. Let your human co-workers spray their fungicides. Finish your internship at DiMarche, but leave the infected plants alone."

"You're joking. Irix, healing plants is part of who I am."

"Then heal plants somewhere else." He pulled over onto the shoulder of the road and put the car in park before turning to me. "You're walking on the edge of a cliff here, Amber. There's a warmonger who needs to continue to believe you're a full succubus. There's an elf working with you that needs to believe you're a human. And now there are two plague demons who need to see you as a full succubus. I know you're a half-elf and that part of you isn't going to be easy to deny, but deny it you must. Work your internship. Fuck some humans. Grow your relationship with Harkel. Just put the plant stuff on hold until we get somewhere safer, somewhere you won't end up being killed either by an elven co-worker or a pair of plague demons."

I ground my teeth and looked out the window. We'd pulled up beside a huge field of immature vines, barely tall enough to reach the first row of wire. Irix didn't understand. What he was asking me to do…it was like asking me to stop breathing for a few months. My whole life, when I'd thought I was human, I'd still nourished plants. I'd had gardens, and orchids, and violets. I'd been the one who had revived the wilted begonias and eased the frostbite on the buds of our cherry blossoms. As a human I'd always thought I had two green thumbs. But now I was supposed to stand by and watch plants wither and die from a plague demon's touch, watch while a stupid, arrogant, useless elf tried to heal them and failed.

Irix was right. I understood the risks. I understood that I wasn't strong enough to go up against two plague demons, that I wasn't strong enough to face a bunch of elves who wanted me dead. But I wasn't sure I was strong enough to deny what the elf inside me demanded I do.

CHAPTER 14

*I*rix drove into Rutherford and pulled up to a pool hall. I shot him a surprised look. "I thought we'd find swingers at somewhere more posh."

"Au contraire, my dear Amber. Swingers are everywhere. Ones at pool halls tend to be a little quicker to get into bed than five star restaurants."

Quicker worked for me. The conversation with the plague demon was still hanging over me, darkening my mood considerably. I wasn't in the mood for this. I wasn't in the mood for anything beyond going back to the trailer and curling up in bed, but I hated to end my day on such a bad note. Besides, I needed the energy, and this might be just the thing to pull me out of my gloom.

We hopped out of the car and I followed Irix in. He grabbed my hand once we were in the door and pulled me close to him as we approached the bar, squeezing between two sets of couples. We ordered drinks, then Irix draped his arm around me, planting a lingering kiss on my lips.

Thoughts of plague demons whacking me in the head, of the DiMarche vineyard a rotted wasteland, of elves who were no more than indentured servants faded away with his kiss. This was exactly what I needed. The crash of billiard balls echoed through the room, drowning out the hum of conversation and clink of glasses and bottles. A group of guys laughed over near the dart boards. A woman shouted, waving her pool cue in the air like a sword, high-fiving her partner. Irix's hand slid from my waist to grip my ass and pull me against him, his forehead touching mine. Then his lips met mine once more, soft and full of promise.

"Go to the bathroom," he whispered against my mouth.

I curled my fingers inside the waistband of his jeans as I pulled away from him, holding on as I walked away, letting go only when my arm had fully extended. I grinned back at him, and felt his eyes watching me as I walked off, putting an extra sway in my step. In the bathroom I went ahead and took care of business, smiling at the other two women who were touching up their make-up as I washed my hands. One of them said her good-byes while the other looked in the mirror and ran a hand over her smooth dark hair.

"How long is the wait for a table?" I asked. "We're new in town. My boyfriend and I were hoping to shoot some pool tonight."

The brunette turned to me, and I saw a glimmer of desire in her eyes. It wasn't unusual. As much as most women liked to claim they were heterosexual, they often weren't. Just because they had a preference didn't mean there weren't the few occasions where they met someone of the same sex they felt that pull of attraction toward.

"It's half an hour at least." She hesitated, digging in her purse and pulling out a lipstick before giving me a bashful smile. "How good are you? We could play together, but I don't really want to have a couple of sharks wipe the floor with us."

I laughed. "I'm lucky if I don't scratch the felt. Irix is

pretty good, but I'll balance out his skill with my less-than-stellar talents."

"Irix? That's a cool name. He's not…" she squirmed, dropping her gaze before forcing it back up to meet mine. "He's not that hot guy at the bar with the wavy dark hair and the light brown eyes, is he? That dude is like an Italian wet dream."

Yes, he was. "Is your boyfriend the blond with the short buzz cut? Military? Girl, you haven't done so bad yourself. He's a whole lot of muscle, there."

"That's Austin." She grinned. "He *is* hot, isn't he?"

Oh yes he was. "Absolutely." I touched up my lipstick with a quick swipe. "If you don't mind my horrible billiard skills, we'd love to share a table with you all."

"I'm Bridget." She stuck out her hand.

"I'm Amber."

"Let's go see how Irix and Austin get along, then maybe we can shoot some pool."

I followed her out the door, knowing full well that Irix would get along with anyone that was a prospective sexual partner, male or female. And Austin might consider himself the most heterosexual man in the state of California, but with one sultry look from my beloved incubus, that was going to change.

Sure enough, we walked out to find Irix next to Austin, the blond man laughing at something the incubus had said. This was promising. And from the anticipation practically vibrating from Bridget, I knew she was hoping the night ended well.

I walked up and Irix slung an arm around my shoulder, giving me a melting kiss.

"Amber, this is Austin. He and his girlfriend are up on holiday from San Diego."

"I met Bridget in the bathroom," I confessed, giving

Austin a warm, but not too warm, smile. "I'm doing an internship at DiMarche, Irix is visiting me from New Orleans."

"Ooo, New Orleans," Bridget squealed, clapping her hands. "I've always wanted to go there. Maybe someday we can go for Mardi Gras."

Irix shook her hand. "You and Austin are welcome to visit us if you do. I have a place just off Lafayette Square. You can see the Mississippi River from my rooftop terrace."

The rooftop terrace where Irix and I had first made love. I caught my breath, involuntarily releasing a small curl of pheromones.

"Hey, we're up," Austin announced as another couple moved away from one of the pool tables. We headed over and grabbed cues. I crushed a square of blue chalk against the tip because that's what I'd seen other people do, then watched while the other three discussed what kind of game we were playing.

The few times I'd played pool I'd been drunk off my ass or trying to get in some guy's pants, so I hadn't really paid attention to the rules. It seemed this time we were in teams, with Irix and me working the solids, and Austin and Bridget the stripes. We alternated shots, which meant Irix and I were probably going to lose.

And that didn't matter, because I got the feeling that no matter how the pool game turned out, we were all going to win.

The game went as expected. Every ball Irix sank was followed up with me just bouncing them around the table. I sank one completely out of luck, but Austin and Bridget easily won. The next round we played guys against gals, and by the end of that round, there were quite a lot of empty beers stacked up on the side table. And the whole time we'd been flirting—me with Austin, Bridget with Irix, me and

Bridget with each other. I saw Austin exchange what seemed like a knowing look with Irix while Bridget and I were laughing over some bad shot, her arm across my shoulder.

"Austin and Amber against me and Bridget," Irix suggested. "Then we probably need to call it a night before they have to roll us out of here."

The other couple seemed on board with that. In fact, they were eager to swap pool partners. Austin teased me about my terrible billiard skills and leaned over me, pressing himself against my ass as he tried to show me how to line up a shot. The whole time Bridget was busy giggling over Irix's Mickey Mouse shirt.

I'm not sure who won that round. Bridget pinched Irix's ass right before a critical shot and he ended up sinking the wrong ball. We were all touching—arms, thighs, a hand tucking someone's hair back.

"This is our last round," Austin announced when the eight ball slid into a corner pocket. He exchanged a quick glance with Bridget who nodded in approval. "Do you both want to come back to our place for drinks? We're only a few blocks away."

We followed them out, Bridget and I leading the way and walking hand-in-hand. She was tipsy, excited, her fingers curling against my palm as she pulled me to her side. We got to their house first and Bridget fumbled with the key, reluctant to let go of my hand.

"There." She turned to me, an uncertain smile on her face.

So I kissed her. My fingers gentle against the edge of her jaw, my lips soft and feather-light against hers. After a brief, teasing touch, I pulled just far enough away that we shared a breath. She leaned toward me, and I took the hint. This time our kiss deepened, tongues touching and exploring. Purses hit the ground and I felt Bridget's touch against my waist, her other hand at the base of my skull, fingers pushing through my hair as she gripped the back of my head.

"Now *that's* totally hot," Austin said. From his voice I could tell he and Irix were only a few feet away on the porch.

Bridget broke our kiss, her hand coming forward to cup my cheek. "Inside?"

Her voice was husky, her eyes on my mouth. "Yes," I told her, making sure she knew that I was saying 'yes' to everything and anything.

Her lips curled into a smile and her eyes briefly met mine. "Shall we let them watch, or make them go away?"

"I want them to watch. And if they're very good boys, maybe we'll let them join in."

She caught her breath. She wasn't the only one. I distinctly heard Austin do the same and Irix's low chuckle. Bridget pushed the door open and pulled me inside, leaving the boys to grab our purses and follow. Five steps in and we were once more in each other's arms, hands and lips everywhere. Clothing made its way to the floor piece by piece, all while we edged our way to the bedroom.

Thought blurred into sensation as we collapsed onto the bed, exploring each other. I was barely aware of Austin and Irix joining us, their hands caressing our skin and occasionally brushing against each other. Pheromones filled the air, languorous and rich as dark chocolate. I made sure Bridget came, then Irix did the same before we all joined together, finding a different pleasure in each stroke and touch.

It was close to dawn by the time Irix and I got dressed to leave, exchanging contact information with Austin and Bridget before heading out of the apartment and to our car in the empty parking lot of the darkened pool hall.

Irix wrapped his arm around my waist, pulling me next to him and placing a quick kiss on the top of my head as he unlocked the car. "Feel better?"

I was humming with energy. I felt loved, cherished, strong. There was a time when I'd hated my succubus self, and there were still times I lamented that the human world thought me a slut, but tonight wasn't one of those times. Tonight my succubus self shone, and my elven half was happy to rest in the background. There were still troubles ahead with the elves, the plague demons, and the fate of a vineyard, but for now I was floating in happiness.

"Much better. Tonight was amazing."

Irix swatted my ass lightly as I climbed into the car. His golden eyes adoring as he watched me tuck my dress around my legs. "*You* were amazing."

CHAPTER 15

J waited to be last in line to get my assignment the next morning and pulled Jorge aside.

"You're up in front of the winery today," he told me. "There are some big tours coming in this weekend and Richard wants all the annuals replaced with fresh begonias and impatiens. Everything has to be lush and in bloom. Eat lunch inside, then afterward spend the rest of the day with the production group in the winery."

It was exactly what I'd wanted, what I'd been silently grousing about not doing. But now that I'd been offered the opportunity to experience the other parts of the vineyard and winery, I found myself reluctant to leave the fields and the plants I'd come to consider mine.

But this was what my internship was supposed to be about—gaining knowledge and experience in all the facets of large-scale, commercial wine production facilities from vines to bottle to marketing and sales. And this would make it so much easier to follow Irix's mandate. I wouldn't be tempted at every turn to heal a sick vine if I didn't have them right in front of my nose eight hours per day.

I glanced over at Manny, Rosa, Henry, and Scotty laughing and joking together as they got into the golf carts to make their way to their respective fields for the day. My friends. Hopefully I'd see them again and that I'd like the staff in the winery just as much as I had these guys. Either way, I was going to seriously miss Rosa's empanadas.

"Will do." I reluctantly handed Jorge my clipboard. "I know I wasn't supposed to be here after my shift, but I need to let you know that I was checking some of the vines the night before last and someone came up and hit me on the back of the head."

"What?" Jorge's eyes widened. "Why didn't you tell someone? Are you hurt? You'll need to file a worker's comp claim."

"No, I'm fine. Really. I just wanted to tell you. I saw Hallwyn working late too, and with the vandalism the other night, I'm thinking we need more security cameras."

Security cameras that might catch an elf or a plague demon sabotaging the harvest.

"We will definitely get those up. I'll let Hallwyn know, too. She didn't say anything yesterday, so I'm guessing she left before whoever assaulted you got there."

Or she was the one who assaulted me, although after our conversation with Txipa yesterday, I believed it was one of the plague demons who had whacked me in the back of the head. Either way, cameras would be a big help. And the next time I stayed late and tried to heal vines, I was going to make sure I stayed aware of my surroundings.

"I also wanted to ask, is Boone continuing to have the same issues with their vines as we are? I was down there the other day for a tasting and got to wondering, since they're so close. The manager didn't seem to think their elf was eradicating the vine diseases as quickly and effectively as they'd expected."

Jorge blinked in surprise. "You know, I'll have to call them and see. I spoke to Sean over there a few months ago and he said they were bringing in an elf to take care of a stubborn downy mildew issue. I'd assumed that was the only problem they were having. And I figured they weren't having *any* problems since they hired their elf. Between them, Santor, and Boone Valley, Richard was considering bringing an elf of our own on board. Once we started really having problems in the field, he was convinced, and we had Hallwyn within a few days. Sean seemed pretty happy with theirs, and we'd been having reoccurring cases of black measles, bunch rot, downy mildew, and more."

"I wonder how effective their elf is compared to the pesticides and other methods," I mused. Was the elf at Boone Valley just as much of a fraud as Hallwyn? Sean had hinted that he wasn't completely convinced the elf was worth the money, but maybe his expectations were too high. Maybe Hallwyn just really sucked.

But elven incompetence didn't explain why *we* were being hit with every single disease and pest known to vintnering at the same time.

Jorge shrugged. "I'll ask. I know they're competition and all that, but I hope they're not having the black measles and Phomopsis and cutworms and leafrollers like we are. Although we weren't having those issues either until a month ago."

At least the diseases hadn't coincided with my arrival and I didn't find myself being blamed for the failed crops. Jorge's words did give me something to think about, though. Was Boone Valley lucky enough to get an elf that actually knew what the heck she was doing, or maybe they were keeping mum about the significant issues they were continuing to have with their plants and crops.

Either way, I'd need to wait to find out. Right now I had

begonias and impatiens to plant and winery production staff to talk to. "Thanks, Jorge. See you tomorrow?"

He shook my hand. "Report to Nancy in the winery tomorrow morning. I think you'll be there for the next week or so. Although if someone gets sick or we get slammed out here, I may ask for you back. You're one heck of a botanist, Amber. I don't know whether you'll decide to pursue field work or chemistry, or production, but I'm hoping you wind up back in my crew before your internship ends. I've never met someone right out of college that has your knowledge of plants, diseases, and pests. You've got quite a future ahead of you."

"Thank you." I was glowing at his praise, and smiled the whole way up to the winery. Here I'd been grumbling about being stuck in the field to do manual labor, feeling that no one appreciated my talents or my potential, and all the time Jorge had been noticing. It made me feel good. It made me wonder if I wouldn't possibly consider a career in the wine industry. Although I was equally excited about working on the wetlands with Jordan. Could I do both?

Wait. I was a half-elf/half-succubus. I'd live for tens of thousands of years. I most certainly could do both. I could do anything I wanted. And that thought made me smile even more.

I walked to the winery and came face-to-face with Hall-wyn. I nearly collided with her, both of us stopping abruptly and staring while doing that dance to try and get around each other. After a few steps she stopped, blocking my way down the hall.

"It wasn't me."

I blinked at her, not sure what to make of her words. She wasn't looking at me as if I were a horrible half-elf monster than she needed to kill, or even as if I were an insolent human who had insulted her. She looked worried, and…concerned.

"It wasn't me."

"Yeah, you said that. Wasn't you what?"

Her shoulders slumped, her face relaxing in relief. "I thought you'd blame me. I was angry, and I know I said that I should kill you for calling me a fraud, but I wouldn't have done it. And I wouldn't have snuck back and hit you in the head either. Jorge told me what happened, warned me to be careful if I was working after hours. I ran up here because I figured you had assumed I was the one who had assaulted you."

I'd been healing a vine at the time I'd been whacked in the head. If it had been Hallwyn, we'd be having a much different conversation right now. Obviously it wasn't her or she'd be trying to stab me or fry me with a fireball to erase my distasteful impure genetic existence.

"I'll admit I did suspect you. You threatened me. And you clearly don't like me. Not that you seem to like any of us."

"Of course I don't like any of you. I can hear you making fun of me. I know you hate me. We enslaved you. We're smarter, more beautiful, more evolved than you are. We elves are in every way your superior. Of course you hate me. I don't expect any of you to like me, but I won't stoop to physically assaulting you. Even if the angels hadn't forbidden us, I wouldn't harm a human. You're base creatures who can't help being two evolutionary steps from primordial ooze."

And now I did hate her. "You're a bitch. None of us like you because you're a horrible, nasty bitch who thinks she's better than all of us and that humans have nothing of value to offer you or the world. And guess what? That means you're going to be really lonely here. This isn't Hel. You don't have a pretty forest kingdom to dance and sing in and congratulate yourselves on how wonderful you all are. You're going to need to drive our metal cars, work for us, eat our food, live next door to us. And if you don't stop being a stuck-up jerk, you're going to spend every night of your very long life all alone in a ratty-ass apartment eating Ramen noodles and watching Three's Company re-runs. You won't have any friends. No one will care if someone robs you on the street corner, or if you fall down the subway stairs, or get hit by a bus." I leaned closer. "And no one will care if a demon hits you in the back of the head one night while you're out in the vineyard. Jorge was concerned when I told him what happened to me. My co-workers would be concerned about me, would be crushed if I'd ended up in the hospital or dead. But you? No one would even go to your funeral. So stick that in your pipe and smoke it."

I pushed past her and stomped down the hall, not caring if she attacked me for insulting her. She *was* a bitch. And I'd had it with her bullshit. Any sympathy she'd gained the other day eating alone in the golf cart was gone. She deserved to lose her job. She deserved to have some plague demon smash her head in. She deserved to get fired for incompetence and sent back to Elf Island where she could rot for the rest of her life.

But there was one problem with my anger-fueled internal tirade. DiMarche didn't deserve to fall apart. And those vines in the field didn't deserve to die.

As horrible as Hallwyn was, as much as I wanted to wash my hands of the whole thing and let that stupid elf crash and burn, I couldn't. Because I couldn't let this company or those innocent plants suffer.

Which meant if I wanted to help this vineyard, I was going to have to go head-to-head against a pair of pissed-off plague demons.

CHAPTER 16

The begonias and impatiens were easy work. The sun was shining. My hands were dark with the rich, loamy soil. The smell of flowers in bloom mixed with the fresh scent of dirt and the tang of mulch filled my nose. When the last plant was set, I went in to wash my hands and join the rest of the production and tasting-room staff for lunch.

There was a bus load of tourists arriving for a tasting at one, so the retail staff were rushing to finish and be back by then. The production folks were a bit more leisurely about their lunch time, discussing various sports teams as well as some reality show that was rumored to be setting up the next town over. I saw someone sit down next to me and turned, not surprised to see Matthieu.

He gave me a dazzling smile. "You're the intern. I saw you a few weeks back, but then you vanished. They must have stuck you in the fields."

Obviously I hadn't been in the winery long enough for my turn on the rotation or I would have already received the "tour". "Yes, I'm Amber Lowry, the summer intern. Jorge has had me trimming and tying in the field for the last two weeks, but I'll be here for at least the next week or so learning the production and retail end."

"Do you have a passion for wine, Amber?"

I'd never seen such a practiced come-hither look before. It was difficult to keep from laughing. If I'd been a normal twenty-two-year-old intern, I might have swooned at his sexy good looks and attention, but I was a half-succubus who made this guy look like an amateur. I'd probably screwed more humans in the last week than he had in the last two months. At least. And besides, as sexy as he might be, Matthieu had nothing on Irix. But then again, it was hardly fair to compare a human player to a sex demon.

Still, Matthieu was amazingly good-looking with warm, golden brown hair that hung around his head in thick waves, dark brown sultry eyes, high cheekbones and a sculpted jaw with full, slightly pouty lips. He was broad shouldered, slim but obviously very fit with long-fingered hands and muscled arms. I wondered how much of his value at DiMarche was in his ability to taste and judge the quality of wine and how much was due to his striking good looks.

Didn't matter. I was totally going to fuck this guy. And unlike the rest of the girls he'd given his "tour" to, I'd be one he'd never forget. Ever. For the rest of his life.

"I have a passion for many things," I told him with a knowing smile. "I like to think of myself as a hedonist. Music. Art. Wine. Food." I hesitated a split second. "Love."

His pupils dilated, his breath catching. This was so easy. I didn't even have to use pheromones. Gotta love a player.

"Meet me here when you're off work and I'll give you the tour," Matthieu said, getting up from the lunch table, and giving me a knowing smile before heading back to the tasting room.

Damn straight he was going to give me a tour, and he was going to love every minute of it.

I temporarily forgot about Matthieu as I worked in the production area staring into huge vats of smashed up grapes while I learned about yeasts and residual sugars and the different fermentation techniques. I'll admit the huge machines that were for de-stemming the grapes, crushing them, fermenting, straining, aging, and bottling were impressive. It was a far cry from the little plastic barrels my friends had used to make their kitchen-sink Merlot. As fascinating as it all was, by the time my shift had ended, I knew I could never make a career at this end of the business. I needed to be in the fields with the plants. Hopefully after a week or so here I could convince Jorge to take me back in the field where I could do what I did best…. Well, what I did but no one realized.

After work I went back to the tasting room and met Matthieu. He smiled at me and wiggled his eyebrows. "Ready for the tour?"

I let myself admire him once more, from his sculptured good-looks, to the way his slim, toned body filled out the dark gray silk pants and soft white shirt. He'd unbuttoned the collar of his shirt and I eyed the smooth tan column of skin.

"Ready," I replied. Boy was I ever ready. Grab a hit of energy from this guy, then, against all better judgement, go out into the fields and see if I could heal a row or two before heading back to the trailer. I was willing to bet Matthieu had the sort of sex drive that would not only give me a rush today, but would continue to supply me for decades. He probably had sex five or six times a week if not more. This was exactly the kind of guy I liked to feast on, the kind that I didn't mind siphoning energy from and firmly tying to me. I wouldn't turn the guy into a babbling fool, but I'd make sure he never forgot me, and that he sent a gift of energy my way each time he got lucky.

Sandy shot Matthieu a narrowed glance, stabbing at her planner with a pencil. "Huge corporate retreat tasting and presentation in an hour, Matthieu. Don't be late."

He eyed me. "I'll be back in half an hour, tops."

It should have been embarrassing having her and everyone else who saw us, know exactly what we were going to be doing down in the cellars as well as the fact that Matthieu was thinking he'd have me done-and-gone in half an hour, but I didn't care. The employees here probably already thought me some kind of slut after having seen me now with Kai, Harkel, and Irix. Might as well give them something else to talk about.

Matthieu led me through the store much as Sean had at Boone Valley, pointing out which wines were their specialties, and what awards they'd won. Unlike the neighboring vineyard, DiMarche used a greater variety of grapes including Semillon and Gewurztraminer, some of which we weren't able to grow in our Napa Valley climate as efficiently as other locales. I knew Jorge took a lot of pride in our Chardonnay and Riesling grapes as well as our Syrah, but it was interesting to see the final products of those grapes and what seemed to be the more successful and acclaimed wines produced at DiMarche.

Then we went through a huge set of doors to a chilled area with cases stacked on pallets, then down a set of stairs into the darkness. Matthieu took my hand, stairs creaking under our feet as we descended into the cool air of the cellar. At the bottom, Matthieu flipped a switch and the whole area was bathed in a low golden light.

"It's important to keep it dim down here. No sunlight. No vibration from people walking around or trucks coming and going. Temperature is kept a constant fifty-five degrees. We make sure it never fluctuates more than two or three degrees from that setting. There are humidifiers throughout the cellar to keep the humidity at seventy to seventy-five percent."

"So the corks don't dry out, shrink, and allow air and bacteria into the wine bottles," I added.

He nodded. "The advent of synthetic corks has meant that dryness is less of an issue than it used to be, but we still like to keep it constant. Besides, we occasionally will use natural cork if we've got a truly special reserve batch that we're aging."

Matthieu walked over and pulled a few bottles from a shelf, wiping them with a rag and peering at the labels. Then he set them on a tall wooden bench and reached underneath to pull out a box. Inside were a variety of glasses and a corkscrew. It made me wonder how often he came down here to re-stock his glasses. Was this "tour" just for attractive female employees, or did he occasionally offer his special services to tasting room patrons? It worked to my advantage if he was getting it on with the customers, but I was curious about the logistics.

"The first one we have here is our 2011 Estate Merlot. All wines list their appellation on the label—whether the grapes are all grown in California, or California and Argentina, etc. A wine needs to have at least seventy-five percent of the grapes grown in Napa Valley to use that specific identifier, and estate wines mean all the grapes that go into the wine are grown on the winery's vineyards. So this bottle I'm about to open was produced using Merlot grapes from our own fields."

It was cool thinking that the vines I'd been working with the last two weeks had gone into what Matthieu was pouring.

"Didn't the California Merlot market crash in 2004 in

favor of Pinot Noir?" I asked, taking a glass and eyeing the deep red-purple liquid in the low light. I tended to steer toward Syrah wines and Pinot Grigio and couldn't recall the last time I'd had a Merlot.

"Trends come and go, but there are always fans that continue to like certain wines. It might not be the gold-rush it was fifteen years ago, but there's still a market for high quality Merlot."

We chatted about cabs and red zin and how sweet wines were making a comeback—and not just as dessert wines either. California had once been famous for their Riesling, only to shift to Chardonnay once that style went out of favor. Matthieu was predicting a comeback of crisp, clear, sweet wines, and I was totally on board with that.

I was also seeing the man in a different light. He was an unrepentant player, but he wasn't creepy. I got the feeling that if I'd said no or acted uninterested, he wouldn't have pushed it.

"What do you think about the elf, Hallwyn?" I asked, wondering if he'd tried to hit on her and choking back a laugh at the thought.

He blinked in surprise at the change of topic. "I really don't know. I mean, I don't get too involved in the day-to-day stuff in the field. It's not my area of expertise. I know Jorge has been ready to pull his hair out this year. I haven't heard anything positive or negative about her work."

That wasn't quite what I was getting at. "No, I mean what do you think of her knowledge of wine? Elves are supposed to be experts there, too."

"Well, I'm not fearing for my job, if that's what you mean." He scowled down into his wine glass. "She doesn't under-stand our varietals, or our processes. She doesn't like our food. She doesn't like our wine. She doesn't seem to like humans, whether it's a business relationship...or more."

Ah, cold shoulder from the elf. Not surprising. But the rest was. "How could she not like our wine? Yeah, a lot of what DiMarche produces isn't high-end, but we do have our estate and specialty wines."

He nodded. "This Merlot we're drinking retails for twenty-three a bottle. Not rich-man stuff, but not something an elf should turn her nose up at."

Matthieu nodded and I followed his lead, swirling the wine, looking at how it coated the inside of the glass. We buried our noses into the glasses, inhaling the aroma, then swirling it once more before sampling a mouthful. This ritual was new to me. In college, we were drinking box wine out of whatever cheap glasses we could find. There was no letting the wine rest or aerate. There was no savoring the bouquet. Even if we weren't partying it up, and the wine was for a dinner with friends, we were just drinking it.

But this wine was worth savoring. And it was well worth twenty-three dollars. I made a note to hint to friends and family that I might like some of this for my birthday. Did Irix have a wine cellar in New Orleans? Given the high water table there, I doubted he even had a cellar. Maybe an above-ground one?

"Red plum and black cherry flavors with a slight tobacco note," Matthieu was saying. "Not peppery like the cabs, and not as earthy as the Pinot Noir, but rich and lush. A quality Merlot should be fruity and complex with smooth tannins and an easy, soft finish."

"And it's been aged for how many years?" 2011. Sheesh, I'd never be able to wait that long before drinking something.

"Actually it's oak barrel aged for twenty-four months, but this was a particularly good year and an award winner, so we're keeping it as long as we can."

I nodded, still thinking this stuff would have been gone within a year of bottling at my house. "So twenty-four months aged to reduce the tannin bite? And oak? I don't taste oak like I do with our chardonnay."

He grinned. "You're good. You've got a better palate than that snobby elf. In this wine, the oak barrel aging is less about the tannins and more about giving the wine a more solid structure. Merlot in this region is more fruit-forward. It's an interesting wine. Grapes from colder climates like Chile are more structured with higher tannin off the vine. They're often similar to Cabernet Sauvignon grapes. In a warmer climate like Napa Valley, the grapes have a different flavor, and the use of oak barrels in aging helps give the wine a more cab-like body."

I was fascinated, and I was suddenly drawing exciting parallels between those beloved vines in the field and this amazing wine in my hand.

"Merlot grapes are thin-skinned and fragile," I commented. "They ripen earlier than the cab grapes and you've got to time the harvest perfectly because a heavy rain is going to mean choosing between over-ripe grapes or ones swollen and diluted in flavor. Plus, it's important to trim back a significant portion of the vine so the grapes don't get a woody or grassy taste, but over-trim and too much direct sun will burst your grapes and ruin a big portion of your harvest."

He tilted his head. "See? I didn't know that. I knew they were thin-skinned grapes and the dangers of getting a grassy, off-flavor, but not about how sensitive they are to direct sunlight."

"The more you know…" I teased, taking another sip.

"Indeed."

Even though I was down here on this tour for about the same thing he was, I could tell that he was enjoying the fact that I actually appreciated wine and did more than nod politely as he discussed his favorite subject.

We moved on to a sweet red, and by the time I'd finished my next glass I was feeling tipsy and ready to rip some clothes off Matthieu. Didn't he have a big tasting like now? Darn this might end up being quicker than I'd hoped. As much as I wanted to be thorough with Matthieu, I didn't want him getting fired. Maybe I'd need to make an exception and give the guy a round two tomorrow after work to make up for what was likely to be a quickie here.

And, as much as I liked sex and wanted to get it on with this guy, all the wine stuff was cool. Matthieu was a font of information, and in less than an hour I'd gone from just liking wine in general to being able to detect differences in the subtle flavors and textures. I was a half-elf. Could I train myself to dive down into the grapes behind the wine and determine the varieties and growing conditions just from one sip? That would be cool, but I'd need more than my elf-senses, I'd need training.

"How do you get to be a sommelier? I'm a botany major, and my future is pretty much going to be in the fields, either with a vineyard or studying the wetlands along the Gulf, but I'm curious." I was more than curious. It might never be a career, but this could be an amazing hobby.

"You may not have the ability to pair food and beverages to the extent needed to be a professional sommelier, but it's still something you should study. And I think you might find your calling as an enologist."

"A what?" I sipped the wine, wondering if this was part of his seduction routine.

"Enologist. They're the ones who work with the raw grapes to determine exactly the type of wines a winery should make from that harvest. Knowing the flavor profiles and how small changes in temperature, soil, and rainfall can affect the wine leads to better decisions in the field, which is critical in that job. It's one thing to be skilled at agriculture, but to also be a bit of a chemist, a bit of a connoisseur, and to wrap all that together to make decisions about the fruit growth and harvest is to be an enologist. And if you're good, then you'll be in demand by the top vineyards. You may not be able to control the weather, but if you understand what qualities your harvest is likely to have, and are able to guide the winery in their product decisions and strategy, your skills and knowledge would be invaluable."

I'd made the mistake of assuming Matthieu was just a pretty face. And I might not be able to manipulate weather, but there were elves who could. And my palate was far more sensitive than this man would ever know.

"So is there an enologist class I take? Is it an apprenticeship? What chance would I have of getting into such a thing as a recent grad with a botany degree?"

What was I thinking? Wetlands with Jordan. That was my future. Yet suddenly my mind was filled with visions of producing the perfect wine, of carefully guiding the process from vine to bottle to ensure the release of a product that rivaled the elixirs of the gods.

He hesitated. "Most usually start with basic wine classes at a local restaurant or winery, or even continuing education classes at a community college. Read. Enjoy. Take notes and study and go to as many tastings as possible. Always ask questions. Work with other enologists, production staff, and vineyard managers. It's a long learning curve."

I took the glass he'd handed me and swirled it, eyeing the thick sheen of light gold coating the sides of the goblet and streaking in the broad lines he'd called "legs".

"Tell me what you think," he urged.

"A lot of residual sugar," I noted, then buried my nose in the top of the glass. "Crisp and clear. Sharp like a knife at the onset, then cold apples and honey. And magnolia."

He nodded, his face impassive as I took a sip. And made a horrible face.

"I thought it was an ice-wine, but it's too sweet. And there's a weird musty taste at the finish, like someone wrapped cotton candy in an old sock and stuck it in a hot attic for a few months."

He laughed, then pulled out the bottle and showed me the label. I recognized it from my youth. It was that fruity-sweet stuff that was every teenager's first alcoholic beverage. Well, every teenager except me. Yuck.

I rubbed my tongue on my shirt sleeve trying to get the taste out of my mouth. "Why do you even have that down here? That's got to be a contaminant for all the decent wines."

"Because sometimes I bring a pretty woman down here and want to see if she really knows anything about wine or is just reciting what she read in the brochures. They might be a bit more circumspect in their description than you were, but the real wine lovers can't keep from making a face."

"And the ones who don't?" I wondered if this was his screening criteria, if only the ones who made the cut got shagged behind the casks? From Matthieu's reputation, I figured he screwed every woman he brought down here.

He shrugged. "I just don't have much conversation with those who don't."

Ah. Wine smart got a bit of a chat before fucking, where they others were bang-and-go. I was so not going to regret this.

"How much conversation?" I made my voice husky and low. "Because as much as I enjoy discussing wine, there are other pleasures."

That ended all discussion. Matthieu removed my wine glass from my hand and moved in for the action. He was skilled, his fantasies pretty straightforward. Sex with him was fun. Safe. He didn't sprout claws, or come at me with something that looked like it should be attached to a much larger mammal. Afterwards he reached over behind me head and pulled another bottle from the shelf.

"I don't usually get into this one, but I think you might enjoy it.

With a quick kiss, he got up to open the bottle, sitting back down beside me after he'd poured the wine. We were naked, sprawled against the casks. He handed me a glass, then gently tapped the edge of mine with his own. I sipped and smiled, realizing that this time Matthieu hadn't given me the nasty teenager crap.

"Blackberry. Hickory. Hint of dark chocolate in the midnotes," I mused. "Not bitter, but rich and deep."

His hand touched my leg, fingers skirting up my inner thigh. "I want to recommend you to a contest put on by the Italian Enology Association. This year it's at a vineyard outside of Bergamo—about thirty miles northeast of Milan. There are classes and tastings, and a lucky few will receive an offer to apprentice with the biggest houses in Europe. It's where I got my big break. I think I can get you in. If you really are interested in becoming an enologist, it's a great way to get the knowledge and experience needed to break into the field."

Oh wow. "Is that because I just fucked your brains out?" I teased.

His fingers reached the apex of my thighs, gently exploring. I saw him stir and wondered if he had another condom. Not that he needed condoms with me.

"It's because you're brilliant and a natural at this. I've never met anyone with your ability. That plus your understanding of varietals, genetic modifications, pests and diseases...all that and you're probably barely in your twenties. You're better than that elf Richard hired. It's like you're the supernatural and she's some imposter. If you're this good at your age, what will you be at thirty or forty? I can't stand the thought of your talents going to waste."

Hallwyn wasn't an imposter, I was just beginning to think she'd lied about her abilities and was in way over her head. Other than that, Matthieu was pretty close to hitting the mark.

"And your other talents are pretty otherworldly as well." He leaned over and kissed me, his tongue brushing my lips as he pulled back. "I'm normally a one-time only guy, but one taste of you and I'm completely addicted."

Yep. No surprise there. What was a surprise, though, was that I was on board for a repeat. I guess it was the wine and the novelty of combining two of my favorite things. And his flattering comments probably had as much to do with my interest as anything. Hey, what girl doesn't like being called brilliant?

"I'm normally a one-time only gal as well, except when it comes to a select few." I took a sip of wine, eyeing him over the glass. "Occasionally something is so tasty that I'll decide to have a second glass."

"Tomorrow?" he murmured.

I smiled. "Tomorrow."

We dressed and cleaned up the glasses and wine bottles Matthieu and I came out of the cellar to a crowd of people. It seems the tasting room was in full swing with several groups of people milling about eating cheese on little toothpicks and holding empty glasses of wine.

Oops. Matthieu was late—very late. I'd clocked out, but he clearly was expected to host this shindig, and the woman running the tour looked rather frazzled.

"Hey, I grabbed his hand before he dashed off to talk wine and flirt with the patrons. "Do you know anything about what's going on over at Boone Valley? Are they having the same struggles in the field as we are, or did we just get hit with the unlucky stick?"

He sniffed. "We're worse off than they are, but they've got issues. It's why the hired that elf woman. She's no miracle worker, though. If she can't turn things around faster than she's doing, they're going to have to buy most of their grapes this year."

Which would kill profits as well as limit what wines they could produce under an estate label.

"The weird thing? The small boutique vineyards aren't affected. Same with farms. McMillian and Sons Orchard was looking at bankruptcy before they hired their elf, but Tom Henry's place right next to them didn't have so much as a brown spot on their apples."

Huh. Good thing those smaller farms were okay since they wouldn't have the money to hire an elf. I had no idea what Hallwyn was making, but I assumed as an expert and as a member of a race that was probably about to be in high demand, she was getting upper management wages.

"Anyway, gotta run." He squeezed my hand. "Tomorrow lunch? Or after work?"

Yeah. This was the problem when I fed at work. I really had no interest in further sexual encounters with most of my conquests, but I had to work with Matthieu, and he was offering to get me into this shindig in Italy, and he was a fun guy to screw. Normally I would have let him down easy and pretended to have my period or something, but this time I was intrigued enough to want to meet up with him again.

"After work. Unless I'm in the field or they have something else for me to do."

He took that as a yes and headed off to the relief of the tour woman. I walked back to my trailer and thought about what Matthieu had said. Big operations were having these problems. Were they more susceptible because of the use of hybrid plants and pesticides? It couldn't be a biodiversity issue since even small farms tended produce high-demand varieties and those where high yields maximized profits.

I couldn't miss the convenient fact that the businesses affected had the funds to hire an elf, and all of them had. The pestilence demon had said she wasn't to blame and maybe she wasn't, but she still could have been indirectly responsible. Had someone asked her to curse the fields? The only ones who seemed to be coming out ahead in this were the elves. But the one at Boone Valley was on the edge of losing her job, and Hallwyn would have most likely been sacked already if I hadn't been healing the plants myself. If they'd been savvy enough to pay a pestilence demon to bring them a form of job security, then they should have been savvy enough to bargain with her for a way out. Diseased crops. An elf gets hired. The elf heals everything and saves the day. No more Elf Island. They'd be supporting themselves and assisting the humans, just as the angels demanded they do. It might not be an ideal job, but it got the angels off their backs and, no doubt, made them a lot of money.

I eyed the acres of vines, rows of green in the early evening sun, and thought that Matthieu's continued attentions weren't the only reason I needed to get back into the field. I needed to heal a few vines…and I also needed to make a phone call.

CHAPTER 17

"Sam? It's Amber."

I was tromping through the fields, doing a sweep to see what rows I could heal and not end up with two pissed off plague demons on my head. This whole thing was bothering me. Why were two demons so determined to grind Napa Valley beneath their heels? I know plague and pestilence was what they did, but I hadn't heard of such a determined effort since the Dark Ages. There had to be something else going on. Were the demons being paid to hit this area hard, and make sure it didn't recover?

If this had to do with Magical Interventions, if the placement company was using the plague demons to drive a need for elven employees, then why didn't the demons stop once the elves were hired? This had to be something else, something unrelated.

And what was up with Magical Interventions? Were the elves going behind the angel's backs to get off the island as quickly as possible? Was some greed demon looking to make a quick fortune as a placement company? Or a greedy human?

I was at a dead end unless I could find why Apixt and Txipa were involved and what was going on with the elven job placements. And no one blew through dead ends like the imp who held the sword of the Iblis.

"Hey. Make it fast because I'm trying to time this anvil-dropping thing just right. What's terminal velocity with our gravity outside of Hel?"

Oh sheesh. "No idea. Hey, I need a favor."

"Ask Harkel. Or Irix. I'm busy. There's a roadrunner I need to squish."

I ignored that. "I'm pretty sure that someone is infesting crops in a scheme to get elves employed at large-scale commercial agribusinesses and off Elf Island."

There was a scraping noise. A pause. Sam shouting "Fuck!" into the phone.

"Sam?"

"Yeah. Damned motherfucking bird. What about the elves? None of them should be off the island yet. Asshole-angel promised me they'd be on some five-year indoctrination schedule."

"One is working at my vineyard. And the other two vineyards down the street. And the big vegetable farm in central California as well as three orchards. That's just this state. I'm sure there are a ton of them dancing around wheat fields in Iowa and cattle ranches in Texas as we speak. There's someone who is doing placement services between the angels running Elf Island and the human world. I think he, or she, is artificially creating a need then providing elven employees at a premium, if you know what I mean."

She was silent a moment and I heard more scraping noises.

"Sam? You there?"

"Yeah. I missed the roadrunner, but there's a Benz SUV that I think I can hit if I hurry.

Was I a bad person that I wasn't terribly concerned about the Benz? It wasn't like Sam had a particularly good aim—with a gun, or arrows, or anvils.

"Another thing—Apixt is hanging around here along with her sister Txipa. They're infesting humans and commercial farms and vineyards in Napa Valley. One of them hit me over the head the other day because I was healing one of the vines they'd infected. Txipa threatened me with worse if I didn't stop messing with her work and healing plants at the vineyard."

"Fuck! Is this cliff two hundred feet or one eighty up from the road? I can't fucking tell. So what do you want me to do? Kill Apixt and Txipa? Kill the elves? Because I can't even seem to kill a fucking bird right now."

Oh for crying out loud. Dealing with her was like dealing with a two-year-old on a sugar high.

"Can you find out who on Elf Island in in charge of job placement? And who their contact is—the one who lets them know about human opportunities and coordinates getting elves their jobs and getting them settled in? And get Apixt and her sister to back off. Ideally I'd like them to leave the area, but at a minimum can you convince them to stay out of DiMarche? And not assault me again?"

"That's a lot of work. I'm trying to kill a roadrunner here, or at the very least an SUV with two adults and three kids. What you're asking of me is a significant favor."

Roadrunner and SUV full of people aside, I'd learned this was a common way of bargaining with demons. "Don't be ridiculous, Sam. It will take you one phone call to get the information, and possibly two more to get the plague demons off my back. That's not significant. And need I remind you that the job in Libertytown turned out to involve far more than some minor crop modifications. If you expect me to expand that deal to include repeated visits every six months or so, then I certainly need more than just immunity for Irix."

"Hey, that was a big favor, far greater in value than fixing some carrots and potatoes in Hel. If anything, *you* owe *me*."

I rolled my eyes even though no one could see me. "Bullshit. I know the angels have a war going on, Sam. Hunting down demons this side of the gates is pretty low on their priority list right now. If two plague demons could cross the gates and wander around Napa Valley doing their thing, then no angel is going to bother with a sex demon getting it on and occasionally repairing his injuries. Even so, with who you're fucking, it probably took you all of five seconds to get that deal. You got Irix clearance to cross the gates when Leethu asked. His immunity was a *minor* favor. I've provided a significant favor, and am continuing to provide one. So don't give me any shit about how this request puts you out or inconveniences you at all, especially if you're dicking around throwing anvils at birds and luxury SUVs."

"Damn girl, you're a hard-ass. Okay, here's the deal. I find all that info out and put in a firmly worded request for Apixt and Txipa to vacate the area. You continue to assist the humans in Hel whenever necessary, plus provide a case of wine from that place you're working. Make sure it's the good shit because angels like wine and I want some for Asshole's born-day party. Oh, and you need to make that seven-layer bean dip again. And the family-recipe red velvet cake that Wyatt likes."

"I'll agree to that as long as you also provide an additional favor to me that I can redeem at a later date and time of my choosing."

"Agreed as long as the favor does not conflict with any previously made vow or agreement."

Standard terms and conditions. Gah, I was beginning to

sound just like a demon. And considering I didn't even know they existed until a few years ago, that was surprising.

"Deal. And Sam, this is a priority. It won't do me any good if I find this stuff out five years from now."

"Fine. Fine. A day or two max. Now let me go so I can set up the next anvil. There's a bunch of dudes on Harleys coming down the road. I'm bound to at least nail one of them."

I hung up, less concerned about the safety of the guys on Harleys than what would happen to Sam if she actually managed to hit one of them with the anvil. Standing in the vineyard, I found myself literally at a crossroads. Should I try to heal one of the vines, or go back to the trailer? I shifted my weight from foot to foot, trying to decide. I'd been attacked at night, so Irix would be worried if I got back late. As much as I hated to turn my back on the vineyard, I knew what I had to do. Go home. Eat dinner. Spend some quality time with my man.

But in the morning… I glanced back over my shoulder at the leaves stirring in the evening breeze.In the morning I'd come out early, and heal a few vines before work.

And hopefully no one, including the two plague demons, would notice.

The next morning I got to the vineyard just after sunup. Looking around, I pulled out my sheet of paper and a pen and got to work. One. I'd heal one vine then go to the winery for my shift. Or maybe two vines. Two tops. I'd be careful that there was no plague demon around to see me doing it, and if Txipa or Apixt confronted me, I'd lie and say it was Hallwyn who'd cured the plant of its disease. After yesterday, I didn't really care if they whacked the elf in the back of the head or not.

I'd done most of the easier stuff before I'd been assaulted, which left the challenging diseases like black measles and Phomopsis. That was what brought me back to that vine in row eight. The sight made me nearly cry.

"Oh poor, baby." I ran my fingers over the brown and black spots on the stems and fruit, touching the yellowed, wilted leaves. I could feel the rot without even trying to go beyond the surface of the plant. "Does no one love you? The sprays aren't working. That elf is useless. You've given up, haven't you, sweetie? Don't worry. I'm here. I'll take care of you."

I should have given up on this vine and moved on to the ones that weren't as affected, but I just couldn't condemn it to die. And die it would. If it didn't improve, Jorge would have it dug up and incinerated in the next few days.

"This is gonna hurt," I muttered. Then I put my hands on the vines and sent myself into them, pulling every bit of disease from the plant to myself. It was a lot and I felt on the verge of either exploding or heaving my internal organs out onto the ground when I'd finished.

Well, finished, but not finished. By the time I managed to destroy the disease I'd just sucked into myself, I was feeling weak and dizzy. But I couldn't leave the vine damaged like this and open to a new disease, so I pulled up whatever reserves of energy I had, drawing from the bonds with Irix and Harkel, and managed to heal the plant before dropping to my knees in the dirt.

"What are you?"

I twisted around, still on my knees, and nearly toppled over. It was Hallwyn. She was staring at me open-mouthed. My heart galloped, thinking I was as good as dead, then I noticed the streaks of tears on her perfect, pale face.

"You're here early," I accused, hoping to avoid her question.

"What are you? That wasn't human magic. It wasn't demon magic." Her eyes narrowed. "Where did you learn to do elven magic? *How* did you learn to do elven magic? Of the thousands of human slaves that we've had in Wythyn, the tens of thousands of slaves throughout all the elven kingdoms, none of them has *ever* been able to do our magic."

"How could you tell? It's not like your glowy-hands crap is doing any good. Why are you here this early? There's no one to impress with your pseudo-magic."

Her face reddened. "Insolent pig. I'm an elf. I have *true*

magic. And I'm here early trying to get ahead of things. There are so many problems in this vineyard that it will take me more than an eight-hour day to fix them."

"Especially when you're *not* fixing them," I couldn't help but retort. "It doesn't matter how much time you spend here, how early you come in, it's not going to make a difference. I don't know what your family did in Hel, but it sure wasn't gardening. You couldn't revive a wilted daisy."

Her eyes narrowed. "Well, you don't seem to have that problem. Jorge was going to have that vine dug up this morning but now it's the picture of health." She took a step toward me. "I saw you. I saw what you did. How did you do that? What are you?"

Hopefully I'd inherited the ability to lie from my demon side, because I was about to tell a whopper. "I'm a human. I just happen to have a talent in healing plants. Every now and then there is a human born who can lay-on hands and heal a person, or heal disease in plants and animals. Every now and then there is a human born who can divine the future, command the elements, astral project. We can't let our skills be widely known for our own protection, but that doesn't mean we don't do what we can to make the world a better place."

"I've never known a human who has these skills. Never. I'm hundreds of years old. We had many human slaves in Hel, and none of them had these types of skills. They might have talents that allowed us to train them in some forms of magic, but none were gifted like this. Your skills are just like those the elves have."

"So what I do is similar to elves? Huh. And as for why you've never seen a human with these skills before, well maybe you were just kidnapping the wrong humans." I couldn't help but be snarky. Every time I thought of what

Nyalla went through, what those humans in Libertytown went through, I got a bit pissed off.

"Do it again," she urged. The look in her eyes worried me. She didn't appear to have any weaponry, but I knew elves could do fireballs and other stuff. Although if Hallwyn was as skilled at fighting as she was at healing, I wouldn't have to worry.

"I can't," I told her in all honesty. "That was a really bad case of Phomopsis and I'm worn out. I don't think I'll be able to do anything else today. And by anything, I mean I might not even be able to stay awake to do my job."

"Do it again or I'll kill you," she said.

I tamped down my fear and lifted my chin. "Right, because nothing is going to get your ass sent back to Elf Island quicker than killing a co-worker. In fact, you'll probably find yourself tossed through the gates of Hel."

She paled at my words. "I don't believe you. I don't believe you have some natural healing ability. Do it again so I can watch."

Watch and possibly detect that my magic was identical to what the elves did? No way.

"You don't believe me? So you think plant fairies came down from the sky and healed this plant? Or maybe that I've bargained my soul away to a demon so I could heal a bunch of vines? Or the Monsanto gods have chosen to bestow their favors upon this vineyard?"

"There is a demi-god here named Monsanto?" She looked around as if she expected some leaf-bedecked dude to spring from the ground. "And plant fairies? I hate this place! I hate it!"

And then she began to cry, making me feel like a total jerk. Although, to be fair, she *had* been threatening to kill me. Still, I couldn't stand to see her cry, so I went over and almost hugged her, at the last moment thinking she might not be the touchy-feely type and instead just patting her on the shoulder.

"No, there are no plant fairies. I made that up. And it's not so bad here. Just give it a chance."

"I don't want to give it a chance, I want to go home," she wailed. "But there is no more home. We've abandoned Hel, and there's no place for us here, and the angels on Elf Island make us eat all sorts of terrible food, and wear gloves and coat our bodies with this nasty gel so we don't get burned if we accidently touch something metal."

I squinted at her. "I thought that was some kind of greasy sunscreen. Ick. But the food here is pretty good, and so is the wine. Did you get a chance to try that 2011 Estate Merlot? Oh, of course you didn't because then you would have had to get naked with Matthieu and I doubt you'd be up for that."

She shuddered. "There is no way I would ever lower myself to such a thing. And the food…the fruits and vegetables all taste strange. The wine tastes strange. Even the water tastes strange. I work all day and barely have enough to pay for enough food to survive and that horrible dwelling I've been assigned to. I'm now the slave, being forced to do whatever my human master demands or be sent back to that horrible island."

Oh, the drama. "Yeah, well welcome to paradise. It's not *that* bad. Jorge is really nice. He's a good boss. And from what I'm told you're making about three times what most of us make, if not more. Didn't those angels teach you how to budget your money? What the heck are you spending it all on, glitter and rainbows?"

"It's not…I mean, Jorge is rather nice for a human. Actually everyone has been kind, although I hear them talk about me. I have very good hearing, and I know they don't like me, but they are always respectful and provide the assistance I need to do my job."

There was clearly something she wasn't saying. "Then what's wrong? Why are you acting like you're some kind of indentured servant forced to eat Ramen and drink from the toilet?"

She hesitated, biting her lip.

"You're going to be surrounded by humans for the rest of your life," I told her. "We outnumber you. There might be an elf or two down the road for you to have an occasional beer with, but most of your days are going to be spent with humans. It's about time you started trusting at least a few of us. And, who else would be better to help you in adapting to life here besides humans? Do you seriously think the angels know what the heck they're doing? Or the other elves? If you need to figure out how to work the toaster or buy a plane ticket online, or play Candy Crush on your phone, you're going to need to start making human friends. Or at least human acquaintances."

"I'm afraid to touch the toaster," she confessed. "It's metal, and even when I put on gloves, I'm too scared to go near it."

"Well, maybe the toaster later. Right now tell me why you're here when you clearly can't do the job you were hired to do? I'm not trying to get you fired or anything, I just can't understand how with an island full of elves, someone thought you were the one to heal a diseased vineyard."

She sighed and plopped down in the dirt beside me, picking at the sorrel that was beginning to pop up along the pathway. "I didn't know what kind of job I was being sent for. If I had known it was this, I would have passed and waited for another opportunity." She looked up at me and shook her head. "Actually that's a lie. I would have taken any job to get off that island. When you pay the placement fee and agree to the contract, you do whatever the Jobber wants you to do, whether you have the skills or not."

"Jobber? Who is this Jobber?"

"They're going to fire me," Hallwyn's voice cracked. "If I can't heal this vineyard and lose my job, I'll be in violation of the contract. They'll send me back to Elf Island or worse. I'll never be able to pay the Jobber back. Actually, he'll offer to clear my debt if I…but I can't do that. Although I'll have to do that because I can't pay him back without employment."

She was bordering on hysterics. I sat quietly and waited for her to work through her strange disjointed monologue. Finally, she wiped away her tears and looked up at me once more.

"I knew *someone* was healing the plants. It wasn't the chemicals, and it wasn't me. I thought maybe one of the elves working on a neighboring farm had taken pity on me and was coming over in the evening hours to help, but they all have problems of their own. That's why I was here early, to try to heal what I could, but also so I could catch whoever was helping and beg them for additional assistance."

Why did I feel like one of the shoemaker's elves all of a sudden? "It was me, but I don't have enough energy to do more than a little bit here and there."

She nodded. "I'll tell you what's going on if you keep healing the plants and if you help me learn how to do it. I can't lose my job here, I just can't."

I was going to heal the plants anyway, but she didn't have to know that. "So we're friends?"

I got a side-eye for that. "No, we're not friends. But if you help me out, I'll answer your questions."

It was as good of a deal as I was going to get. "Okay. Tell me about this Jobber first."

"There is someone that we call the Jobber. I assume he's human, but I don't really know because no one has ever seen him. He sends a list of jobs to the angels running Elf Island. This Jobber goes around and scouts out jobs where elves might have an advantage and be uniquely suited to help the humans, then he convinces the humans to agree to hire an elf. He sends the list of employment opportunities to the angels, then they post it. We're encouraged to submit our qualifications for the openings, and if the Jobber picks us, we're able to leave the island under certain restrictions."

Sounded pretty much like going through a recruiting firm. Except for the restrictions, that is.

"We *have* to retain gainful employment in order to leave and remain off Elf Island. The Jobber is our only way out of there unless we decide to go back to Hel. And once the angels send us to Hel, we're not allowed to return here again."

"So this Jobber basically holds all of your lives in his hands," I mused.

She nodded. "Yes, and word went around that for a fee, you'd be given a priority slot. If you paid the fee and signed a contract with the Jobber, you'd be given employment some-where. I didn't realize the job would be one I was completely unskilled to perform. But it's not like there would be many openings in my family's skill area. The angels demand that we take positions that assist humanity in their positive evolution, so most of the posted jobs are in healthcare, agri-culture, and the arts."

"And your family…?"

She grimaced. "Administrators in public policy. My father was the mayor of one of the small cities in Wythyn. My mother was on the council. We're trained to deal with budgets and planning, large-scale projects, determining skills and number of elven and human workers needed for these projects, management of public service departments. Outside of that group in Iceland who managed to get some kind of exemption, we're not allowed to hold public office or operate in any kind of management capacity."

Basically she had no transferrable skills to apply for an angelic-approved job. If she hadn't bought her way off the island, I wasn't sure she ever would have left. Well, at least until they managed to teach her to watercolor or something.

"How much was this placement fee?" And how did she manage to pay it? I couldn't imagine the elves came here from Hel with a stash of human cash or bitcoin credit. Plus, hadn't Jorge said DiMarche had paid a placement fee to the recruiting company? If so, this Jobber was double-dipping.

Hallwyn told me a sum that had my jaw nearly hitting the ground. "Of course, we don't have the money to pay it up front and the Jobber doesn't take elven currency, so we have to sign a contract. We pay the fee plus interest over the course of our employment. In addition to the fee, the Jobber gets a percentage of each paycheck."

"That's horrible." I calculated what Hallwyn would have left out of her paycheck and winced.

"And we don't have money for the security deposit and first month's rent on an apartment, or a vehicle, or appropriate human-style clothing to wear, or the cell phones that we need to ensure our new employers can reach us if necessary."

I was getting a horrible picture of this whole thing. "Let me guess, the Jobber provides all that at a grossly inflated price and 'loans' you the money to purchase it. And you pay back that loan with interest out of your paycheck?"

She nodded, tears once more glistening in her eyes. "I won't have my debt paid off for at least eighty years, more if my car breaks down or I need to purchase something else. And if I lose my job, I'll be in default on that loan."

"Which will put you right back in Elf Island, as well as

ruining any future chances at getting employment through this Jobber."

"That would be the best-case scenario." Her shoulders dropped. "My father was desperate for me to get off the island and get established, hoping that if I had a good job, he could convince the angels to let him and my mother leave and live with me, that I could vouch for them and support them. I can't even support myself right now. And if I default…the shame of returning would be just as bad as the knowledge that I lost my only chance of ever getting off that island."

"You said there was something worse," I prodded. "You mentioned that the Jobber had offered you a way to clear your debt."

She took a deep breath. "The debt doesn't go away if I lose my job and get sent back to the island. The Jobber will continue to make me repay it, with added interest and penalties, by doing small tasks here and there for him while on the island. If I die, my family is responsible for my debt. But he has hinted that there is a special opportunity that would clear me of all my debt."

I didn't like the sound of this one bit. "Like if you become his sex slave? Bear his children? Give yourself over to a lab where they perform experiments on you until you die? Throw you in a gladiator ring with other elves where the only way out is to kill each other?"

Her eyes were huge, and she flinched at each of my suggestions. "I have thought of every one of those scenarios as well as others equally unpleasant. I don't know what this opportunity is, but I'm scared of it. I don't think I'd come out of it alive."

"And you've never seen this Jobber? You've never seen anyone that works with him? Who escorted you off the island, handed over your car keys and apartment and showed you how to get to work your first day?"

"The angels deliver us to our new homes, and a human rental person meets us there with the keys. Clothing and other furnishings are already inside as is information about the car, the cell phone, and directions as well as other information about our jobs." She shivered. "It was scary. Probably the scariest few days of my entire life, but I made it through okay."

This didn't make sense. "How are you supposed to pay the Jobber back? Are they yanking money out of your checking account? Does Guido show up every month to collect?"

"All the paperwork for my employment at DiMarche was completed before I arrived. There is a bank account with some loaned money in it. When my paycheck is deposited every two weeks, the Jobber has the loan repayment amount automatically withdrawn. The remainder is mine to purchase food, fuel for the automobile, additional clothing."

I smiled, patting Hallwyn's knee. "If he's withdrawing money from your account, there will be an electronic paper trail. And my brother is just the bloodhound to track who's at the end of that trail. Do you have your account information on you?"

She pulled a card and a checkbook out of her purse. I snapped a picture of each with my cell phone and dashed off a quick text to Wyatt with the pics.

"Do you really have enough magic to heal these vines and help me keep my job?" She asked, stuffing the checkbook and bank card back into her wallet.

"I can heal the vines, but the problem is time. I only have so much energy. It could take me six months to heal all the diseased plants, and most of them don't have more than a few weeks." I hesitated thinking about Apixt's threat. I should do as Irix said and back off. I should let go and tell Hallwyn that I just couldn't do it. The infestations were too great for even the pair of us to handle, and there was no sense getting on the bad side of a plague demon for a hopeless case like this.

But then I looked around me and knew I was lost. I'd become attached to these vines. As long as I was here, working at DiMarche, they were my responsibility and I just couldn't stand by and watch them die, no matter what the plague demon had threatened. Still… "I'll do what I can, and hopefully I can train you to help, but unless we can get a group of skilled elves in here, I don't have much hope for the vineyard."

Hallwyn hung her head. "The other elves are having the same problem. Tralian over at Boone Valley is a friend of mine. She actually does have some skill with plants, but even she can't keep up. The others are completely overwhelmed." Hallwyn looked up at me, her eyes worried. "Do you think that's his plan? Does the Jobber want us all to fail so we'll have to accept whatever horrible thing he wants to do with us?"

"I don't know. All this—" I waved my hand at the infected vines "—is a result of a pair of plague demons. I suspect he hired them to drive demand for elven labor on commercial farms, but I don't know whether things just got out of hand, or the Jobber actually *wants* you to fail. It could be that he paid for a small-scale outbreak and the demons got carried away and went too far."

"If we find the plague demons, do you think we could pay him or her to remove the disease?" she asked, her voice hopeful.

I remembered Txipa's expression when Irix and I had been trying to get her and her sister to lay off the vineyard. This was personal for them. I doubted we could bid higher and make any difference at all. Plus, pay her how? Hallwyn had no money. I had no money.

"I met with Txipa the other day and she seems determined to kill off this vineyard. We may need to just let it go. Pick our battles." My stomach turned at the thought. Hallwyn and I might be able to heal a few plants here and there, but I needed to reconcile myself to the fact that we were no match for a pair of plague demons. As horrible as it was, this vineyard was doomed.

Hallwyn whipped her head around to stare at me. "You *met* with her? You, a human with uncanny magical skill tracked down a plague demon and walked away from the conversation alive and with your soul intact?"

"It's a long story." And not one I wanted to tell right now. "Step one is to find this Jobber and put an end to this Company Store-Coal Mine Era scheme." If this Jobber was using Txipa and Apixt to spread disease, then he needed to be put out of business. And although I might not have much love for the elves, it bothered me that they were being taken advantage of this way.

Hallwyn frowned. "But if there is no Jobber, then how will elves find employment? They'll be stuck on Elf Island forever."

"How about a Jobber who doesn't use plague demons to drive demand and doesn't enslave you all with horrible contracts and loan-shark deals? This kind of crap isn't right. I might not be a huge fan of elves, but making you suffer the same fate as your human slaves isn't the answer."

She stood and brushed the dirt from her khaki pants. "I'm beginning to realize that the humans we had as slaves weren't representative of what you are as a race and what you're capable of. Maybe because we didn't allow them to do anything except what we told them. Maybe because, as you said, we'd kidnapped the wrong ones. This world is scary, but it's the best future available to me. If I need to be flexible about my circumstances and learn to lower my standards, to somehow force myself to consider elves as equal with humans, I will. It won't be easy, but I will."

I stood and looked at my phone, realizing that I'd need to hustle to get to the winery in time for my shift.

"I have a quick date with Matthieu after work, but I'll meet you directly after that in field twelve and I'll help you cure a few of the vines. Beyond that, there's not much I can do in the vineyard. I'll do everything I can to get you and the other elves out of this mess with the Jobber, but I really can't go up against a pair of plague demons. I just can't."

The elf sighed. "I guess that will have to do. I'm not going to give up. You are a weak and easily cowed human, but I won't run away from these plague demons. This is my employment. I might not be very good at it, but I made a commitment to do this job, and I will."

I chafed at the dig, but bit back any retort. If she wanted to see me as weak and afraid, fine. She wasn't the one who had been hit over the head and dragged through the vineyard. She wasn't the one who had heard the sincerity in Txipa's threats. I'd heal a plant here and there because I just couldn't help myself, but anything more would be like declaring war on the two plague demons.

I turned to leave, then thought of something else. "And I want you to start socializing with humans. You'll be miserable unless you start to make some friends. You don't have to love us all, just find one or two that you like well enough to go to the movies with or grab a quick drink at happy hour."

She nodded. "Amber? Thank you. I know I've been harsh with you and yet here you are offering to help me. I respect that you had the strength of character to extend the olive branches of peace. If other humans are like you, then I think I might be able to find a friend among them."

"I'm sure you will." The pair of us walked through the vineyard side-by-side.

"Maybe that Rosa—"

"No, not that Rosa," I interrupted hastily. Although it would be funny to watch the elf trying to make friends with the prickly Chilean woman. "Actually, if you don't mind someone who thinks she's superior to you in every way, you might get along with her. She's an amazing cook. And the way to her heart is through grocery store cookies. Don't tell her I said that, though."

Hallwyn shot me a surprised look. "I've seen the elf of Keebler pastries in the grocery store. There are some that are chocolate with chocolate chips and the double M's in them."

"Yes those. Or the ones with coconut."

She nodded. "I have a few dollars left in my purse. I will buy these cookies in hopes that Rosa will maybe have lunch with me tomorrow."

My heart twisted at the image of Hallwyn eating alone in the golf cart, staring at her strawberries as if she didn't quite know what to make of the fruit. She was arrogant, snobby, and possibly the worst horticulturist I'd ever met in my life, but she deserved to have a friend. Everyone deserved to have a friend, even jerks of elves.

I saw the crowd of field hands clustered around the golf carts as Jorge handed out clipboards, the winery a brown speck in the distance. Ugh, I was going to need to run for it.

"See you tonight," I told Hallwyn.

"See you tonight. Oh, and Amber? Is there really a Monsanto god and would it help if I delivered a sacrifice to him as a plea for his assistance?"

I choked back a laugh. "Some people feel the Monsanto god does more harm than good, while others swear he is the key to providing cost-effective, high-yield, sustainable agriculture. I'd suggest you read up on him a bit more before deciding whether to sacrifice a goat."

She nodded, eyes wide. "I will do so, Amber. And thank you again for all of your assistance."

I turned from her and once out of sight of the others, I began to run at elf-speed toward the winery. She could thank me later, much later, because I may have sounded confident, but I wasn't sure I'd be able to help her, the other elves, or the vineyard.

CHAPTER 19

After work and my quick interlude with Matthieu, I headed out to the field, waving at Manny and Rosa as they were heading home. Hallwyn was in field twelve, row twenty, staring with a forlorn face at a plant full of downy mildew.

"Powdery mildew, correct?" she asked.

"Nope. A light case of powdery mildew shows up as white or light yellow spots on the top of the leaves. As it progresses, there will be blotchy areas on the canes and a white web-like covering with white powdery spots. You might think at first it's some kind of spider mite, but if you touch the white stuff, you'll realize it's not webbing or egg sacks, but a mildew. It usually reacts well to spraying, but an advanced case can take over the fruit. And it can remain in the plant over winter in buds, so any infestation needs to be re-treated in the spring."

"This has yellow spots," she countered. "How do you know it's not an early case of powdery mildew?"

"Because there's no powdery white webby stuff. And look, the spots are on the underneath of the leaves. See how these are more furry and less webby? And it's hit the mature leaves in the central part of the plant. Look at the fuzzy gray stuff here. That's a sign of downy mildew. This is one that hides out in leaf debris, so even though a good dose of fungicide usually knocks it out, cleaning up fallen leaves and trimmings is important in order to keep it from springing back up in this or a neighboring vine."

The elf threw up her hands. "I can't remember all this stuff! There are too many diseases and pests for one elf to remember."

"Nonsense. With enough experience, this will all become easy. And you're not likely to have twenty different diseases at once, either. Most of the time it's one or two, and if you don't recognize it right away, you do research. The best part of being with humans is we record everything, and it's all available at the touch of a finger. You'll need to be able to sort out the bullshit from the legitimate information, but research and looking things up is how we get around having to memorize everything about everything."

"Like the archives?" she asked. "But only certain elves are allowed access. Will the humans allow me to read these tomes?"

"Are you kidding?" I pulled out my phone and typed in a URL, turning it around to show it to her. "I hope the angels taught you to read as well as speak English, or you'll have to rely on audio, which isn't as quick to sort through."

She took the phone and swiped down a few times. "There are even pictures."

"Yep. And see how different the downy mildew looks from the powdery mildew?"

"Yes! I wish I'd been given this when I came here. Why did no one tell me this was available?"

I rolled my eyes. "Because humans all know how to find this stuff on their computers and phones and tablets, and even physical libraries. Everyone figured you knew that, too." I was beginning to think the angels probably weren't the best ones to be teaching the elves how to get along in the human world. Most of them probably didn't know how to work the toaster either.

"Let me know your number and I'll text you the links. Just tap them with your finger and they'll take you right to the site. And if there's ever something you're not sure about, take a picture with your phone and send it to me, and I'll help you identify it."

She handed the phone back to me, a huge smile on her face. It was the first time I'd ever seen her smile, the first time I remember ever seeing an elf smile, not that I'd seen many elves in the course of my life. It completely transformed her from this cold, aloof being to someone who glowed with life and breathtaking beauty. When they were happy, elves were pretty darned appealing.

"Thank you," she said.

And it was the first time I'd ever heard that from her. She wasn't treating me like I was dog crap on her shoe, and she'd actually thanked me. Clearly Hel must be experiencing an unexpected frost.

"Knowing how to identify the disease or pest is the first part of the problem. The next step is being able to eradicate it."

She shuddered. "It feels horrible. Every time I try, I feel sick, and I never manage to get it all."

"Because you need to get over the fact that you're going to feel sick. You're pulling the disease from the plant into yourself, because as an elf, you're better equipped to destroy it. If you destroy it while it's still in the plant, the vine won't survive, but a case of downy mildew isn't going to kill you. This is the ick part of your job where you'll just have to buck up and deal with it."

She shook her head. "I need to do this for eight hours a day, five days a week for the rest of my life."

"That or find a different job, or go back to Elf Island. Hey, it's better than cleaning toilets or pumping septic tanks."

Hallwyn straightened her shoulders and shook out her hands, as if she were prepping to sprint the mile. "So what do I do first?"

"Touch the plant, feel the disease, and pull it from the vine. Make sure it's all out of the plant and inside yourself. If you can block the plant while you eradicate the disease within yourself, then you can keep touching it, otherwise disconnect from the plant first. The next step is to heal the plant, but that might be beyond your capabilities. And at this point, I think the management at DiMarche will be satisfied to just have the downy mildew gone."

She grimaced, then put her fingers on the plant. Her hands glowed with a golden light, the fuzzy gray fungus vanished from the leaves, but the leaves still bore spots and were a brownish-yellow. Hallwyn, on the other hand, looked pale and gray, her mouth pinched and stomach heaving. She dropped her fingers from the leaves, and the golden glow extended throughout her body, lighting her up from the inside. Slowly the glow faded and the elf swayed. Then she vomited.

Was I a bad person that I was glad she's spewed her lunch all over the ground? I was only a half-elf and I struggled to keep from puking each time I healed a plant. It was sort of comforting to know a full elf had the same problem.

Attempts to repair the damaged vine weren't as success-ful. Evidently all elves had some ability to heal, but not many could reconstruct the damaged leaves, stems and fruit. I wondered if I'd been given that ability as part of my elven heritage, or my demon side? Either way, Hallwyn being able to at least knock out the fungus and various blights would be a huge help to the vineyard. We also discovered that Hallwyn didn't have the ability to eradicate pests, so the leafrollers and mites would be up to me or the chemicals to take care of. Still—if she could keep the vineyard free from black measles, Phomopsis, and different mildews, it would be a huge help.

We went down the row, checking each plant before circling to the next row. Hallwyn might have been dry heaving with each act of healing, but she had more stamina than I did and we were able to complete four rows before the encroaching darkness forced us to quit.

"I can see very well in the dark," she told me. "Perhaps I can stay and do more."

"Tomorrow. In the morning." I told her. "Don't push yourself too hard this first time. You've got eight hours to do this tomorrow." If she could do the healing, then maybe I could come through and try to repair what vines I could.

She nodded and we walked back to the parking area together, me to head off to my trailer, and her to drive like a blind toddler to whatever rat-hole apartment the Jobber had rented for her, no doubt charging her double the going rate.

"What...what are you eating for dinner?" I couldn't help asking. She looked so darned skinny, and I kept remembering her expression as she ate that strawberry, as if it were potentially poisonous.

She hesitated. "I don't get paid for another two days, so whatever is in the cabinets or the refrigerator."

"And what exactly is in your cabinets and refrigerator?"

"I have a jar of pickled vegetables and some packets of dried fruit."

Irix was going to kill me, but I couldn't let her go home to sweet gherkins and banana chips. I waved for Hallwyn to wait then pulled out my cell phone.

"Babe? What's for dinner?"

He sighed. "When you call me 'babe' I know you're about

to tell me something unpleasant. I grabbed a sausage and pepper quiche, and a salad on the way back to the trailer. Am I eating alone tonight? If so, I hope it's because you're out getting laid."

Crap. I was pretty sure Hallwyn heard the last part with her excellent elven hearing because she looked rather uncomfortable at Irix's last statement.

"Um, no. I'm bringing a friend back for dinner tonight."

"A threesome? One of your co-workers?"

"I better get going," Hallwyn said, edging backward toward her car.

"He's teasing," I told her before turning back to my phone. "No, it's Hallwyn, the elf I told you about. All she has at her place is pickles and a bag of dried fruit until she gets paid. I'm bringing her home for dinner—I mean to share dinner with us, because we're not going to eat her or anything." I beckoned to Hallwyn who was still taking slow steps toward her car.

"Amber." Irix's voice held a stern warning. "It's bad enough that you're working with an elf. You don't have to bring one home for dinner. She's not a stray puppy. You know this is a horrible idea."

But Hallwyn *was* a sort of stray puppy from my point of view. She thought I was a human with a magical gift, and one dinner wasn't going to cause her to suddenly realize I was a half-elf.

"Hallwyn, don't go. Wait. It's quiche and salad, and if I know Irix there's something amazing for dessert. I promise it's just dinner, then you can go home."

"Amber!" Irix snarled over the phone.

"I don't know what quiche is," Hallwyn told me, knotting her shirt in her hands and eyeing her car a short sprint away.

"I promise you'll love it. Come on. You need to start fitting in with human society, and this is a good way to dip your toes in the water. Plus, quiche and salad is way better than a jar of pickles."

"Amber! Amber, I forbid you from bringing that elf home." I'd pressed the phone against my boobs, hoping that Hallwyn hadn't heard that last bit.

"Okay, but I'm leaving right after dinner. And no one touches me or I will fireball them."

Crap, maybe Irix was right. Although one look at Hallwyn's face and I realized that she was scared. All alone, fresh off Elf Island with only the teachings of a bunch of clueless angels to guide her. Poor thing.

"I promise," I told her. "Irix, we'll be there in a few." I hung up the phone and waited while Hallwyn looked back and forth between me and her car, her face pinched with anxiety and indecision.

"I will dine with you, Amber, and your boyfriend. But there will be no threesomes and no teasing of a sexual nature."

I held up my hand. "I promise. Come on. It's just a short walk away."

The elf walked beside me, still twisting her shirt in her hands. I climbed the rickety steps of my trailer, turning to her just before I opened the door.

"Oh, and FYI, because you probably should know. My boyfriend Irix is an incubus."

Her green eyes were huge and she swallowed hard, glancing backward, no doubt judging the distance between the trailer and her car. "No touching. No discussions of a sexual nature. And no pheromones."

"I promise," I told her, opening the door and ushering her inside. I promised, but that didn't mean Irix would. I'm sure he'd be the absolute gentleman. Unless he thought I was in any danger, then all bets would be off.

CHAPTER 20

$\mathcal{M}$y head was pounding with a headache as I walked to work the next morning. Dinner had been…tense. Hallwyn ate the salad like a half-starved rabbit, no doubt because Irix had gotten the vegetables at a local farmer's stand on the way back from his day of hunting and they were just-picked fresh. The quiche confused her since at first she thought it was a sweet pie, but once she tasted it, she went through three slices. I don't know where she put it all, especially because she had two helpings of oven-warmed apple strudel with ice cream after. And wine. And coffee after dinner.

The whole time Irix glared at her like he was two seconds from ripping her head off. I think if the elf hadn't been so hungry, she would have turned around and run right out the door. As it was, she dashed off right after finishing her second of strudel and coffee. Leaving me with a very pissed-off incubus.

I got a royal ass-chewing, then he stormed out, leaving me to stand amid dishes and empty wine glasses, wondering what to do with the rest of my night. I needed energy. As much as I hated the thought of going out alone and picking up a sexual partner after our fight, it's what I needed to do. After lecturing Hallwyn about how "work" wasn't always fun, I couldn't slack off and add fuel to the fire by expecting Irix to recharge me whenever he got home.

So I cleaned the dishes, grabbed a quick shower, changed, and went to the interstate to find the nearest truck stop and bang some random guy in his cab. My heart wasn't in it, even though my body was, and by the time I got home, Irix was in bed, asleep.

I was just glad he'd come back, so I slid in beside him, careful not to wake him and deal with the cold-shoulder treatment. Then I tossed and turned all night, staring at the ceiling and walls until it was time to get up and go to work.

Jorge was at the sheds, handing out clipboards and assignments. I stopped to say hi to all my co-workers before I headed back to the winery and noticed Rosa munching on a double-chocolate cookie.

"Are you back with us today?" she asked, strolling over with clipboard in hand.

"No, I just came by to say hi. Where's Hallwyn?"

"That elf?" Rosa shrugged. "No idea. She usually arrives in the pickup with Jorge. Maybe she got in early and headed out, or maybe she's sick today. Don't know. Don't care."

"Where'd you get the cookies?" There was no way Rosa would be caught dead buying those things, and as far as I knew I was her only supplier here in the field.

"Hush." The woman quickly looked around. "They were in my golf-cart this morning, all wrapped up in a plastic grocery-store bag. It was one of those small packs that you get at the convenience stores. Do you think Manny knows?"

About her cookie addiction? "Probably not. Maybe it's a

secret admirer." Remembering what I'd said last night, I assumed that Hallwyn had come in early to work and left the offering in Rosa's golf cart. The elf was more observant that I'd thought, and clearly had a good memory. Maybe Irix was right and I should be more careful.

She snorted. "Right. That sommelier hasn't looked twice at me, and the guys in the field are all married."

I shrugged, looking down at my phone as it vibrated in my hand. Rosa peered over my shoulder at the message.

"You've got the elf in your phone contacts? Are you trying to add her to your conquest list? Is she the next one we'll see coming and going from your trailer?"

Yeah, everyone thought I was a total slut. Figures. "No. I helped her out with something the other day and I think we're kind of friends. She's not so bad."

"Well, she wants you in field twenty, row twelve. Need a lift? I'm going by there."

I'd been worried how I was going to get there and back in time for my shift to start, but Rosa's offer solved half that problem. And I wanted to get there, because that was exactly where we'd been working last night. Was she trying again to repair the damaged plants? Did she need me to take care of those leafrollers ?

"I'd appreciate a lift, thanks."

I climbed in beside Rosa and held onto the frame of the golf cart as she raced down the narrow dirt path that separated the fields, pulling the cart over as we reached the correct row. Instead of continuing on, Rosa climbed out of the cart with me and headed toward Hallwyn, who was hugging herself and pacing back and forth. Drat. With Rosa along, I could hardly work any of my own magic. Maybe after we spoke to Hallwyn, I could convince her to go away.

"Amber, it's back. It's back." Hallwyn had been crying again. Was she one of those who cried all the time? That sort of thing drove me nuts. And the fact that the elf's face wasn't blotchy and red as she sobbed annoyed me even more.

"Wow, those vines are even worse than they were last night," Rosa commented. "What did you do to them? You're supposed to be helping, not causing the disease to go into overdrive."

And now Hallwyn was crying even more. "I didn't! There was no disease left at all in these plants last night. None. Why is it back? What happened? I'll never be able to get rid of it. I'll be fired and have to go back to Elf Island or become a sex-slave breeder for a hideous hairy human with bad breath and warts on his skin."

Rosa and I exchanged astonished glances. "Is she always like this?" the woman asked me.

"I've got no idea," I responded. "I've only known her a few days and we're not exactly besties or anything."

"Stop crying." Rosa patted the elf awkwardly on the shoulder. "Maybe if you try again it will work. Here, have a cookie."

Hallwyn choked back her sobs and took the offered cookie, gagging and spitting out the bite she took. "It's too sweet and tastes like chemicals."

"I think I hate her," Rosa commented, eyeing the elf's reaction to the coveted treats.

"The downy mildew was gone," I assured Hallwyn. "I checked myself, and it was gone. Apixt or her sister must have come back and re-infected the plant."

"What, what, what?" Rosa's head swiveled back and forth between us at whiplash speed. "What do you mean 'Apixt or her sister'? Are you saying there are two women walking around with a box of fungus and leafrollers and slapping it on our vines, *on purpose?*"

I really wished Rosa would go away. "Since when have you ever seen all these diseases and pests, many of which require completely opposite conditions to thrive, infecting a vineyard all at once and to this degree? Yes, it's on purpose. And it's not some women, it's a pair of plague demons doing this."

Rosa stared at me, then munched thoughtfully on another cookie. "Two years ago I would have thought you were crazy, but since I'm working side-by-side with pointy-ears here, I believe you. So do these plague demons just show up out of nowhere?"

"No, they come from Hel," Hallwyn chimed in. "That's where the demons live, and up until a few months ago, that's where we elves used to live."

Rosa crammed the rest of the cookie in her mouth. "Great. Did you bring them over with you? Why are they here now? And why DiMarche?"

I went to reply, but Hallwyn beat me to it. "Demons have always come across the gates, but these two were most likely summoned or hired under contract."

The woman's eyebrows shot up. "A *contract*? Who would put out a hit on DiMarche? Boone Valley? Santor? One of those snobby French wineries? And why are they using demons instead of a hostile stock takeover like every other business in the world?"

I frowned at Hallwyn, warning her to keep quiet. I was reluctant to air all the elven dirty laundry, and if Rosa and the others thought Hallwyn had gotten her job through a sort of plague-demon sabotage, they'd never come to see her as a friend.

"I don't know. It might be for some other reason. I have my suspicions, but no proof."

"You told Jorge yet?" Rosa asked.

I shook my head "No, because I thought we were taking care of it. I mean, *Hallwyn* was taking care of it. But the plague demons are coming back here and re-infecting everything we—she heals." Again I felt torn. Should I give up the vineyard as a lost cause? Let Apixt and Txipa take it and rot every vine to the ground? Hallwyn was fighting a losing battle, but maybe if I managed to somehow get enough energy, and she got her elven friends to help…

No. I couldn't win this one. I'd help the elves with this shit-head Jobber, and maybe Sam would come through for me and get the plague demons to back off the vineyard, but that was it. That was the best I could do.

"They keep coming back?" Rosa narrowed her eyes at Hallwyn. "Guess you've got your work cut out for you. No vineyard, no job. And happy as I'd be to see you tossed back on that island, I really don't want to be out of a job myself, so hustle your butt up and put those glowy-hands of yours on some vines. Get to work, elf-scum. Stop your crying and get to work."

Rosa spun around and headed to her go-cart.

"You're not a nice human, and I'm not bringing you any more cookies," Hallwyn yelled. Then she kicked a clod of dirt. I had to smother a laugh, because at that moment she seemed very non-elf-like.

"She's right, you know. I mean, not about you being sent back to the island, but the rest. You'll need to work your ass off clearing away as much disease as possible. Our only hope is to stay a bit ahead of the pestilence demons until they get bored and go away." Or until Sam managed to convince them to go away.

"Wonderful. I work myself to exhaustion, only to come back the next day and find it all undone."

She was right, but we had no other choice.

I left Hallwyn in the field and ran as fast as I could to the winery, earning a grumpy look from Nancy for being late. The day turned worse when I realized my assignment was to follow her around and check the various fermentation tanks, then spend the afternoon cleaning and sanitizing equipment. By the time my day was over, my hands were raw from the abrasive cleaners, and my clothes were wet. I waved off Matthieu's attempts to drag me down in the cellars for a quickie, and headed out.

When I reached the equipment sheds, I stopped and bit my lip, trying to make a decision. Should I head out into the field and help Hallwyn heal some plants? I'd been coming home every night drained of energy, and the quick scores I was picking up here and there weren't enough to replace what I was expending. I'd been relying too much on Irix and what Harkel had given me, but that wasn't fair. I needed a night off to recharge, and to spend some time trying to make things right with Irix. I shot a reluctant glance over to the fields, sent Hallwyn a quick text, then headed for my trailer.

There was no home-cooked meal when I got home. There wasn't even a quiche and salad. Irix was there at least, but he greeted me with a frosty "hello", never lifting his eyes from the book he was reading.

I dug in the fridge for some leftovers, then pulled out the bottle of rum, hoping a drink would help the situation.

"I didn't bring a stray puppy home tonight," I told him, handing him a rum and ginger.

"Huh." Irix took a sip, the ice clinking in the glass.

I sat beside him and waited, but there was no further comment. "She thinks I'm a human with weird magic skills. It's okay. I don't even work with her anymore. They have me in the winery."

"Good."

This was going to be a very long, tension-filled night. I eyed my glass, wondering if I should have just drunk the rum straight. "The plant with the mildew that Hallwyn healed last night had it again this morning. It was even worse. The plague demons must be coming back in the middle of the night and re-infecting everything she heals."

"Which is another good reason for you to stay away from that elf. Let her deal with the vines and the plague demons. It's her job, not yours."

He still sounded pissed, but at least he was communicating in more than grunts and one-word sentences.

I scooted closer to him. "There's some Jobber guy, I don't know if he's an elf or a human, who's making the elves sign these horrible contracts and pay to get them a job and off Elf Island. He's inflating the costs and loaning them money for everything at a crippling rate. It's usury. It's predatory lending."

"It's none of your business."

"Hallwyn says they have no say over what job they get, and that she's completely unqualified for this one."

"Then she should get a new job. Or go back to Elf Island and tell the angels what this guy is doing."

"She'll be stuck there forever because the angels will never allow her to get a job in public policy administration. They're only approving jobs in agriculture, the medical fields, and the arts."

"Then maybe she can take the Elf Island equivalent of continuing education classes."

"And she'll still owe this Jobber guy. The interest will pile up, and on the island she won't have any way to earn money to pay him back. The alternative is some unnamed work for the Jobber. What do you think it is? Selling her organs? Prostitution? Some kind of elven-magic sweatshop?"

"Guess she shouldn't have signed that contract." Irix put his drink and book down on the table and turned to look at me. "It's not like the angels are whipping them. Elves are a bunch of whiny pansy-asses. They need to make the best of a less-than-ideal situation, learn what the angels are trying to teach them, be patient, and stop trying to buy and bribe their way off the island. It's her own fault. If they're stupid enough to sign onto horrible debt and questionable default clauses with this Jobber, then they need to deal with the consequences. Don't fall for her helpless big-eyed elf routine, Amber. She had a choice. She could have stayed on the island. Instead she made a bad deal. Not your problem. Not my problem. Not anyone's problem but Hallwyn's."

"But they don't understand the human world. The angels don't understand the human world. I know elves are shitheads and she shouldn't have signed that contract, but it seems like one of those situations where they're vulnerable to scams like this."

Irix shrugged. "They have kidnapped and enslaved humans for thousands of years. They weren't the easiest neighbors in Hel, although I'll admit they were occasionally entertaining. They chose to come here, with bad intentions. They made this mess, and now they have to live with it."

I stared down at my drink, knowing he was right. I'd been a hero in New Orleans, in Maui, and in Hel. I wanted to be the hero here as well. If I couldn't save the vineyard, maybe I could save the elves.

But did they really need saving? They were in the human world now. Maybe I needed to just refer Hallwyn to a good bankruptcy attorney or contract lawyer and wash my hands of the whole thing.

My phone beeped and I frowned looking down at the text.

"No." Irix demanded, reading over my shoulder. "No. Not happening. Tell her that you're busy."

Every cell of my being chafed at the tone in his voice. He was right, but still…

He took the phone from my hands. "You're not going.

She's a grown elf. She can handle this herself. It's her job, and she's just putting in overtime. She doesn't need you."

Probably not, but I kept thinking of the downy mildew that had returned overnight. "She's not very good at this. I could just show her how to heal the black measles case, then leave her to take care of it."

"Show her, then heal a few vines, then wind up out there all night with her, risking that Txipa or Apixt sees you and decides to take your head off for interfering."

A chill ran through me at the thought of Hallwyn in the field, distracted and at the mercy of the plague demons. But she was an elf. She had skills of her own, and she knew to be careful.

"I promise. I'll just show her how to eradicate the black measles, then I'll come right back."

"You're not going out there."

"You can come with me. I promise, a half an hour max."

"No."

I heard the finality in Irix's voice and snatched my phone back, typing in a note that I wasn't able to help tonight. Then I quickly added a second text, reminding Hallwyn about the plague demons and that she should just go home for the night, that I'd show her how to fix the black measles in the morning. "There. Satisfied?" I showed Irix the screen. He still didn't look happy.

"Yes. Now go out and hunt. You're hungry."

I winced. There was no loving offer to share, no wicked little smile and proposal that we hunt together. Was an elf going to tear us apart? Although it was wrong to blame Hallwyn for this. It was *me* that was going to tear us apart. I did things Irix felt were risky and foolish. He was a demon. He didn't get my need to help others, to save the day, to be a hero. In his world, there were very few things worth risking your life over. Ethics, ideals, commercial vineyards, and random elves weren't on that list.

But they were on *my* list. I'd risked my life to help down in New Orleans. I'd risked my life to help in Maui. I'd risked my life to go to Hel and help the humans. I'd risked my life to gain him immunity from the angels. Would I risk my life to help Hallwyn and a winery that I didn't even own stock in? It was me that would break us apart, but could I change who I was?

I couldn't change, but at least I could pick my battles. He was right. Hallwyn was a grown elf. I was doing what I could to find this Jobber and put a stop to his scheme. I was doing what I could to shift Apixt and her sister's focus away from DiMarche. I didn't need to drain myself dry out in the fields in the middle of the night healing vines next to an elf.

I put my hand on Irix's chest and looked up at him. "Please come with me?"

He made a "harrumph" noise. "I spent all day hunting. I'm full. And you don't need me to attract a sexual partner."

"No, but I want you there. Maybe you can watch, or just have a drink while I bang some guy out back behind the bar. We fought last night and never made up. We're still fighting. I didn't sleep all night. I can't hunt with you mad at me. Well, I can but I don't want to, and if I walk out of here now, you'll be asleep by the time I get home and I'll spend another restless night knowing you're still angry with me."

"I *am* still angry with you, Amber."

He was, but the golden brown in his eyes had softened with my words.

"Please?" I rubbed my hand down his chest and looped my fingers in the waistband of his pants. "I'll let you pick my prey. Then afterward I'll fulfill *your* every fantasy."

"Blow job?" he asked. "Then anal?"

Men. "Sure, I'll strap a dildo on if you want."

He chuckled. I felt a thrill run through me to have gotten that out of him. "No. Me in your ass. After me in your mouth."

As long as it wasn't the reverse order, because that would be gross. "I'm all yours, baby."

He smiled, and gold flecks came to light in his eyes. "I know. And I'm all *yours*, baby."

Trix had picked out a particularly challenging mark for me, but I'd managed to score. We were on our way home, the full moon casting a path of light along the road, the neat rows of vines on either side lit up to a shadowy gray. We turned down the drive to the trailers, and I frowned, seeing something at the edge of a row that was out of place this early in the morning.

"Stop. There's a golf-cart down there."

His arms tensed, hands tight on the wheel as a muscle jerked in his jaw, but Irix slowed the car.

"Some kids joyriding. Or maybe that elf pulled an all-nighter. It's not your business, Amber."

Something told me it was. "Let's walk down. If Hallwyn's working straight through the night, we'll leave. If it's an abandoned golf cart, I'll let Jorge know in the morning where it is so he can send someone out to retrieve it."

Irix sighed and pulled the car over to the side of the drive. "We're just going to check the cart. We're not searching all over a thousand acres to check up on that elf. Got it?"

"Yes, sir," I teased.

We got out of the car and I waited for Irix to come around to join me before heading down the row of vines. It had been so hot during the day that the evening air felt chilly and I rubbed the goose bumps on my arms. It wasn't just the cool night air that had me on edge. The vineyard was creepy in the dark. The leaves rustled softly in the breeze. The moon was darting in and out of wispy clouds, flickering the dim light around us and sending shadows across the path like an army of invisible soldiers marching forward across the ground.

The golf cart didn't look as though it had been vandalized. The keys were in the ignition, and there was a bag of dried pineapple on the seat. I guess Hallwyn *was* working late.

"Okay? Let's go."

Although where was Hallwyn? I wasn't seeing any glow from her magic, and I hadn't heard anyone in the rows nearby. Elves moved silently, but Irix and I hadn't tried to be quiet as we'd approached. If she was nearby, she would have heard us and come to see who was here. Perhaps she had worked her way down the row and was farther up in the field.

Irix turned and took two steps down the row and froze. "Stay here," he hissed.

He backed up a step then edged two rows down, his face grim. I disobeyed and crept up behind him, crying out when I saw a figure with long blond hair and pointed ears sprawled on the ground. I ran toward her, my hands shaking as I turned the body over. Her skin was cold and damp, her hair tangled over her face, dirt staining the white shirt and khaki pants. No. No.

I should have been here. I could have helped her fight back. Jumping up, I turned and smashed into Irix's chest. His arms came around my shoulders and I felt everything inside me break as I began to cry.

"It's your fault. Yours," I shouted at him. "I wanted to go and help her. I should have been here to help her. You forced me to choose between you and something I knew was right. I picked you and she died. She died because you're a selfish controlling asshole. She died because of you."

Irix flinched at each of my words, but never let me go, his arms tight around me, his cheek against the top of my head. Even when I managed to pull my hands free and punch him in the chest he held me.

"You would have died here with her. She made the choice to stay out here, and it was a foolish choice. If you had been here with her, your body would be next to hers on the ground. I need you to be safe, Amber. I can't let you die because of some stupid, reckless urge to save everyone you meet."

This time I punched him hard. "The two of us might have been able to fight back, or to get away. And even if we both died, at least we would have died fighting together. She wouldn't have died all alone out in a field. She wouldn't have died in a strange world, surrounded by strange customs and humans, feeling trapped and desperate. She was here because she was afraid of losing her job. She wasn't out doing something stupid, she was trying to do her job."

I yanked away from Irix, resisting the urge to slug him across the face.

"I don't care," he told me, his eyes nearly black in the dim light. "That was her choice. I'm not having you die because some elf stupidly signed a contract and took a job she wasn't qualified for. I'm not having you die because an idiot elf got herself in trouble."

"It's not your right to decide when and how I die. It's not your right to tell me what my priorities are or who is worth risking my life for. I love you, but I'm not some fragile doll for you to lock in an unbreakable case and put on a shelf. I'm me. I'm a half-elf, half-succubus, and my life is *mine* to live, not yours."

"You're a *what*?"

My heart nearly left my chest at the whispered voice, and I could tell by Irix's expression that he was equally startled. I spun around, my mouth dropping open. Hallwyn stood behind me, her hair a snarled mess that hung down past her hips. Her clothing was torn and scorched. Her face marred with a jagged red cut that went from her forehead diagonally to her chin. As I watched another elf materialized from behind the row of vines. She had the same white button-down and khaki pants as Hallwyn and the body at my feet, and hers were in the same disrepair. Whoever this Jobber was that had provided them with clothing, he must have gotten a bulk deal from Old Navy.

"You're alive!" I stupidly announced. Then I looked down at the body.

"We were able to get away." Hallwyn choked back a sob. "Callia wasn't. There were two of them. They came at us out of nowhere and attacked us while we were trying to heal the vines. They were too strong, and had weapons."

Callia. I bent down and smoothed the tangled blond hair away from the elf's face, realizing that although all three women bore a striking resemblance, this dead elf wasn't Hallwyn.

"They had weapons?" Irix asked. "Human weapons, like guns and knives?" He knelt down beside me, looking over the body.

"Not knives. One had some kind of metal thing that shot little fireballs. They were demons, but not using lightning attacks. They used energy attacks, and the mini fireballs. One hit Callia and she just dropped."

Irix smoothed away the girl's hair and showed me the bullet wound in the side of her head. I felt sick. That alone was enough to kill a human, but with the elves' allergy to the metals, it would definitely have been a fatal wound.

"You couldn't come," Hallwyn said, her voice more than a little accusatory. "You couldn't come to help, so I called Callia and Tralian, they're the elves that work at Boone Valley and at Santor Winery. We've been meeting once a week to discuss our jobs and trade information. They said they would help me tonight. We were going to spend each evening at a different one of our vineyards until we had this thing beat."

I'd let Hallwyn down and one of her friends had gotten killed. I might not have been able to make much of a difference if I'd have been here, but I could have maybe held the attackers back so they all could have gotten away. I smoothed Callia's hair, mourning her death even though I'd never met her. She was so pretty, so ethereal as all the elves were.

And she also had an advanced case of the mumps.

"Hallwyn, did you all get vaccinated on Elf Island?"

She blinked at me. "I don't know what this means."

"Did someone inject you with a series of dead viruses so you wouldn't be susceptible to human diseases that you've most likely never been in contact with before?"

She exchanged a puzzled glance with the other elf. "No, we don't get human diseases. Some of the humans who fell through the traps were sick. We healed them, but never contracted those illnesses."

That didn't mean they were immune to *every* human disease. Or that some diseases wouldn't mutate to a form that would infect the elves.

"Did Callia complain of feeling unwell? Did she have a fever, headaches, loss of appetite?"

"No. Why?" Hallwyn came closer.

"Did her cheeks always look like this? Because mumps affects the glands in the cheeks and makes them swell."

"No!"

The other elf approached and both stared down at Callia in shock. Hallwyn reached down and touched her friend's face, then jumped backward, nearly falling on her rear in her haste to get away.

"She didn't have that when she came here tonight. And that's not a normal human disease, it's one that's demon spread." Her voice wavered. "That plague demon touched Callia. She shot her with the mini fireballs, then touched her and violated her body with this foul disease."

"Txipa. She's the twin that specializes in human and animal diseases while Apixt spreads blight among plants. And bringing a gun…" Irix shot me a worried glance. "They came here not just to reinfect the plants but to kill the person who was healing them. Amber, that bullet was meant for you."

Tralian shook her head. "Why would they need a gun to kill a human? Unless Amber also has special healing powers, one touch should have stricken her with a disease that would have killed her within seconds."

"I'm fast, and they would have had to catch me to touch me. A gun can kill me from a distance, and I'm just as susceptible to those mini-fireballs as your friend Callia was."

Hallwyn's eyes narrowed and she took a step back from me. "But I heard you. I heard you say you were a half-elf and a half-succubus."

"You misunderstood me," I told her. "I know our languages are new to you. What I said was that I was similar to an elf and a succubus."

She stared at me intently. "There was an elf who was put to death not long ago, a high elf related to the High Lord of

Wythyn. She had been accused of lying with a sex demon and conceiving a child through that union."

I tried to look shocked. "But you told me elves would never have sex with a non-elf, that they'd never bear a half-breed child."

"This elven woman denied it to her death, but there were rumors that it was true. Are you…could you…?"

"I think my human mother would slap you in the face to hear such an accusation. Do I look like a half-elf to you?" Hopefully the answer was no.

She tilted her head and the other elf did the same.

"She does have an amazing symmetry of features that is lacking among the humans," Tralian noted.

"But those ears…" Hallwyn added.

"Yes, those are hideous ears. No elf, even one born from such a disgraceful union would have those ugly ears." Tralian wrinkled her nose in distaste.

I'd never been so grateful for my succubus half.

"And her body is not like an elf's," Hallwyn continued. "Her posterior is too big. And her breasts are disgustingly large."

I clamped my teeth together to keep silent and not respond to such insults.

"I agree," Tralian said. "She is merely an attractive human who has magic and has sold her soul to this incubus. I've always believed the half-elf story to be fantasy anyway. No elf would so lower herself, especially a high elf."

Good. Now that we were done discussing my unattractive physical attributes, we should turn our attention back to the matter at hand. "Hallwyn, you'll need to call the police about your friend, as well as Jorge. And for the future, I think everyone should keep their healing activities to daytime hours."

I looked over at Irix, and knew from his grim expression

that he was thinking the same thing I was. Apixt and Txipa weren't going to back off, and they were serious enough about laying waste to this vineyard that they were willing to kill me or any elf that got in their way. DiMarche today, Santor and Boone Valley tomorrow, then what? Txipa had said she was spreading human diseases. This was more than just about the vineyards, and I got the feeling it wasn't a personal vendetta against Napa Valley. The farms, humans, and now this elf were just collateral damage in what I was beginning to believe was some kind of feud between the Jobber and the two plague demons.

The Jobber needed to go, but clearly I wouldn't be able to just stand by and let the plague demons decimate Northern California in the meantime. Irix might not like it, but I needed to help. But the question was how best to approach this situation? I wasn't strong enough to face down two plague demons, even with Irix's help, so my best chance at fixing this mess seemed to be through tracking down this Jobber and hoping we could resolve whatever was going on with the plague demons that way.

CHAPTER 22

"Sorry it took me a while to get back to you. A dozen bikers beat the crap out of me and threw me off a cliff with an anvil tied around my neck. Took me a while to deal with that."

I wasn't surprised that Sam had gotten beaten up for her antics, but I was surprised it took her more than five seconds to repair her injuries and hunt down the bikers. "I assume there are a dozen dead guys with a twisted up mess of Harleys in the middle of the desert somewhere?"

"Are you fucking kidding me? Do you know how many reports that is? I almost had to fill one out for the guy I hit with the anvil, but I got down there in time and was able to heal him. They didn't take kindly to that—either me dropping an anvil on their friend, *or* giving him my angelic-style mouth-to-mouth."

I'm pretty sure it was the anvil and not the mouth-to-mouth that had incurred the wrath of the bikers, but with Sam, who knew?

"So, bad news first. Apixt and Txipa say to fuck off. And to stay out of their business or they'll fill you full of lead. Or boils. I'm not sure which. Both Apixt and her revolting sister are really pissed off at you right now because you're 'fucking up their shit'. Their words, not mine. Although I have been known to use similar words."

Damn. It's not like I'd had much faith Sam would be successful in intervening with the plague demons. I'd need to turn my attention to the Jobber, and get to the demons through him. And to do that, I'd need to either ask Wyatt to trace the money, or work this through the angels on Elf Island. Or both.

"Good news: I found out how the placement process works on Elf Island. Asshole is pissed off that they're letting elves out this early, and thinks an angel there might be on the take, so he's sending in some trusted angels to clean house. This Magical Interventions placement company? Get this— it's run by an elf. Which is another reason Asshole is pissed. The elf gives the angels a list of jobs, then picks from the applicants. Right now, all the jobs are in Northern California, so he's there, working with a human who meets with clients while the elf, no doubt, creates a demand for the elves he's placing by using those plague demons."

So a human and elf team. If they hadn't expanded beyond Northern California, I should be able to catch them.

"I'm sending you a list of all the employed elves and where they're working to help you track it down. The elf goes by Gallette. No idea on the human, but I'm sure if you talk to these businesses, they'll know who they paid the referral fee to."

"I've got the company name and I'm asking Wyatt to start tracing the money," I told her. "Do you think the plague demons are off their leash? I assumed they were supposed to stop infecting the crops once an elf was hired, so the place-ment company could build a good reputation, but they're not. Things are getting worse, anything the elves do to heal the crops is being reversed, and three elves were attacked last night. One was killed."

"Yeah. Apixt and her sister are really pissed at someone, which is why they weren't amenable to shifting their efforts to a different area, even with some rather lavish bribes. I'd assume something was going on between Gallette and the two demons, and the deal went bad. Demons generally don't go crazy and start shooting elves and threatening other demons unless they're worked up about something. Txipa and Apixt are both lazy. They wouldn't try to take out vineyards, commercial farms, and a few hospitals. If they wanted to destroy Northern California, they'd go for a processing plant and *E.coli* or rot millions of dollars of product and cause a worldwide famine or plague. This is personal. And these particular farms, vineyards, and hospitals mean something important in their revenge plot."

"Do you think the elf stiffed them? That he didn't keep up his end of the bargain?" I asked.

"That or they really hate wine, apples, and zucchini. I'd suggest you check with the other employers on the list. If they're all continuing to have the same escalating infestations, then the demons are angry at the elf. If not, then it's someone else they're pissed at. And I gotta warn you, they work closely together, in pairs. If someone has slighted Apixt, Txipa is gonna back her up. If the elf made good by Txipa, but didn't hold up his end of the bargain with Apixt, then he's got two plague demons gunning for him, not just one."

Which explained why there was mumps on the dead elf. "Thanks. And Sam? The plague demons aren't the only ones running around here, performing their work blatantly in the open. Harkel came across the gates to see me, and he said the word is it's open season here. The demons know that the angels are busy with their own problems and aren't as vigi-lant as they usually are. The henhouse is unguarded."

"And a shit-ton of foxes are about to line up for dinner. Great. Just fucking great. How's things with Harkel, by the way? Color me impressed, girl. You preggers yet? Wearing his ring?"

I immediately envisioned myself wearing Irix's ring, pregnant with his child. "Nope. We had some fun and I think we have a threesome relationship going on, but it seems that he's transferring his request for a breeding incident to Irix."

The imp snorted. "A threesome, huh? I'm not surprised that he's taken a shine to Irix as well. You're too fragile for demon sex, especially with a warmonger. Huh. Hopefully you can leverage that relationship in the future, but it's prob-ably good that Irix is involved. Wyatt and I might not be an item any more, but he'd blow my brains out if I let anything happen to you."

Yes, he would. I so loved my big brother. "Thanks again, Sam. I'll be home in time for your shindig."

"Damn straight. Bean dip. Don't forget the bean dip. And the red velvet cake."

I assured her that I'd be bringing the coveted bean dip and cake, and hung up. Sure enough, the second I hung up my phone beeped and there was a text with an attachment. Twelve businesses, all in Northern California, all with elves hired in the last two months, all of them some kind of agribusiness.

There was no way I could drive all over the upper part of the state to talk to these places, not when I had to be at work in half an hour.

Irix stirred beside me, rolling over to wrap an arm around my waist and pull me against him.

"You had to call her from bed, did you?" he murmured, his voice sleepy.

I didn't want to leave his side. Last night's events had shaken me. I'd thought Hallwyn was dead, and I'd begun to like her a bit. I'd thought she was dead, and I'd blamed Irix. He'd never mentioned my meltdown or my accusations, and I wasn't sure how to broach the topic. Should I just let it rest? Not mention it? I'd hit him, blamed him, accused him of not letting me be me. And I was right, but over the last year he'd been obviously trying. Each time he'd forced himself to pull back his overprotective instincts and give me space. But each of those times he'd insisted on being right beside me, helping me and protecting me. As much as I loved him, as much as I appreciated his greater skill and power and loved that he'd do anything to protect me, I needed to spread my wings. I'd done that in Hel. I'd gone there alone, and as frightening as some of that trip was, I grew there. I learned things about myself and my abilities and limits that I hadn't with Irix's protective wing around me.

I didn't want to die. I didn't want to leave him. But I needed to find my way. And I needed to feel skilled and powerful in my own right. I needed him to respect me and not treat me as if I were a fragile helpless infant in need of his constant protection.

But I wasn't stupid enough to ignore when I was in over my head.

"I'll call the farms on the list," he said, his hand caressing my stomach. "Forward me the text and while you're working, I'll check with them all. If Apixt is on some rampage of revenge because Gallette didn't uphold his end of the bargain, then Sam's right and Txipa is right by her side. I don't want what happened to that elf to happen to you. I'll call the farms. I'll help you track down the Jobber elf and the two demons, but promise me you won't do it alone. Promise me you won't make one step without me by your side."

I hesitated a second too long and his arm tightened like a vise around me.

"I love you, Amber. I can't lose you. You're powerful in ways I'll never be, but you're still young and you don't understand demons like I do. I get that these vineyards and these elves are somehow important to you. If you want to risk yourself to help them, fine. I can't stop you, but I sure as hell can make sure I'm by your side to protect you when shit goes down and bullets start flying."

"Mini fireballs," I teased, snuggling my ass against him. "I promise."

Once more Irix was helping with something he didn't give a flying fuck about, just because it was important to me. And because he didn't want me to be the one dead in the vineyard with a bullet hole in my head and an advanced case of mumps.

I turned in his arms and buried my face against his chest, feeling the rise and fall of his breath and the solid thump of his heart. "I love you. I'm so sorry for what I said last night."

"Hush. You were upset. Hallwyn might not be a lifelong friend, but I think you've sort of temporarily adopted her. She's your stray puppy. She's your mentee, and you felt responsible for her. I'm still glad you didn't go last night, and I don't think it's your responsibility to protect an adult elf who is centuries older than you are, but I get it. And I get that you were lashing out at me from guilt and grief."

"Forgiven?" I kissed his skin and felt his pectoral muscle jump under my lips.

"Yes, forgiven. Although you still owe me that blow job and anal action."

I laughed. "Raincheck? I need to get going or I'll be late for work."

"Raincheck." He smacked my ass and pulled away from me. "Get going, or you *will* be late for work."

Everyone, both at the winery and in the field, were shocked over what had happened last night. Richard was putting up security cameras near the shed and drive. No one was allowed to be out in the field after dark, and those who had to work late in the tasting room or production facility were to be escorted to their cars when leaving. There was a huge meeting where Richard reiterated DiMarche's full cooperation with law enforcement on finding the attackers.

Hallwyn's face was streaked with tears, her mouth trembling and eyes full of grief as everyone expressed both their condolences over the loss of her friend as well as shock and sympathy for what she'd suffered in the attack. Her injuries had already healed, but watching a friend get shot left scars that lasted a lifetime. As the vineyard employees headed out to the field, I saw Rosa come up to her, pat her on the back, and slip her a small brown paper bag. My mouth watered at the thought of what it held. Hallwyn must have made an impression if Rosa was giving her empanadas.

I found out later how much of an impression she made. Everyone was talking about the attack in the vineyard, and everyone was talking about how dedicated Hallwyn was, working all through the night to try to turn things around out there, even bringing in two other elves from the neighboring vineyards. They'd gone from wary dislike of the elf to admiration overnight. Elves were suddenly team-players, selfless and hardworking, giving a hundred-and-ten-percent to get the job done. And they weren't above pitching in and helping each other out, even if they were employed by a rival winery.

Elves were now saints. And I wasn't sure how I felt about that. I didn't want the Jobber preying on their inexperience and desperation, but I didn't really want the elves to become the heroes of the human world, especially knowing what they'd done to the humans in Hel and what they'd intended on doing to the humans here when they'd migrated. I'm sure elves like Hallwyn would end up being productive and helpful members of society, but there would still be elves like this Jobber who only wanted what was best for themselves. Not all elves were saints, and I hoped that the humans weren't so fascinated by their new co-workers that they completely let their guard down.

I was working with Richard today, getting an idea of how things worked at the management end of the winery, and he waxed poetic all morning about how wonderful elves were and that if he'd hired Hallwyn months ago, the vineyard wouldn't be in such bad shape that she'd needed to risk her life working all through the night. By quitting time, I had the mother of all headaches, wanting nothing more than to get away from all the talk of amazing, helpful, wonderful elves. Once more I brushed off Matthieu's advances, and headed out.

"I managed to call all of the farms on the list," Irix told me as I walked through the door. At the same time my phone buzzed and I looked to see a lengthy text from Wyatt, giving me the information I'd requested.

That's right. It was payday, and he'd been tracing the transfer of money from Hallwyn's account. A sum went to the landlord, then nearly the entire rest of the paycheck went to one bank account. Magical Interventions, a division of Banks's Placement Services was listed as the account owner along with an address, phone number. Then my brother had dug deeper and found the name of the person who'd organized the DBA. Aaron Banks was either a human or the elf had stolen the man's identity because the man had a paper trail going back for nearly twenty years. He'd worked for temporary placement firms, managed a few, then opened up a boutique recruitment firm specializing in accounting positions, of all things.

A human and an elf working together. One human having the knowledge of how to get businesses to contract with him to fill job openings, the other an elf who knew how to work things with his angel contact on Elf Island, as well as prep the elven side of the equation. And the elf would have most likely been the one who contracted with the plague demons to ensure businesses were receptive to Aaron's proposal.

I had no idea how the elf had pissed off the demons, or how tight his relationship was to this Aaron, but I needed to find them both and stop their business in its tracks. And if they couldn't call off the demons, then I'd need to deal with that issue separately. I glanced over at Irix as I typed my thanks to Wyatt. We'd need to deal with that issue separately, because there was no way I was going up against two demons without some significant backup.

"Ready for my news?" Irix handed me a glass of wine and motioned for me to sit. I plopped down on the sofa, worried what he had to say that necessitated both an alcoholic beverage and not standing.

"All the farms met with someone named Aaron Banks with Magical Interventions. A few had worked with him before through Banks's Placement Services getting admin and accounting staff, so they knew him and were happy to share his company's address and phone number with me. A few months ago, he started asking them about the need for elven employees, touting their special skills and telling them this new division specialized in these sorts of placements. Every single farm said they hadn't been interested at first because the fee was expensive and the wages for the elves were high. No one had it in the budget for this year, and they weren't convinced that the elves really had any sort of super-natural powers that would be of value to them. No one wanted to spend a ton of money and look the fool."

"Magical Interventions is the company who is getting the

money transfers from Hallwyn's account." I quickly told Irix about Wyatt's text and waited for him to continue.

"No one wanted to hire the elves, but then things started to go wrong with crops—blights that nothing cured, insects that no amount of spraying killed off. Each day that went by, things got worse and worse until the farms were desperate. The first few who hired elves had seen dramatic improvements, but every single one of them has seen a reversal in the last week—so drastic that two farms had been on the verge of firing their elves."

"Did they?" I asked.

"No. I guess the elves saw the writing on the wall and were just as terrified as Hallwyn about what would happen if they lost their jobs. They took off. Vanished. No one has any idea what happened to them. They didn't show up for work one day, didn't even come in to collect their things."

I felt a chill run down my back. Had they run off, abandoning everything to go off grid in the mountains and hide from the wrath of both the angels and the Jobber, or had this Jobber taken preemptive action when he discovered their employment was in jeopardy?

Irix pulled the wine glass from my hand, drank down the contents, then held a hand out for me. "Come on. If we hustle we can get to this placement service before five."

I jumped up, knowing we'd have to hurry, and knowing that Irix was thrilled to have this opportunity to break every speed limit between here and Sonoma.

"Fast food for dinner?" I asked, grabbing my purse.

"Depends. If we can catch Aaron Banks at work, we might have time afterwards to find a good restaurant."

CHAPTER 23

We pulled up outside of the address that both Wyatt and the farms had given for Banks's Placement Service, and checked the directory. The building was a squat row house with a brick façade and a coffee shop in the lower level. Up a narrow set of stairs were two doors, one was ironically an investigative agency, the other the placement firm.

I knocked, because that was the polite thing to do even when dealing with potential criminals, then opened the door. The office was cleared out. A few filing cabinets stood open and empty in the corner, a huge executive-style U-shaped desk off to the side, some discarded paper clips and chewed pens scattered on the surface. The trash cans were emptied, and there was nothing that would indicate the firm had moved their operations elsewhere.

Irix and I left, and this time he knocked on the PI's door, swinging it open at the disembodied voice tell in us to come in.

The inside of this office was in stark contrast to the one across the hall. One wall was lined with file cabinets that barely shut around the contents bulging from the top. This U-shaped desk was battered and so full of file folders that I couldn't see the occupant seated behind them.

"Can I help you?" A woman popped her head above the folders. Her gray hair had a streak of blue and was cut in a stylish bob. She wore cat-eye glasses, and instead of feeling old-fashioned they seemed a hip harkening back to the late fifties.

"What's up with your neighbors across the hall?" I asked. "When did they leave?"

She sniffed. "Yesterday. Banks Placement Services, although a few months ago Aaron put a little addition to the name on the door that said Magical Interventions. No idea what the heck that was about. Maybe he'd decided to become a part-time psychic or something. The placement company seemed to be doing a good business, so I was surprised."

"Why did they move?" Irix asked.

Clearly they were still getting funds transferred into their bank account. Maybe their lease had run out, but I suspected Aaron Banks had a different motive to pulling up shop.

"I assumed they were getting a bigger place or a better address, but when I asked where they were going, they said they were temporarily closing up shop."

"They?" I asked.

"Aaron took on a partner about the time that stupid Magical Interventions sign went on the door."

Irix and I exchanged knowing glances.

"You guys the cops?" the woman asked.

Irix's eyebrows shot up. "No, why?"

"Because I think maybe they were up to something. Aaron's been in business for seven years, renting that office space over there and he's always done okay, but then he gets this new partner and suddenly they're flush with cash. Then abruptly they're throwing files and furniture into a rental truck, and running like the devil himself is after them. Embezzlement? Organized crime connections? Got on the wrong side of a gang?"

"All of the above," Irix said. "Did you ever meet the partner?"

"Once. Aaron did all the client-facing work from what I could see but the partner came in to meet with him one day. Snooty guy. Tall, thin, long blond hair, accent I couldn't place. I took him for some Eurotrash snob."

"Pointy ears?" I asked.

She laughed. "What, one of those elves everyone's talking about but no one has seen? I didn't see any pointy ears, but the one time I saw him he was wearing a hat. And he did have that long hair."

They were on the run, no doubt from two pissed-off plague demons. But they were greedy, so they'd be leaving an electronic trail to wherever they went. It gave me an idea.

"Do you have any idea where either one lived?" It was a long shot, but I figured she could find out quicker than Wyatt could. She was a PI after all. And there was a good chance at the very least Aaron Banks hadn't completely skipped town yet. He'd been in business in the area for a long time. Even if he didn't have family and kids he'd need to uproot, at the very least he had a house and possessions that he wouldn't want to just abandon, especially if he'd started spending all of that money on cars and boats and flashy clothing.

"No idea on the partner. Heck, I don't even know his name. But I did watch Aaron's cat for a week once." She wrote down an address on a sticky note, ripped it from the stack and handed me the hot-pink paper. "It's for sale, but I'm sure the real estate agent knows how to get in contact with him."

We thanked her and headed out to the car, then I looked up the address on Zillow and called the agent. The property was vacant and still for sale, I set up a showing that I had no intention of going to, and when I enquired about why the previous owner had moved, she claimed he'd bought something larger out in the suburbs.

Property search with the registrar of deeds in the two adjacent counties within a six-month time frame, and bingo. Address for a property purchased by Aaron Banks three weeks ago. And holy shit, he was moving up in the world. Aaron would be reluctant to run out on a house like that after shelling out a fortune on it. I was betting that he was either still living there and hoping no one could trace him to the new house, or he was keeping a hold on it and hiding out in some hotel. In which case, there would be lawn crew or neighbors who knew how to reach him in case something happened to his beautiful new digs.

"You're just as good as your brother," Irix commented as he watched me work my magic with the cell phone.

"Nah. This is all public record stuff. Wyatt gets the stuff that's not public record. He hacks into bank accounts and medical information, and DMV records and corporate payroll systems."

And that gave me another idea. I sent a quick text asking Wyatt to do something truly illegal—reverse all of the money that had been auto-paid from all accounts to the placement service one, then block any future transfers. If anything was going to get these guys' attention, it was draining their bank account. Plus, it gave me a sense of satisfaction to know that these elves who'd been working their butts off and living on jars of pickles and dried fruit would suddenly have their money back.

Then I gave him Aaron Banks's old and new addresses and asked him to dig through the cell phone services in the area and find his number. I doubted the man would be using a burner phone, since he'd want his clients and friends to be able to get a hold of him. Everyone always envisioned quickly going off the grid and vanishing if bad guys came a-calling, but that was difficult to do on a moment's notice, and darned near impossible to do long-term. Auto registration to keep tags from becoming expired. Driver's licenses. And don't get me started on trying to keep everything cash-under-the-table. Unless a person went and lived in a tent under a bridge and ate out of a garbage can, or set up shop in the middle of the wilderness and grew all their own food, they were going to eventually ping somewhere on the great electronic highway. And I couldn't see Aaron Banks, or any regular person, opting for either of those two scenarios.

Irix and I went to get dinner, and by the time we were done, Wyatt was calling me.

He was laughing when I picked up the phone. "You've got no idea how satisfying that funds reversal was. I'm texting you Aaron Banks's phone number now."

I thanked Wyatt, then looked over at Irix. "We need to make a trip, after I make one quick phone call."

Dialing the number Wyatt had just given me, I left a message. "Hi Aaron. You don't know me but I'm about to save your life. Check your company bank account. You've got no money, and some really bad guys on your ass. We don't want you, we want your elven partner, Gallette." I listed the address of a remote location and told the man to meet us there in thirty minutes. Then I told Irix to drive to Aaron Banks's new home.

"Not the address you just gave him?" Irix asked.

"Nope. He won't show up. He's too scared. But with all of his accounts drained to zero, he's going to need cash. I'm willing to bet he's at least got a few thousand stashed in his house. He'll grab what he can, run away, and hope he can stay away until all this settles down."

Irix shook his head. "You missed your calling. Forget botany, you should have been a PI."

We parked a few houses down and waited until Aaron Banks arrived. The man raced inside, and was back out in five minutes, stuffing something into his pants pocket as he jogged toward his car.

My plan was to follow him in our car, but evidently Irix had another idea. Hopping out of the BMW, the incubus strolled over as if he were a neighbor out for a walk while I hissed for him to get his ass back in the car. Banks hesitated, tensing when he saw Irix. Then the man relaxed, his lips turning up in an odd smile as he returned Irix's wave and pivoted to get into the car.

Pheromones, helping sex demons get laid and make friends everywhere we went. Right behind the man, Irix jumped forward, grabbed him and kissed him soundly, simultaneously sending a jolt of electricity through him.

Yeah, I could clearly see it, and I desperately hoped that other neighbors weren't watching as Aaron Banks twitched and jerked in Irix's arms, his head dropping limp onto the incubus's shoulder when he'd broken their kiss.

Scooping the man up in his arms, Irix dramatically carried him to our car. Then he crammed the man into the back seat, climbed in, shutting the car door and sitting on the human.

"Drive."

I choked back a laugh and slid over to the driver's seat, pulling the car out of the subdivision. Seconds later our captive regained consciousness and began to squirm under Irix's weight, all the while loudly accusing us of kidnapping and offering to pay us anything, do anything as long as we didn't give him to the demons.

He knew. Which meant he knew a lot of other things too

—things that would be very helpful for us in trying to track down the elf responsible for this mess.

It was getting late. From Irix's directions he clearly intended to take our captive back to my little trailer to interrogate. And while we were both fully capable of coaxing this man's secrets from him, I wanted someone else there. I wanted the one person who'd been personally affected by this man's scheme, who had watched a friend die at the hands of plague demons, whose entire future was tied up in this man's company.

About to add to the growing list of illegal things I'd done today, I picked up the phone and called Hallwyn.

CHAPTER 24

"Irix, we can't just kidnap someone like this. What if the neighborhood had security cameras outside? You're going to get arrested," I whispered.

We were back in the trailer with Aaron Banks securely taped to one of my kitchen chairs. The closer we'd gotten to my home, the more I realized we were going to be in serious trouble. Kidnapping. Assault. And what the heck were we going to do with this man once we were done questioning him? We could hardly let him go or kill him, but I didn't like the idea of sleeping just fifteen feet from a human duct-taped to my kitchen chair.

Irix cocked an eyebrow at me. "Seriously? I spend hundreds of years evading angels and you're worried that a bunch of humans is going to haul me off to prison? If they saw anything it was a romantic embrace between two lovers."

"Then they saw you carry an unconscious body to a waiting vehicle, stuff it into the back seat, then climb in and sit on it while I drove off. Lovely."

He grinned. "You're more worried about yourself getting arrested than me, aren't you?"

"Yes. Yes, I am."

"Is this him?" Hallwyn interjected. She'd burst through the door, breathless and practically glowing with anger, then stood, juggling her weight from foot to foot while she waited impatiently for us to stop arguing.

"Yes, this is Aaron Banks, the human half of the placement firm—"

I gasped as Hallwyn backhanded the guy across the face. The blow was forceful enough to rock the man's head to the side. I'll give him credit, he didn't do more than grunt in response.

"Callia is dead because of you," she snapped.

"I don't know who Callia is. I run a legitimate placement firm. All I've done is help a bunch of elves get jobs for a fee. It's legal. And it's a complete win-win. You elves get off that island and get a well-paying job, the businesses get an employee with a special skill set, and we get a placement fee. No different than filling a job opening for an accountant or marketing specialist. Completely legal. Completely above board. Same thing, just a special skill set."

"What special skill set?" I asked. "Hallwyn and the others have no skill in agriculture, yet they've been placed in jobs where they're expected to heal plants and ensure a good harvest."

"That wasn't my job," he argued. "I handled the client side, and Gallette handles the elf side. He told me that he wanted clients who were in healthcare and agribusiness, so that's what I got him. He was in charge of screening the resumes and selecting the applicants."

"Then why were you running?" Irix asked.

He paled. "I'm not running."

"Your office is cleaned out. I'm willing to bet if we knocked on doors around your new home, we'd find you had told the neighbors you were away on an extended vacation. In another two days, your bank account would have been conveniently empty and closed. Luckily we beat you to that last one."

"I *am* going on vacation. And we're relocating the office. I've done nothing illegal. You, on the other hand, have done something illegal. You've stolen money from my accounts, kidnapped me, and are now holding me against my will."

"We haven't killed you." Hallwyn's eyes narrowed. "Yet."

The man paled. "I haven't done anything illegal, I swear it. I'm sorry if you're not happy with the job you have. I'll work to get you something else. Just let me go and I'll get you a different job. I've got a job at an apple orchard, or if you're not into that sort of thing, I can see if you qualify for one of my other openings."

"And how much more would that cost me?" the elf shrieked. "One, two years' salary? And if I end up fired from that job, you'll make me perform disgusting sexual acts for humans or give them my kidneys?"

"No! It's not… It's all legal. I swear it. No prostitution or illegal sales of body parts. I run a placement company. I'll get you another job."

"If everything your company is doing is so above-board and legal, then why were you begging me not to turn you over to the demons?" Irix asked.

His eyes shifted to the right. "What demons? What are you talking about?"

Irix sighed. "When you were yelling in the car about being kidnapped, you offered to pay us, to do anything as long as we didn't turn you over to the demons."

The man set his jaw and clamped his lips together.

"Speak, or I will rip your fingers off one at a time until you do."

I eyed Hallwyn with concern, not certain if the elf truly

meant her threat or was channeling some inner super-spy interrogator.

Aaron glanced up at her in alarm. "Look, I'm just a recruiter. It's my job. I find out what openings businesses have, then find the right people for those jobs. This elf approached me a few months back with a business opportunity. I figured we'd make a good partnership, but no one was interested in hiring elves at this time. I wanted to let it go at that, figuring that eventually we'd find a business willing to take a chance then we'd be off and running, because according to Gallette, elves are the best workers ever."

"Well, we are," Hallwyn said.

"But Gallette couldn't wait, so he made a deal with these two demons to just stir things up a bit, to create a circumstance where companies would want to take a chance and hire an elf. It worked, and business took off. I wasn't thrilled about people getting sick or crops catching mold and stuff, but Gallette told me that it was minor and temporary, that the new employees would soon set things to right and would prove so valuable to these companies that everyone would be demanding an elf of their own. We'd have bidding wars. We'd be rich."

"And what did the demons get out of this deal?" Irix asked.

"I don't know. I didn't have anything to do with them. But I told Gallette that we didn't need them anymore. We're getting traction on the elf placements. I didn't like the idea of using those demons anyway, and there was no further need for them."

Irix sighed and rubbed a hand through his hair. "They were getting cut out of the deal. Whatever Gallette had offered them, they weren't going to get more if they were cut out of any future deals."

Aaron swallowed hard. "All I know is the demons are

pissed. They're screwing things up. We already had two elves on the verge of getting fired because the demons were continuing to mess with those two farms and the companies thought the elves weren't doing their jobs."

"What happened to those elves?" I asked, dreading his answer.

He shrugged. "All I know is the companies are demanding their placement fees back. I guess they quit and took off somewhere."

"They can't quit," Hallwyn snapped. "The Jobber has us so far in debt to him that we're practically slaves. We pay him to get these jobs, pay him to set us up with apartments, a vehicle and furnishings, we pay him a portion of our earnings. If we quit or get fired, we need to pay up or he'll find a way for us to pay it off."

Aaron winced. "I swear I don't know what happened to them. They were on the verge of getting fired. Maybe they ran away rather than have to deal with Gallette or go back to Elf Island."

"Who are they?" Hallwyn demanded. "What are their names?"

"Eller, and Mahal. I didn't hurt them. I wouldn't do that."

Hallwyn typed the two names into her phone. "No, you just turned them over to Gallette to be sent back to Elf Island, or worse."

He shook his head. "I didn't even know they were gone until the companies called me wanting their placement fee back, I offered to get them a different elf. That's usually how we handle placements that don't work out, but these companies didn't want us to fill the job. They were really unhappy with the quality of the elven work, said that the employees didn't have the skills that they were supposed to have. Gallette and I had a huge falling out over it. He's in charge of screening the applicants and selecting the right elf for the job. His screwing that up was tarnishing our company's reputation. It wasn't just having to refund the fee, that kind of word gets out, and no one will do business with me—either Magical Interventions *or* Banks's Placement Services."

"The right elf is the one that pays the most for the job," Hallwyn interjected. "That's how he's selecting them, and we're so desperate to get off the island we'll take anything, sign anything."

"Your company is going to go out of business," I warned him. "Gallette's taking bribes and selling the jobs to the highest bidding elf, and now, with the plague demons angry at him, even the elves who could do the job they were hired to do are going to fail. Every vine Hallwyn heals at DiMarche is dead of rot the next day. The vineyard is going to go under, and they'll fire her before they do. Your business will be ruined, your reputation ruined, and along the way these plague demons are laying waste to Northern California."

"He said he's taking care of that," Aaron protested. "Gallette said we needed to close shop and lay low. The demons would get bored and leave or be caught by the angels, then the elves can work their magic. Two months tops, then we'd be back in business. And he promised me that he'd do a better job of screening the applicants."

Such bullshit. The plague demons wouldn't leave until everything, and everyone, was dead, just out of revenge against Gallette, and with the angels busy, there was no guarantee they'd be stopped in time. The elf would just start over in a new town with a new placement firm partner, leaving this portion of the state destroyed, elven lives destroyed, and Aaron Banks's business destroyed. We didn't have time to wait.

"We need to find Gallette," I told Aaron. "This area is going to be wiped off the map with plague and pestilence, and you're going to go down with the rest of it. You'll never see him again."

He hesitated. "But he promised. He's got money tied up in this, too. It's his reputation, too."

"No, it's not. He's got the contacts with the angels. It would be easy for him to start working with someone else and just fill job openings in Virginia, or Texas, or even Iowa with elven employees. He doesn't need you. And if he's learned enough about your end of the business, he might not even need a human partner."

"I've lived here my whole life," Aaron confessed. "I've built this business up from the ground floor, made it into something I could be proud of. I didn't like the idea of using the plague demons, but it was just supposed to be temporary. Gallette was supposed to have everything under control." The man shook his head. "I should have never trusted him, but it seemed like such a great and innovative business opportunity, and the money was pouring in. I didn't realize he was defrauding my clients, or putting the whole northern part of the state in danger."

"It's not enough to stop the demons," I told him. "We need to stop Gallette. It's one thing to find elves a job that suitable to their skills and earn a placement fee, but it's horrible to put these elves so far in debt that they'll never get out, and it's not fair to the companies or the elves to put unqualified applicants into these jobs, to fill the openings based on who pays the biggest bribes. We need to stop him."

Aaron's eyes narrowed. "But there's still a need for finding these elves jobs, right?"

"Of course," Hallwyn said. "It's the only way we can get off Elf Island. We need to find employment that allows us to be of service to the humans and assist in their positive evolution. And every one of us wants to get off that island."

"Then I have a proposal here. I'll work with you, I'll tell

you everything I know about Gallette and the demons. I'll help you, and in return I'll be the primary placement firm for the elves."

"How about you tell us everything and we don't kill you?" Irix asked.

"No, he has a point," Hallwyn said. "We do need a Jobber, but we need one who understands the human world, understands what human companies want and need in employees. If he agrees to do this with only the placement fee, and ensures that elves are given employment opportunities in line with their skills, then I am willing to make a deal with this man."

Aaron looked over at Irix and me for confirmation.

"It's up to her," Irix said. "As I've said from the beginning, it's not our problem. If she wants to make a deal with this man, then I'll go along with it."

"Okay. Deal. I'll need to figure out who Gallette's contact is on Elf Island because I think they're going to be shuffling some angels around, but you'll be the go-to guy for job placements. If at any time you're not holding up your end of the deal, or if it's discovered that you're skimming off the top or not being honest, then the deal is off. Got it?"

He nodded. "I'll need my phone."

Irix cut the duct tape around Aaron's hands and I handed him the cell phone we'd confiscated from his pants. He sent a quick text and seconds later the phone rang.

"It's all gone," Aaron said without any greeting. "Our bank account is cleaned out to zero. I need to meet you."

There was the murmur of Gallette's response.

"No, I need to meet you. There's no money. I can't 'lay low' for two months without any money, and I doubt you can either. It's payday. All the transfers from the elves were supposed to happen today. As soon as they hit, the money was yanked out. We need these plague demons off our backs.

Whether they're the ones behind the embezzlement or not, they need to stop messing with our clients right now, not in two months."

Gallette responded and Aaron shot us a grimace. I held my breath, afraid to say anything because I knew how sensitive elven hearing was.

"I'll work with the bank to try to find out what happened to the money, but in the meantime we need to deal with these plague demons. What do they want? A bigger cut? What?"

Aaron nodded as Gallette's voice rattled on. I looked to Hallwyn, knowing she could hear the other end of the conversation and saw her lip curl into a sneer. I'd initially thought her a snobby jerk, then someone who cried at every obstacle, but now I was seeing the violent side of the elf. Was she crazy? These mood swings of hers were worrying me a bit.

"I need to meet you. I don't care, I want to meet you in person so we can figure out what to do." Aaron hung up and turned to us. "Gallette is going to make a few calls and see if he can't get rid of the plague demons. He'll call me in the next two days and let me know what's going on."

I shook my head in frustration. We needed to get our hands on Gallette. Irix duct taped the man once more, gagging him with a dishtowel to still his protests. Then he waved for Hallwyn and me to step outside the cabin.

"This has got to be the most poorly planned project in all my life," he scolded, waving a finger at me.

"Hey, I wasn't the one who *kidnapped* the guy. I'd just wanted to follow him and see if he'd lead us to Gallette."

"And do what? Are you going to try to kill Gallette?" he asked.

"Yes," Hallwyn said.

"No," I responded at the same time. The elf glared at me.

"I've got a good idea how things worked in Hel, but that's not the way the humans run things here. We don't just kill people. Or elves."

"Then put him in jail," Hallwyn retorted. "I don't care if he's dead or in prison, I just don't want him taking all of our money, and threatening us with a return to Elf Island or becoming a nasty human's sex toy if we lose our jobs or can't pay him."

I narrowed my eyes in thought, but couldn't come up with anything that Gallette had done that would get him arrested. Predatory lending was more of a civil and contract law kind of thing, not the sort of crime that would put him in jail. Which meant someone besides the humans needed to deliver the punishment.

"I'll ask Sam to send one of the angels from Elf Island to take him away. He's running around loose without their permission. He's doing things I'm pretty sure most angels would object to. They can take him back and deal with him."

Hallwyn stared at me as though I were an idiot. "He's dealing with an angel on Elf Island. That's how he gets the jobs posted and arranges to have the employed elves allowed off the island. They're all working together."

"I've got a feeling there are a few rotten apples in the angel barrel that are working with him. If not, they still won't be pleased that he's working with plague demons, placing unqualified elves in positions, and selling jobs to the highest bidder. Let alone the sex-slave thing."

Although I wasn't sure if the sex-slave thing was true or something out of Hallwyn's very vivid imagination.

"So we ask for an angel to take Gallette away once the guy in there can finally arrange a meeting," Irix summed up. "After he's out of the picture, that Aaron guy takes over the placements and somehow deals with the angels on Elf Island. And the plague demons wander off back to Hel since the elf they're pissed at is now in the hands of the angels. Am I missing anything here?"

I glanced at Hallwyn, then back to Irix. "Uh, no. Sounds pretty much what I had in mind."

Irix folded his arms across his chest. "Lovely. And the guy we have duct taped to a chair? What do we do with him in the meantime? Leave him there for the next two days until Gallette gets back to us? Trust him not to sell us out and let him go?"

"We can't let him go." I bit my lip. "I guess we just leave him taped to the chair?"

Irix pulled his keys out of his pocket and headed for the car. "Hey," I called out. "Where are you going?"

"To get dinner for us—all of us. And to make a phone call. I love you Amber, but your plan has more holes in it than a fire-balled Low. I promised I'd trust you, that I'd treat you like an adult and respect your need to do things on your own, but just in case all this shit falls apart, I'm putting together a backup plan."

"I'm not adverse to a backup plan," I shouted as he opened the door to the BMW.

"Good," he shouted back.

Hallwyn and I watched him drive away. "Should we go back in?" I asked, worried that Aaron may have some hidden James Bond abilities that meant he was right now sawing through the duct tape with his fingernails or something.

"Can we punch him a few times?" Hallwyn eyed the door.

Sheesh. Crying one day, wanting to beat up everyone the next. This stray-puppy elf of mine was weird. "No, we can't punch him, but I've got an idea for what we can do."

CHAPTER 25

My idea of torture was making Aaron watch endless Spongebob Squarepants cartoons, but unfortunately that meant that Hallwyn and I also needed to watch them, so as soon as Irix returned, we turned off the television and dug into the containers of Chinese food. Hallwyn proved to be a quick learner with the chopsticks, and we let Aaron loose to stretch his limbs and eat with us after warning him that Hallwyn was elf-fast and if he tried to escape, she'd be on him before he was two steps out the door.

It was late and I wanted to go to bed, but that posed yet another problem.

"Duct tape him to the chair again," Hallwyn proposed. "I'll take the first shift on the couch, and we can alternate."

"I'm not taking a shift," Irix said, making his way back to the bedroom. "You two work it out."

I gave Hallwyn my most pitiful look. "I didn't get any sleep at all last night. As in zero hours of sleep." I didn't really want to tell her that my sleepless night was due to some hot swinger action with a couple in the neighboring town.

"I won't be able to work tomorrow if I stay up all night and watch this stupid human," she protested.

"I can watch myself," Aaron suggested. "In fact, if you let me sleep on the sofa and not duct tape me to the chair, I promise I won't run away."

"No." I scowled at him, wondering if I should use the dish towel gag again. "You don't get to go free until Gallette is gone and we're sure you won't betray us."

"Fine," Hallwyn scowled. "I'll stay up and watch him tonight, but tomorrow night is your turn. And no having sex with that demon tonight. I have very good hearing and I don't want to have to sit here and listen to the pair of you fornicating like animals."

I was tempted to have noisy, hair-pulling, screaming-orgasm sex with Irix just to annoy her, but I was too tired. "Deal."

When I got up at dawn to shower and get ready for work, I found both Hallwyn and Aaron asleep. Aaron looked horribly uncomfortable slumped in his chair, but Hallwyn was curled up in a ball on the sofa, a bath towel wrapped around her like a blanket.

"Hey," I whispered, gently shaking her shoulder. "I'm heading out. Feel free to use the shower."

She sat up, rubbing her eyes. "Your couch smells like blood and semen."

Yeah, well there was a good reason for that.

"I'll run home after work to shower," she continued. "Your bathroom has too much metal in it. I'm afraid to touch anything."

I grabbed a box of donuts from the kitchen for us to eat on the walk to the vineyard, and poured some coffee to-go for the pair of us. As we were getting ready to leave, Irix stumbled into the room, sleepy-eyed with bed head—and completely naked. Hallwyn rolled her eyes but didn't seem phased at his nudity. I guess it was the sex acts she was offended by and not the actual body parts involved.

"You're not leaving," he told us, his voice rough with sleep.

"We're going to work," I replied. "We'll be back around three."

"No, you won't. I'm not sitting here and watching this guy all day for you. I need to go out and hunt. Besides, this is your project, not mine. I made all those phone calls yesterday, kidnapped the guy for you and went out to get Chinese food last night. That's the extent of my contribution. I'm leaving. I'd suggest one of you either stay here to watch him, or figure out something else."

Jerk.

"We could kill him," Hallwyn suggested. "But then I guess we wouldn't be able to find Gallette."

"I promise I'll stay here." Aaron twisted his neck and I heard it pop. The guy had to be stiff as a block of cement after being duct taped to a chair for six hours.

Of the pair of us, I had to be in to work later. "Go on," I told Hallwyn. "I'll stay behind."

That way I could let Aaron stretch his legs, and perhaps work some begging, pleading, blow job action on Irix and get him to at least take watch duty for half the day.

Hallwyn grabbed a donut from the box I was holding, then we all froze as a cell phone rang. Shit. Shit! It was Aaron's and his hands were duct taped. We all scurried around, me cutting the tape from the guy's hands and throwing the scraps onto the growing pile on the floor while Hallwyn grabbed his phone and pushed the answer button, holding it to his ear as he shook out his numb hands.

There was a mumble of words. Aaron and Hallwyn's eyes grew big. The elf shook her head.

"No. It's too early to meet at the bank," Aaron replied.

"They're not open and I'm not even in Sonoma. Meet me at Santor Winery. Their elf died and they need me to fill out some paperwork."

More mumbling, although this time it sounded like mumbled shouting.

"Look, we're broke. There's no money in the bank and two of our clients won't work with us again. Santor wants us to place another elf with them. We need their business. And they have some life insurance thing on their employees. I need to get it to the dead elf's next-of-kin to fill out."

There were a half-second of silence, then thoughtful mumbling.

Aaron rolled his eyes. "Yes, it's a lot of money. And obviously you need to take the form with you since you're the only one who knows who the elf's next-of-kin is. I'll meet you there, get you the form, and we'll discuss this situation."

Aaron pushed a button on the phone and handed it back to Hallwyn.

"Is that true?" I asked him.

"Yeah, actually it is. I was going to have Santor Winery just mail the forms to me, but I figured it would be a good way to flush Gallette out of hiding. They do want another elf placed there, and I'd planned to swing by today on my way out of town."

Life insurance. I was willing to bet Gallette had never thought of such a thing. We really needed to get him in the custody of the angels, because once he figured this out, he was likely to go killing off every elf he placed, just to collect on the policies.

"What time?" Hallwyn asked, setting the phone on the counter and taking a bite out of the donut.

"We've got an hour. We're meeting in one of their fields."

"I'm coming along." Hallwyn crammed the remaining part

of the donut into her mouth. "I'll call in and tell Jorge I need the day off."

Good, because I got the feeling the elf would come in handy in a fight against Gallette.

"I'm coming, too." Irix scowled. "Let me get a shower first. And I'm driving."

I handed him a donut and my coffee, giving him a quick kiss. "Thank you."

"Yeah, right. Like I'd let you face this guy with only an elf to protect you."

Irix headed into the bathroom. Hallwyn stepped outside. I freed Aaron and offered him a donut. Then I called in to work, and sat down to make one more call.

"Sam? I need an angel. And yes, this satisfies the extra favor you owed me."

* * *

"WHERE'S THE FORM? I'm still working on the plague demons, but maybe I can manage to fill this spot at Santor in the meantime." Gallette looked at me then did a double take, staring at my ears.

"This is my girlfriend, Amber," Aaron said, smiling weakly. His hands were sweating all over the life insurance forms.

The elf shook his head. "For two hundred thousand, I could have gotten you a real elf, instead of this ugly human lookalike."

"I don't want a real elf." Aaron switched the papers to his other hand, wiping the one on his pants leg. "Is that what happened to the other two elves? The ones that were about to be canned but went missing?"

Gallette laughed. "I wish. I went by their place as soon as you told me they were losing their jobs, but they'd already run away. They'll eventually turn up. Now, the death-payment papers...what do I need to fill out to get the money?"

Where was the angel Sam was sending? I wasn't sure Aaron could drag this meeting out much longer.

"Here. The next-of-kin needs to fill this out. I'm not sure how quick the process will be since elves don't have the paperwork that human insurance companies require. I guess the elves will help?"

He took the papers, grimacing at the sweat stains. "No, humans will help. I'll give them a cut, and in a few days I'll be..." he glanced at the papers, "...I'll be Callia's brother, or husband, or father. I wish I'd have known about this earlier. These elves are worth more dead than alive."

Asshole. Gallette turned to leave and I panicked.. He needed to stay just a bit longer, just until the angel got here.

"You need to die."

The elf stopped, his head swiveling slowly to the side. Aaron's and mine did the same. A few feet away stood Hallwyn, her body shaking with rage.

"You place us in jobs where we have no skills. You drain us of all our income, basically enslaving us. You turn plague demons loose on our employers, threatening both our jobs and our lives. Callia died because of you, and here you are to steal what should rightfully go to her family."

Gallette grinned. "No one forced you to sign that contract. And Callia died owing me a lot of money. Her debt doesn't go away when she dies. This,"... he waved the papers, "...this will help pay it off. The rest will continue to accrue interest until her family can manage to get jobs and work off her debt in addition to their own."

Hallwyn's hands formed fists. "You have no loyalty, no honor. I, Hallwyn of Wythyn, sentence you to death."

He laughed. "Try, little one. You'll never take me alone,

and when I kill you, that will just be one more life insurance policy I can collect on."

Aaron turned and ran. Irix appeared by my side to grab me and pull me backward. I struggled, not wanting to leave Hallwyn to face this asshole alone, to most certainly die in this fight.

"But I am not alone," Hallwyn spat out. All around us elves materialized from the grapevines. This time I did let Irix yank me backward, out of the circle they were forming.

For an instant, Gallette looked shaken, then he stood tall, tucking the papers into the back of his waistband and bringing his hands forward. Fireballs shot from his fingers, deflected by the two elves in front of him. The dirt at our feet rumbled and shifted, a hole forming right where Gallette stood. He pushed his hands downward, a silvery light flowing from them.

The ground pulsed, and the elves closed in, tightening their circle and chanting. Roots emerged like tentacles to wrap around Gallette and pull him downward. He struggled, silver light burning the roots to ash as they tightened on his body and firmed the ground at his feet. I held my breath, safe in Irix's arms as I watched a dozen elves continue to work their magic, slowly overwhelming Gallette's counter attack until all I could see was a mass of dark brown roots, like a cocoon, with bursts of silver light coming from the center.

There was a muffled scream and a crunching sound, then the silvery light faded and all that remained was the giant cocoon of roots.

Two of the elves put out the embers from the deflected fireball, then they all vanished into the vines, leaving Irix and Hallwyn and me.

The elf walked over to the cocoon of roots and punched it, sending it toppling to the ground. "There. I've been wanting to do that since I got here."

"How did…where did…" I stammered.

Hallwyn turned to smile at me, brushing the dirt from her hands. "The day I came to work and realized that I was unable to perform my job, I began to track down all the elves in the area. We need to stick together, to help each other. That's the only way we're going to be able to make it in this human world. I know you want me to make human friends, but I also think we need to form an elven community, to come together to discuss challenges and think of solutions. And to take care of problems like this piece of durft dung here." She motioned to the cocoon.

I wasn't sure how I felt about this. Elves coming together as a community sounded fine, but it was one step from elves banding together to attempt another overthrow of the human world. But that was a problem for the angels.

And speaking of angels. "I'm really pissed at Sam. She promised me an angel would be here."

There was a flash of light, and before us stood a being with huge wings, the feathers a gradient of purple hues. He was pretty—really, really pretty. Like, pretty enough to be a male model in a magazine.

He bowed, and I caught a flash of mischief in his violet eyes before his dark hair spilled over them.

"I'm here to collect a naughty elf."

"Well, you're ten minutes late," I told him. Nicely, because he *was* an angel and I didn't want to piss him off, late or not.

A watch suddenly appeared on his wrist and he frowned at it. "Sam said nine forty-five. I'm actually here five minutes early, which is a miracle. I'm never early to anything except dinner."

I'd told Sam nine thirty. That imp was so owing me another favor for this.

Hallwyn waved a hand at the cocoon. "The elf is in there. Actually, I'd appreciate it if you took him away since I don't know how the winery will react to having a dead, entombed elf in their vineyard."

The angel approached the cocoon and shuddered. "Eww. You squashed him. Oh well, makes him easier to transport." He looked around at the three of us. "Well then, I'm off."

He waved a hand at the cocoon, and with a flash of light, they were gone.

Hallwyn sighed, her shoulders drooping. "I'm glad that's over with."

But it wasn't. The Jobber was gone, and these elves were no longer bound under his draconian contracts. But we still had two plague demons to deal with, and I wasn't sure Gallette's demise would be enough to stop their efforts to lay waste to DiMarche and all of Northern California.

CHAPTER 26

Hallwyn and I both went into work late. I succumbed to Matthieu's advances after work, just so I could pull additional energy from him through our tie, then detoured through the vineyard on my way back to the trailer, hoping to catch Hallwyn before she staggered home.

Her car was still in the parking lot, a golf cart visible out in a distant field.

"Hey," I called to her, jogging up the row of vines. "Thought you would have left by now."

"I wanted to catch up, since I came in so late." The elf looked horrible, dark circles under her eyes, bits of hair loose from her usually neat braids and tangled around her ears. "Besides, with Gallette gone, I'm hoping the plague demons will leave and I'll be able to actually make progress in healing these vines."

I eyed the angle of the sun. "Promise me you'll leave at sunset? I don't want you to get caught out here alone in case the plague demons don't leave."

Actually I didn't want her out here alone right now either,

but I knew how stubborn she could be. And yep, there was the iron set to her jaw as she looked up at me.

"I cannot promise that. I'll work until I'm tired, then I'll go home."

She was tired now. "Can I at least bring you some dinner?"

That perked her up. "If there is any of that noodle and vegetable dish from last night, I would truly enjoy some of that. And the rolls of egg."

I jogged back home, raiding through the refrigerator and heating up the leftovers. I was just putting them all in a box to carry along with a few bottles of water when Irix came through the door. He sighed when he saw what I was doing.

"Stray puppy?"

"She's working late. She was up all night guarding Aaron, then fought Gallette, then went straight into work. I don't think she's eaten more than a donut today. She's hungry and exhausted."

He took the box from my hands. "Well, come on then. Let's go feed her."

We walked to the fields, the green leaves rustling in the breeze, the fruit full and thick on the vines. It was going to be okay. It was all going to be okay. I kept telling myself that, repeating it like a mantra just to make sure it was true.

"Do you think Txipa and Apixt went back to Hel? Or went somewhere else to spread their ick?"

I wanted to believe it was all going to be okay, but there was something deep inside me that knew the plague demons were still out there, that feared they were having too much fun, that this had become more than revenge to them, it had become an obsessive hobby.

"I don't know. I spread the word around town that Gallette was dead, and that his human partner had taken off. I even stopped by the ice cream shop. No one has seen them since last night. That's a good sign, but we won't know for a week or two."

If Hallwyn's healing wasn't reversed, if all the blight and the epidemics lessened, knocked back by human medicines, then we'd know they were gone. But I still wanted Hallwyn to be out of this field by nightfall.

The elf was thrilled to see us, sitting on the ground and devouring the leftovers while Irix and I kept her company. After she'd finished every last scrap, I packed the box with the garbage and gave her a stern shake of my finger.

"Now go home and get some sleep. These vines will be waiting for you in the morning. It won't do either you or them any good to keep working as exhausted as you are."

She gave me a soft smile, her eyelids half-shut already. "I'll finish this last plant, then I'll head home."

"Pinky promise?"

"I have no idea what that means, but yes, pinky promise."

I shook my finger again, just for good measure. "Text me when you get home so I know you're safe, okay?"

"Bossy human," she teased. "Yes, I will text you."

We left her to her vines—her vines, not my vines. As much as I still felt a responsibility toward this vineyard, I'd recognized that these plants were now hers. I was just an intern. I'd leave at the end of the summer while she'd remain behind to finish out the harvest, prune back the vines for winter, and continue to nurture them through another year.

Irix pulled the box from my hands and put it up on his shoulder, freeing one arm to drape around my shoulders. "You're good at this stray puppy thing."

It was a mothering thing. And that thought twisted my heart.

"Once we get settled in New Orleans, maybe we'll get a dog," Irix teased.

Was that one step away from a child? I didn't want to

push him. I didn't want to be *that* girlfriend, always hounding him for a ring, a wedding, kids.

"Maybe we could have a baby?" I couldn't help it. He and Harkel would most likely be having a demon together. Why not us? Why not *me*?

Irix sucked in a deep breath. "Our child would be three-quarters demon, Amber. We do pretty well walking among the humans as a couple, but it would be very difficult to raise a demon-child here. The first time he electrocuted one of the neighbors, or burned down a church, or at the age of five seduced his Kindergarten teacher…?"

I remembered my own childhood, how I'd killed my human father accidently on purpose because I was five and angry and had no idea what power I'd held inside of myself. The memory, the guilt, still haunted me. Irix was right, but I still felt the sting of tears at the thought that we'd never share that bond of raising a child together—our child.

"Maybe a dog then—"

"If you want a child with me, then we'll make it happen. Someday. In the future once we figure out how we can make it work, or we can go to Hel and raise it among the demons."

My heart jumped with hope. "No dwarven nannies? No demon foster-care?"

He chuckled. "No demon foster-care, although trust me, you'll probably be begging me for a dwarven nanny after the first week. Demon children are a handful."

Yes, but this would be *our* demon child. "Thank you for not saying no."

He sat the box beside the trailer door and took me in his arms. "I have a very hard time saying no to you. And honestly, I love the idea of creating with you. I love the thought of us planning what we want for our child, the long gestation period to anticipate, the joy of a being that is a part of you and a part of me. I just want to make sure that you're aware of all the challenges, and the way a demon-child would change our lives."

I reached up to twine my arms around him. "Not now. Later. I do want to have a child with you eventually, but for a while, I'd like to have you all to myself."

He fitted me against him, his hands tangling in my hair. "Good, because I'd like to have you all to myself. Starting right now."

CHAPTER 27

It was the fifth time I'd checked my phone, and still no word from Hallwyn. Irix and I had dozed off after making love, and I'd woken around ten at night, an hour after sunset, worried that I hadn't heard the familiar beep of my phone receiving a text. I'd sent her a message, then waited, then sent another message.

If I woke Irix, he'd tell me to go back to sleep. He'd tell me that Hallwyn was a grown elf, fully capable to taking care of herself. He'd tell me that she probably got home and fell asleep before her head hit the pillow, forgetting to text me. He'd forbid me from going out in the dark of the vineyards to look for her.

So I didn't wake him. Putting his cell phone next to him on the pillow and turning the volume up so he'd hear it if I called for help, I snuck out to find Hallwyn, walking up and down the rows and tracking her to the far end of the vineyard. The night was overcast, and with the lack of lighting in the field, I was barely able to see more than a few feet ahead of me. Hallwyn could easily navigate the vineyard with her elven eyesight, but I stumbled over rocks and roots, cursing softly under my breath each time.

"Be quiet, noisy human," Hallwyn hissed. "You could wake the dead with the stomping of your elephant feet and loud mouth. How could I have ever thought you might have elven blood?"

I jumped to hear her voice so close to me, grabbing the front of my shirt. Damned elf nearly gave me a heart attack. "You were supposed to go home," I hissed back. "You pinky promised."

"I felt better after I ate and just kept going." She looked up at the sky and wrinkled her nose. "It's dark. I've got very good hearing, and outside of you tromping through the rows and cursing, I haven't heard anyone else. I think the demons are gone."

"Please come with me, get in your car and go home," I pleaded. "Or come back and sleep on my couch. Irix will kill me if he knows I'm out here, but I can't leave you alone. I really don't want to show up tomorrow morning and find you dead next to a rotted vine."

She sighed. "Fine. But I am not sleeping on your couch again. That thing stinks. It smells like you were having sex and sacrificing goats on it."

That was pretty close to the truth. "Then let me walk you back to your car."

Hallwyn nodded and led the way. I followed closely, grateful for her superior eyesight. I was following so closely that I ran into her back when she came to an abrupt stop.

"Shh." She held up her hand.

I froze and listened. I could hear footsteps. Then voices cursing as they tripped over stakes and ran into vines. The demons. Shit it had to be the demons. I looked at Hallwyn, her expression just as panicked as I'm sure mine was.

"Run," she whispered, grabbing my hand. Then she

sprinted, half-dragging me through the rows as we zig-zagged our way toward the parking area. I was fast, but as a full elf, she was faster, and it was all I could do to keep up. All the while I heard the crashing of the demons.

The clouds parted, the waning moon lighting the fields in shades of gray. A figure stepped out into the path in front of us and raised her arm. Hallwyn gasped and dove to the side, but not fast enough. I heard the gunshot, heard her scream, then felt a burning sensation, like someone has shoved a red-hot knife through my upper arm.

Hallwyn let go of my hand, falling to the ground. She was holding her shoulder and writhing in the dirt. The metal bullets. I knew elves had an allergy to certain metals this side of the gates, but I didn't know how serious an in-and-out wound would be. Could she go into anaphylactic shock? Lose her arm? Die?

I heard footsteps and knelt down in front of Hallwyn, ready to do whatever necessary to protect the pair of us.

"You're lucky we don't kill you, too," Apixt said waving her gun at me as she approached. I knew it was her because she was fingering one of the leaves of the grapevine, withering it with her touch.

"Gallette's dead," I told her. "Your deal with him is over. You've done enough damage here, it's time for you to move on elsewhere."

Txipa walked out of a row to walk in step beside her sister. "Did you not hear me before? We're not leaving until our work here is done, and you interfering with our work is pissing us off. We gave you a courtesy warning. Now move aside and let us finish off this elf, or we'll shoot you as well."

"No. I'm not letting you kill her. Let us go and…and I'll take her with me. We'll leave Napa Valley."

"We warned you, and we warned her, too," Apixt said. "The elf only gets one warning. You get another pass because we like sex demons, although if you're not out of here by the time I count to ten, I'll change my mind."

"She's mine," I shouted, trying to think of a demon negotiation tactic that would get both Hallwyn and me out of this. "She's mine and I won't let you have her."

"One. Two."

"I'll trade you something for her. A favor to be redeemed at a later time, or something else." Eww. I hoped they didn't want me to have sex with them.

"Three. Four."

I shot a bolt of lightning at Txipa who easily deflected it.

"Five. Six."

"Let us go or I'll kill both of you." My voice wavered, far distant from the tough-bitch I wanted to portray right now.

"Seven. Eight."

I summoned every bit of energy and threw it into the vines closest to the plague demons. Stems and leaves shot into being, elongating and expanding as they filled the space between the rows like a wall of green. Apixt yelped, grabbing vines and withering them as quickly as I could grow them. I heard a gunshot and shifted my focus, twisting thick leaves and vines around Txipa and her gun while trying to shield Hallwyn from any stray bullets. We were at a stalemate, the demons killing off the vines at the same pace that I was creating them. The only difference was that I was tiring fast, while I got the impression that they had deep energy reserves. I wasn't sure I could hold them off enough to get my phone out and call Irix for help, and I didn't know how much time Hallwyn had before she'd succumb to her wounds. Was she already dead? I didn't dare break my concentration to turn around and check on the elf.

The vineyard suddenly exploded in light. "Did I miss anything? I dislike it when I miss all the good battles."

I turned around in surprise and saw Harkel and Irix

standing behind Hallwyn and me. The cavalry had arrived, and without a moment to spare. I felt my strength falter, my vines withering under the plague demons' attack. Txipa pulled her gun free from the vines and aimed it, only to throw it in frustration when she realized that the magazine was empty. Something inside me snapped, and all the vines fell away. Apixt launched herself toward me and I raised my arms, trying to protect Hallwyn.

That was when Harkel strode into the middle of the fray, lifted his hands to the sky then pushed them down in a quick sharp motion.

The sonic boom deafened me. Whatever the warmonger had done it extinguished all of the fire and sent both demons crashing to the ground. Spikes rose up from the dirt, surrounding the three of them and keeping the plague demons from Hallwyn and me. I felt Irix's arms around me.

"Idiot." The word lacked heat. In fact, he sounded rather shaken. "When I woke and found you gone, I had a feeling this is what was going to go down. So I enacted my backup plan."

Which was Harkel. I wondered what Irix had promised to get him to leave his activities in Central America and come racing back here?

The warmonger stood before the two demons, scowling. "You dare attack a member of my household? A succubus that I have petitioned with a breeding contract?"

I had been under the impression he'd withdrawn that, but maybe there was a formality that hadn't yet been taken?

The two plague demons rose. "We have claimed this vineyard. She and the elves keep reversing our work. We've warned them," Apixt said.

Harkel's eyes glowed an eerie orange. "One demon type cannot claim exclusive territory in this world against another demon type. You may lay waste to fields and sicken the populace, but I still have a right to come in and cause a revolution. A sex demon still has the right to come in and seduce. An imp has the right to come in and cause mischief."

"She wasn't seducing," Txipa complained. "She was healing the vines we'd infected. It was a direct slight. And those rights don't extend to elves."

Harkel laughed. "You are paltry plague demons if a *succubus* can reverse your work. I suggest you slink away lest word of this get back to Hel. And as for the elf, if the succubus Amber Shania Lowry says she has claimed her, then the elf is hers and not yours to harm. Leave now. My patience with the two of you has come to an end."

Both demons shot bolts of lightning at Harkel who absorbed them with ease. In return, he blasted a beam of bright red light toward the pair, blowing holes through their abdomens.

Txipa and Apixt screamed, falling to the ground, the holes expanding, blackening flesh all down their torsos.

"You are both lucky that I am in an excellent mood from my activities this week." Harkel walked over, placing an elf button inside the smoking holes that were just under the two demons's rib cages. "*Glah ham, shoceacan*," he announced. And then they were gone. I glanced over at Irix. I'm sure my mouth was hanging open with shock.

The iron spikes dissolved and the warmonger walked over to me, shoving a finger into the wound in my arm. I gritted my teeth, trying not to pass out from the pain.

"You wear your wounds with pride, Amber. Yes, you are quite an amazing succubus. I need to return to my rebellion, but perhaps next week…"

"I would love to see you next week," I gasped, grateful when he finally removed his finger from the hole in my arm. "Thank you for coming. I don't know how I can possibly repay you for your assistance."

Harkel seemed perplexed at my statement. "Of course I came. That's what the head of a household does when one of his demons has been threatened or is being attacked. As for repayment…" He grinned, and it was a naughty-boy grin that rivaled Irix's. "Perhaps anal sex when I return. I promise I will use the mouse cock for you."

Men. Didn't matter if they were human or demon, it was all about the ass. "I would be delighted," I told him, turning to Hallwyn as soon as the warmonger was gone.

She was alive, but pale, gasping and holding her arm. I pulled my shirt off and made a makeshift bandage around the wound. "Are you going to be okay?"

She nodded. "This really hurts, but I'm slowly healing it. It's going to take weeks, and I'll have a scar." The elf burst into tears. "I'll have a scar. A scar on my beautiful skin. Oh, Amber, I'll be ugly, just like you."

And that was the thanks I got for saving her life. I helped her to her feet, and with some pleading, convinced Irix to carry her back to our trailer where we put her on my sofa and covered her with the towel she'd used last night. As tired and hurt as she was, she didn't even complain about the smell before dropping off to sleep. I was thrilled to hear her snore. Huh. So much for perfect elves.

Irix led me to the bathroom and cleaned my wounds, jumpstarting my healing with one of his panty-soaking kisses. Then he washed the rest of me and led me off to bed, curling in beside me and spooning against my back, taking care not to jostle my arm.

"Sex?" he asked.

"Not with the stray-puppy-with-excellent-hearing on the couch." I laughed. "Tomorrow morning, after she's gone to work we'll get nasty."

"I'm still waiting on that blow job and anal," he teased.

"Speaking of anal. Thank you for calling in Harkel."

He brushed his hand down my thigh. "I thought we could use some backup."

"And what did you have to promise him for this favor?"

Irix grinned. "That, my dear girl, is none of your business. I'm not an incubus who kisses and tells."

"Yes you are." I turned over and gave him a quick kiss on the cheek. "But thank you."

He wrapped a leg around mine, pulling my hips tight to his. "Anytime, elf-girl. Anytime."

I opened up the envelope and let out a squeal.

"What? What is it?" Irix tried to grab the paper from my hands, but I was waving it in the air and dancing around. I'd spent the day packing because this was the last week of my internship. I'd go home for a few weeks, visit with my human mother, Wyatt, and Nyalla, and make bean dip and red velvet cake for Sam's shindig, then I'd start sorting through all of my belongings in preparation for my move to New Orleans.

It was exciting, scary, and strangely depressing all at the same time. I'd be living with Irix in his amazing home, in a city that I loved, surrounded by friends. I'd be filling out grant paperwork and working odd jobs until Jordan and I could get our non-profit organized and ready to go. It was what I'd been dreaming about for the last year, but there was this wiggly-worm of doubt that wouldn't let me be completely happy, completely satisfied with the course of my immediate future.

Something felt off. And then, out of nowhere, came this letter.

"Amber, give it to me." Irix snatched the paper from my hands and scanned it. I couldn't read the expression on his face, and that dampened my enthusiasm.

I was at a fork in the road, and I wasn't sure which path to take.

"Should I go?" I asked him. "It's just for two weeks, and I might not even get the apprenticeship. I mean, I'll be competing against people whose families have been enologists for generations, who grew up in vineyards and wineries."

"But you won't know unless you try." He handed the paper back to me. "If you go and you get the offer, then you'll have a decision to make. If you go and don't get the offer, well then at least you tried. If you don't go, you'll never know what course your life may have taken."

I bit my lip. "But I'm a half-succubus. I'll live for tens of thousands of years. I could always do this some other time."

"But the offer is now. Go. Explore. And see what happens."

I looked up at him, searching his eyes for some sort of answer. "Will you be mad if I don't go to New Orleans this fall? We had plans... And Jordan..."

"Jordan really wants to work with you, but she'll understand. And no, I won't be mad. Actually I'd like to come with you. I haven't been to Italy in centuries. We could stay in Lake Como, and mix business with pleasure."

I eyed the paper and smiled. "I'd need to be there for the courses, and take some time to study. Then there's the competition/exam. But it seems like we'd have lots of free time to explore. Mmmm, villas, and statues, and artwork, and wine."

"And sex." He laughed. "Let's do it. Think of it as an extension of your internship. And at the end of two weeks, if they offer you an apprenticeship, then you can decide which direction you'd like to go."

I loved how Irix supported everything I wanted to do, how he was always willing, and excited, to come with me on these adventures.

He took the papers from my hand and tossed them on the table, pulling me into his arms. "Let's do it."

"Do it as in sex? Or do it as in Italy?" I teased.

His chest rumbled with laughter. "Both. Sex now. Italy after."

Unholy Pleasures

City of Lust (Fall 2017)

* * *

<u>Imp World Novels</u>

No Man's Land

Stolen Souls

Three Wishes

Northern Lights

Far From Center

ACKNOWLEDGMENTS

A huge thanks to my copyeditors Kimberly Cannon and Jennifer Cosham whose eagle eyes catch all my typos and keep my comma problem in line, and to Damonza for cover design.

Most of all, thanks to my children, who have suffered many nights of microwaved chicken nuggets and take-out pizza so that Mommy can follow her dream.

Debra lives in a little house in the woods of Maryland with her sons and two slobbery bloodhounds. On a good day, she jogs and horseback rides, hopefully managing to keep the horse between herself and the ground. Her only known super power is 'Identify Roadkill'.

For more information:
www.debradunbar.com